Sunset at Embthwaite Farm

Sunset at Embthwaite Farm

A Mowbray Sisters Romance

Kate Hewitt

TULE
PUBLISHING

Sunset at Embthwaite Farm

Tule Publishing First Printing, March 2024

The Tule Publishing, Inc.

First Publication by Tule Publishing 2024

Cover design by Rhian

ISBN: 978-1-962707-53-4

Chapter One

ANNA MOWBRAY DUG her thumb deep down into the compost, enjoying, somewhat perversely, the feel of the soil sinking underneath her nail. There was something satisfying about doing work that got you dirty. Something wonderful about planting a seed, letting it grow.

She dropped the seed into the tiny well she'd made and then covered it with more compost, patted it down. It was the fifteenth she'd done that morning, all the little pots lined up on the potting bench, her breath coming out in frosty puffs as she worked.

The greenhouse at Embthwaite Farm hadn't been used in ages, probably not since she'd left, thirteen years ago. She'd wandered into its cobwebby interior when she'd first returned a few weeks ago, completely at a loss at being back at the place that held so many painful memories, which she'd walked away from in something of a stupor, not that Anna could explain that to the people who mattered most—her two grown-up daughters.

A soft sigh escaped her, and she reached for another pot and began to fill it with compost. There was something both miraculous and natural about planting something, she reflected. It amazed her every time she saw the first tiny green seedling shooting up through the soil, truly a miracle, and yet the way the whole world worked.

It made her draw rather unfortunate parallels to motherhood, which was also both natural and miraculous, or at least was meant to be, if you believed the greeting cards, the parenting books, the Instagram feeds. It hadn't been either for Anna, which was why she was out here, on a freezing January morning, instead of inside with her children, making memories. Good ones.

After being away for so many years, she'd been back at Embthwaite Farm for just two weeks. She'd come when her older daughter Rachel had texted her to say her father, Anna's ex-husband Peter, was dying of a brain tumour. Both Rachel and her sister Harriet were tending to him, and Rachel had written, rather repressively, that she'd only texted because she thought Anna ought to know. Her oldest daughter hadn't invited her back, not specifically; her attitude had been more one of simply relaying factual information. And yet Anna had come.

Two weeks later, she was continuing to wonder why. It had not been an easy landing, but then she hadn't expected it to be. You couldn't more or less abandon your children—even if they had been nearly eighteen and nineteen years of age—for so long and not expect some painful repercussions. Hostility, even hatred, or cool indifference, which in its own way hurt even more.

Anna felt as if she'd experienced the whole range of those unpleasant emotions since she'd been back—the indifference from Rachel, the hostility from Harriet. The situation had thawed a *little* bit over Christmas, or at least Anna had felt as if it had, when they'd celebrated the opening of the hotel owned by Harriet's boyfriend Quinn. Harriet had made cookies for the Christmas party and had been buzzing with orders ever since. Rachel, who had relocated to the farm when Peter had first taken ill, was starting her own investment management company; her office was the dining room, and she was often with their neighbour Ben Mackey, with whom she'd recently started a relationship.

They both seemed busy and happy, and Anna was delighted that their lives had turned out so well. She just wished she could be a part of it all, instead of hiding out here in the greenhouse. She'd come back ostensibly to help care for Peter, but her daughters had insisted they could manage on their own. She'd barely seen her ex-husband since she'd arrived; admittedly, he'd been sleeping a lot, but when she'd dared to peek in his bedroom, he'd simply glanced at her, harrumphed, and then looked away.

Well, had she really expected any other kind of response? It was more than he'd given her for most of their marriage, although maybe that was unfair. It was so easy to let your mind snag on the painful memories rather than the good ones, the way your jumper might get caught by brambles. Tugging yourself free hurt, and usually ended up with something being wrecked.

Anna didn't want that to happen this time, which was why she was still here, two weeks on, with her daughters stepping around her like she was a stranger, or maybe even a statue. A guest they didn't want to stay, at any rate, and yet she hadn't gone because if she left now, she feared they would never reconcile. She would lose her daughters forever, something she couldn't bear to think about, even though they'd already been lost to her, more in the case of Harriet and a little less for Rachel, for thirteen years already.

Still, as long as she was here, there was hope…or so she kept telling herself. She continued with the planting for another half hour, filling pot after pot with compost, pushing the snapdragon seeds down into it. She wasn't even sure why she was doing it; the state of the greenhouse and garden suggested no one had planted a thing since she'd left, and she most likely wouldn't be here long enough to nurture these seedlings, plant them out and watch them grow.

There was another parallel there and one Anna didn't want to make, yet her mind inexorably went there, stayed. *You didn't stay to see your daughters grow. You didn't help them with their struggles. You are the most unnatural mother in the world.*

She drew a breath that was only a little bit ragged and then pushed her neat, silvery hair behind her ears. Her fingers were freezing, and she was desperate for a coffee. She was simply going to have to brave going back to the house and bearding the two lionesses in their homely den.

Anna slipped out of the greenhouse, her boots crunching on the frost-tipped grass. On this January morning, the world looked magical, the mist drifting up in ghostly shreds that caught on the hills rising sharply behind the farmhouse, the sun filtering through the white cloud that would most likely melt away by midday. Everything that could be was rimed in frost—every leaf, every twig, every blade of grass, a world outlined in sparkling white, glinting under the sunlight.

She took a moment simply to stand there and breathe it all in, remember just what she'd loved about this place, before it had all gone wrong...although, realistically, it had all gone wrong before anything had even started. She just hadn't realised it at the time. Still, she *had* loved this place, once upon a time. It had felt magical, especially after a childhood in the bleak and boring suburbs of Reading, living in a brick semi-detached with two parents who had worked all the time, not seeing the point of anything outside of academia. Coming to a place where you could breathe properly, and see the world around you, and set your own hours, and start to dream...it had felt wonderful, for a little while.

The light in the kitchen at the back of the house was on, and Anna could see someone moving around. Harriet or Rachel? Her girls looked so similar—dark hair and eyes, Rachel willowy, Harriet a bit curvier. Both of them resembled their father so much in his colouring—so unlike Anna's fair, now silver, hair and pale blue eyes—that it amazed her that Harriet had been convinced she wasn't Peter Mowbray's biological daughter. It was understandable, of course, because *he'd* been convinced of that fact...even though it was as obvious as the snub nose on Harriet's face, the same as her father's, that it couldn't possibly be true.

Even if you said it was?

Yet another regret, piled on top of so many others, an immovable heap in the middle of Anna's heart, a heaviness she carried with her everywhere, so she sometimes felt as if she were dragging something behind her, or maybe on her back, haggard and limping from the effort.

At the back door, she eased off her welly boots and left them upside down on the boot rack before she opened the door and stepped into the warm, welcoming kitchen. The rumble of the Rayburn, the smell of fresh coffee and yesterday's baking, the laundry drying on the rack hoisted above the stove…it all felt so *homely*, and for a second, Anna could remember when she'd felt happy here, or at least convinced herself, for a short while, that she was.

Then she saw Rachel standing by the kettle, about to pour herself a cup of coffee, the relaxed look on her face turning instantly guarded as she caught sight of her mother.

"Good morning," Anna greeted her as lightly as she could. It took so much effort to keep sounding relaxed and friendly when she wasn't getting a single thing back; after two weeks, she felt positively drained from it. "Did you sleep well?"

"Yes, I suppose." Rachel lifted the French press, about to pour out some coffee, and then glanced at Anna. "Would you like some coffee?" It sounded as if it had cost her something, to ask such a simple question, and as if she'd really rather Anna said no, she didn't.

"I'd love some, thank you," Anna replied as warmly as she could without sounding desperate or deranged, both of which she sometimes felt. She wanted her daughters to forgive her, to accept her, to open up and talk honestly. So far, it hadn't happened. "It's really cold out there," she remarked as she took off her coat. "Beautiful, but cold."

Rachel took another cup from its hook and began to pour. "What were you doing outside so early? Going for a walk?"

Anna hesitated and then said, "No, I was in the greenhouse, planting up some snapdragons."

Rachel raised her eyebrows, a look of surprise as well as blatant scepticism on her face. Clearly, she didn't see the point in her mother doing such a thing, and Anna couldn't really blame her.

"How long will those take to grow?" she asked, and Anna struggled not to wince at the implication—the same thought she had, that she wouldn't be around to plant them out.

"About seven to fourteen days for the first seedlings to sprout," she replied. "But they'll stay in the greenhouse until the danger of frost has passed."

Rachel shook her head slowly as she splashed milk into two cups. "I don't think anyone has stepped foot in the greenhouse in years," she said, and then glanced at her mother in something like challenge. "Not since you left."

"No, I don't suppose anyone has," Anna replied. "It doesn't look as if anyone has, at any rate." Still with the light tone, although it pained her. Yet how else could she be? She'd already had an attempt at a heart-to-heart with Harriet a few days after she'd first arrived, when Harriet had been practically pulsing with pain from her father's rejection. Anna had tried to explain what had happened all those years ago without actually giving much away, because she didn't feel like the story was hers alone, or maybe she was just being cowardly.

In any case, while the conversation had reassured Harriet that she was Peter's biological daughter, it hadn't seemed to move her and Anna's relationship forward. Harriet still avoided her, or threw her fulminating glances over the dinner table, and Anna was at a loss at how to proceed. She didn't want to force herself on her daughters…and yet she was still here.

"No, we couldn't really see the point of the greenhouse, I suppose," Rachel stated rather flatly, and Anna felt herself stiffen. There was something accusatory about the way her daughter had made the remark, as if it was her fault that they hadn't planted a garden or made use of the greenhouse, the way she had when she'd lived here.

"And I suppose you were busy at university," she pointed out mildly, only to have Rachel glare at her.

"Yes, I'm well aware of that," she replied shortly, and thrust a coffee cup towards her so Anna had to grab it, hot liquid sloshing onto her fingers.

Rachel turned and walked out of the room without a word while Anna stared after her blankly. What had she said that made Rachel so prickly? Rachel had been, over the years, the more reasonable one; they'd met up every so often—less and less, it was true, as the years had gone—for stilted conversations over lunch in some London restaurant. Anna had loved and hated those afternoons in equal measure; she wanted to see her daughter, but she hated the strained silence, the way Rachel treated her like an acquaintance, the palpable relief her daughter felt when she finally rose from the table. *Well, I guess I'd better be going…*

As for Harriet…she hadn't spoken to Anna at all, for thirteen long years. Anna had called her, a few months after she'd first left, hoping to build bridges, only to have Harriet hang up on her. They hadn't spoken since, although Anna had tried on various occasions, but admittedly not as hard as she could have. What were a few voicemails and texts when you were somebody's *mother*?

And yet each ensuing rejection had felt like a kick to the teeth; how long could you keep putting yourself through that kind of masochistic torture? Eventually she'd stopped, for her own sanity.

Still, something had clearly nettled Rachel about her remark; Anna just didn't know what it was, and she didn't know her daughters well enough anymore to guess.

She sat down at the table, nursing her mug of coffee, trying not to feel entirely disconsolate. Perhaps she'd drive to the garden centre outside the nearby town of Mathering, or take dear old Fred, now sprawled in his usual place in front of the Rayburn, for a walk. The fresh air might clear her head, even if she already knew it wouldn't help heal her heart.

"What do you think, Fred?" Anna asked, and the spaniel's plumed tail beat against the slate floor as he looked up at her with his droopy eyes. Ben had bought him for Rachel about a year before Anna had left; he'd still been a puppyish ball of energy when she'd walked out the door. "Shall we go for a walk?" she asked. His tail beat harder, but he didn't move so much as an inch from his place on the worn carpet by the warm stove. Anna smiled faintly. "I don't blame you," she told the dog. "It's cold out there."

She couldn't help but acknowledge that the most significant interactions she'd had in the last week were with the dog. Suppressing a sigh, Anna sipped her coffee—just as she heard footsteps down the front stairs, and then Harriet came into the kitchen, checking herself at the door.

Her daughter was dressed in her usual eclectic mix of brightly coloured wool and corduroy—in this case, a green jumper splotched with bright yellow sunflowers and an aqua-blue corduroy skirt with matching tights. Her curly hair was pulled up on top of her head, and she wore a pair of fuzzy slippers on her feet. Anna's heart ached to see the closed look come over Harriet's face as she caught sight of her.

She'd really hoped, after their conversation just before Christmas, Harriet might have thawed a bit towards her. Anna had felt as if she had, during the Christmas party at Quinn's hotel, when Harriet had thrown her a few cautious smiles across the room, each one feeling like an olive branch. Anna had hoped it would lead to more conversations, more healing, but it hadn't.

Whatever festive bonhomie her daughter had been feeling then had hardened into the usual stoic silence in the new year. They hadn't spoken properly, or even at all, in over a week, and the conversation where Anna had reassured Harriet she was Peter Mowbray's biological daughter seemed a long time ago now. It was clear she still hadn't been forgiven…for anything.

"Would you like some coffee?" Anna asked when Harriet didn't seem as if she was going to move from the kitchen doorway. "Rachel just made some, and I think there's a bit left in the pot." Anna started to rise to check, but Harriet shook her head firmly as she came into the kitchen.

"I'll have tea," she stated as she switched on the kettle, and Anna sat back down in her chair. She watched warily as Harriet moved around the kitchen, making tea and then putting oats in a pot on the Rayburn, adding milk, her movements all a little brisker than normal. The crack of the teapot being placed firmly on the counter made Anna wince.

"Would you like some help?" she offered humbly. "I could stir the oats, if you like." She sounded desperate, she knew she did, but she couldn't help herself. She didn't know how else to show her daughters that she cared. She'd *always* cared...even if they refused to believe that.

Harriet drew a breath as if to reply, and then she placed her hands flat on the counter, her head bowed as she slowly breathed out. Anna watched apprehensively, unsure what was coming next.

"I'm sorry, but I can't do this," Harriet stated flatly, her head still bowed. She straightened and turned to face Anna, folding her arms. "I can't play happy families with you right now, like we don't have *decades* of history between us. I can't, and I won't." She stared her down, her dark eyes simmering with what looked like fury, while Anna's mind spun, trying to think how to reply.

I just wanted to make the porridge didn't seem like a helpful answer right then.

"I don't want to pretend, Harriet," she finally said, her voice quiet and a bit croaky. "I want to..." She hesitated, unsure how to finish that sentence.

Harriet arched her eyebrows, looking as sceptical as Rachel had about the snapdragons. More. "You want to *what*?"

"Make things better," Anna replied after a moment. "If I can."

Harriet appraised her coolly for a long moment. "I'm not sure you can," she finally said. "There might be too much water under the bridge."

"Okay," Anna answered after a pause. She wasn't sure what else to say. She didn't want to ask Harriet if she wanted her to go, because she didn't *want* to go. Not yet. Not before she'd done…something. Something more, although she wasn't sure what that was. What her daughter would let it be.

"Look," she said at last. "I know you're angry and you have every right to be. I'm not trying to push anything. But I'm here, and I can be helpful. At least let me help in some way…with your father."

Harriet's lips twisted. "Why do you care about him now?"

"I was married to him for twenty years, Harriet," Anna replied quietly. "That did mean something, you know." Even if it hadn't to him.

"It didn't seem to mean much to you, in the end," Harriet tossed back, her tone caught between flippancy and jagged pain.

Anna resisted the urge to close her eyes, will it all away. Of course Harriet was lashing out. She understood that. She really did. She just wanted it to stop…eventually. "You're very busy with your baking enterprise," she said steadily. "And Rachel's trying to get her own business going. I'm here, kicking around, wanting to do something. Will you let me?"

Harriet shrugged. "No one's stopping you."

Actually, they more or less had, always fobbing her off, telling her they could manage, taking Peter his meal trays and medication, checking on him throughout the day. That had come more from Rachel than Harriet, it was true, but there still had been a definite sense from both of them that she wasn't needed.

"All right, then," she said, trying for a smile, determined not to cause an argument. "I'll take him his breakfast when he wakes."

Harriet hesitated, and then shrugged again. "Fine. He likes a fried egg, runny in the middle, and toast with marmalade, no butter."

Anna had to press her lips together to stop the instinctive reply. *I made your father breakfast just about every morning for twenty years. I think I know what he likes.* Somehow, her leaving this farmhouse all those years ago had negated, in her daughters' eyes, all the time she'd spent in it. All the meals she'd made, the toilets she'd scrubbed, the Halloween costumes she'd sewn by hand, the birthday cakes she'd decorated, the medicine she'd doled out, the clothes she'd ironed, day after day after day. None of that counted for anything anymore.

"Great," she replied lightly. "I'll get started."

"Fine," Harriet said and, taking her tea, she left the kitchen, leaving the pot of oats on the Rayburn, untouched.

Chapter Two

SINCE THE OATS were there, Anna made porridge, stirring it slowly, recalling all the quiet mornings she'd done just this, before the girls had got up, and Peter had been out in the barn. There had been a peacefulness to it, along with a sorrow, a sense of loss and longing she'd never, in all her marriage, been able to shake.

When the porridge was made, she tiptoed down the hall to ask Rachel if she wanted any; her daughter was sat at the dining room table, frowning at her laptop, a cup of coffee cradled in her hands.

"No thank you," she said, all stiff politeness. "I'm good with coffee."

Harriet must have gone back upstairs, and Anna wasn't brave enough to beard her daughter in her bedroom. She'd leave it on the stove, she decided, and then doled out a bowl for herself, drizzling it with honey.

She ate by herself at the kitchen table, recalling the many mornings her daughters had sat with her, teasing or bickering good-naturedly while she'd savoured her second cup of coffee of the day. Invariably, Peter would have come in at some point, grunting a hello before sitting at the head of the table and waiting for her to put a plate in front of him.

She couldn't blame Peter for who he was, Anna knew—a stoic, somewhat surly Yorkshire farmer, from a generation of men who didn't know how to fry an egg or wield a Hoover and were most certainly not about to learn. A man who didn't *do* emotion, who thought that providing a roof over his family's head was all that was required of him, because it was all he'd been given, and his father before him, on and on, back through the generations.

Admittedly, when they'd first met at a country fair while she'd been on holiday with some uni friends, that rugged, brooding stoicism had been attractive, even sexy—he'd been twenty years older than her, handsome in a taciturn, craggy-faced way that at twenty-one Anna had found exciting. She'd thought him a modern-day Heathcliff, and having actually read *Wuthering Heights* later in life, instead of just hearing about it, she wondered if that was in fact about right. The trouble was no one actually wanted to be *married* to Heathcliff. At least she hadn't, which she'd realised far too late.

Anna had just finished her porridge when she heard the sound of someone moving about upstairs. The heavy footfalls had to be her ex-husband rather than her daughter, and in alarm that he might be trying to get out of bed—according to Rachel, he hadn't been able to do so without assistance since before Anna had arrived—she hurried up the stairs. Harriet poked her head out of her bedroom as Anna rounded the landing, her face alarmingly blotchy, as if she'd been crying.

Anna's steps faltered. "Harriet—"

"Are you seeing to Dad?" Harriet asked abruptly, and Anna nodded.

"Yes—"

Her daughter shut her bedroom with a decisive click. Deciding to tackle that particular problem later, Anna hurried to the door of her old marital bedroom. She'd only been in there once since she'd arrived, and then only very briefly, and now, with her hand on the knob, she felt her heart stutter. She wasn't sure she was ready for this.

And yet she could hear Peter moving around, sounding like a lumbering bear, and she was afraid he might fall and hurt himself if she didn't hurry. She tapped once and then turned the knob.

"Peter?" she asked gently as she came into the room. The curtains were drawn, and she had to blink several times in the gloom before she was able to make him out—he was standing by the bed, hunched over and wearing a worn pair of pyjamas that Anna vaguely remembered from their marriage. His sparse white hair was flattened on one side and sticking up on the other, and his bushy eyebrows drew close in a scowl as he caught sight of her.

"What the hell are you doing here?" he demanded, although the words were so slurred it took Anna a few seconds to realise that was what he was saying.

"I'm here to help, Peter," she replied quietly. She suspected, from the grumpy and confused look on his face, that he didn't remember seeing her from before. Carefully she closed the door behind her. The room smelled stale, of sickness and medicine. Peter's legs trembled as he flung one hand out to the bed to balance himself. "Let me help you back into bed," Anna suggested, taking a step forward.

"Where's Rachel?" Peter demanded querulously. "I want

Rachel!"

Anna reached out to put one arm around her ex-husband; he stiffened at her touch. "Rachel's downstairs working, Peter," she said gently. "Let me help you—"

He flung her arm off with more force than she'd expected, so she took a stumbling step back.

"Damn it, woman, I don't need your help!" he exclaimed in a garbled roar. "I want Rachel, because I need to take a piss!"

Before Anna could reply, the door was flung open and Rachel stood there, managing to look both anxious and accusing as her gaze moved from her father to Anna. "I'm here, Dad," she said, and gave Anna a quick, quelling look. "I can take it from here," she told her, her tone decidedly cool.

Well, so much for helping. Anna couldn't keep from feeling not just rebuffed but also humiliated. What on earth was she still doing at this wretched farm, she wondered, if no one actually wanted her help? If no one wanted her here in the first place?

"Very well," she managed, her tone stiffer than she would have liked, and then, not trusting herself to say anything more, she headed downstairs.

Back in the kitchen, she glanced at the porridge she'd left warming on the stove and then, in what she suspected was no more than a childish fit of pique, she dumped the congealed mass in the bin. She scrubbed the pan out in the sink, using more force than necessary, because the truth was, she was feeling rather furious, and she knew she had to master her emotions before she spoke to Rachel or Harriet again.

A few calming breaths later, with the pot clean and drying on the rack, Anna felt a bit more reasonable about the whole unfortunate episode. All right, yes, she could understand why her ex-husband did not want her helping him use the toilet. She didn't want that particular job, anyway. But it was hard, she realised, *really* hard, to keep feeling like an unwanted guest in what had once been her own home. She'd forfeited all rights to anything here by leaving, Anna knew. She'd accepted that, or thought she had, and yet to be smacked in the face with it at every possible opportunity was certainly starting to sting. Yet what could she do about it?

"He's back in bed."

Anna glanced towards the door, where Rachel stood, her arms folded, her expression obdurate. Lost in her unhappy thoughts, she hadn't heard her come down the stairs.

"Well done," she said as brightly as she could, but that was clearly the wrong thing to say because Rachel simply scowled. "Shall I make his breakfast?" she suggested. "You can bring it up to him if you'd like, if you think seeing me might upset him."

Rachel gave a weary sigh, like she was tired of Anna hassling her. "All right, fine," she replied, clearly a concession. "I need to get back to work but let me know when it's ready."

Yes, madam; very good, madam, Anna thought sardonically, trying not to grit her teeth. She wanted to help, but she still didn't like being treated like some sort of skivvy. There was, she supposed, no winning.

Not for the first time, she wondered if she should just go home. Her cosy little terraced house in Stroud was waiting for her, with its courtyard full of winter aconite and jasmine, its quaint and tiny rooms perfect for one person. She'd bought it after she'd sold her parents' house in Reading, where she'd grown up. It had felt like a new beginning, months after she'd left her husband and children, emerging from the darkness of despair that had been so thick and cloying she'd felt as if she'd forgotten how to breathe, to see.

Running back to that safe and comforting place, where she'd rebuilt herself and learned to heal, even if that had been no more than finding a way to live with the scars, was tempting, treacherously so. And yet if she gave up this time, Anna thought, if she walked away again, even if her daughters were practically *asking* her to, she feared there would be no way back, ever. Right now, there still was, no matter how narrow and precarious a path it was, and she was determined to take it...which meant staying.

She just needed to figure out *how* to stay. How to make this work in a way that moved the three of them forward. She could start, she supposed, by making breakfast.

Ten minutes later, Anna had assembled a fried egg—runny in the middle as Peter liked—and two pieces of toast with marmalade, no butter, on a tray, along with a cup of tea, milky and sweet as she remembered he took it. There was something both poignant and bitter about making breakfast for a husband who had never, not once, said thank you for all the breakfasts she'd made him over the years. He wouldn't this time, either, she supposed, but at least now she knew she could live with it.

She went to the dining room to summon Rachel, who was frowning once more at her laptop.

"I've made the breakfast," she offered hesitantly.

Rachel yanked her gaze up from the computer screen, looking irritated. "Sorry…do you mind taking it up yourself? I'm in the middle of something."

"Of course," Anna replied. So, this time she was allowed? She wouldn't question it. She slipped from the room and went back to the kitchen for the tray before heading upstairs, her heart starting to beat hard with trepidation.

Harriet appeared still to be closeted in her room, the door firmly shut, as Anna crossed the hallway to Peter's bedroom. Balancing the tray on one arm, she tapped once and then pushed open the door. Rachel had tidied the room, and settled Peter in bed, the covers drawn up to his middle as he leaned against several pillows. There was a lap table next to his bed that Anna supposed he used for meals.

"Good morning," she said quietly, keeping her tone friendly but not overly bright. There was too much history between them to attempt to be chipper, and in any case, she didn't think she'd be able to manage it.

"What are you doing here?" Peter demanded. His voice was slurred as before, but Anna could still understand him.

"Bringing you breakfast." She put the breakfast tray on top of the bureau before reaching for the lap table and setting it on the bed, across Peter's middle. He glared at her as she did so, his eyes rheumy and fierce.

"You know I didn't mean that," he said. A bit of drool dribbled from the corner of his mouth, and it filled Anna with a sudden, surprising pity.

"I know," she replied. "But it's all of a piece, really. I'm here to help, Peter."

"I'm managing fine with Rachel," he replied in a growl.

"But Rachel and Harriet aren't managing fine," Anna replied as calmly as she could. "They have jobs and lives, and they need support."

Peter simply shook his head as if to deny the truth of his words as he glared down at his breakfast. Anna recalled Rachel saying he needed help eating and drinking; his hands were too shaky now to manage it on his own.

"Let me help you," she suggested, and reached for his fork.

Peter batted her hand away, hard enough to hurt. She drew back, alarmed, as he glared at her fiercely. "*No.*"

"Why be so stubborn?" she protested, trying to sound reasonable. She knew he had his pride, but his vitriol was hard to take, on top of everything else, especially when they both knew it wasn't deserved. Peter, more than anyone, understood why she had left. The real question was why she hadn't left sooner.

"I...can do it...myself," he forced out, the words coming slowly and painfully, making Anna once more feel that inconvenient rush of pity.

"Peter," she tried again, "I know how hard this must be. But for Rachel and Harriet's sakes, please let me help you. They're too young to manage this kind of thing on their own."

"You did," he pointed out, surprising her, because that was just about the last thing she'd expected him to say right then. Yes, she had, back in her late thirties, when the girls had been teenagers and her mother had been dying of cancer, her father already passed. She'd travelled frequently between North Yorkshire and Reading, a five-hour journey, going back and forth because the girls couldn't manage alone, not with Peter working all hours on the farm.

A sigh escaped her, full of sorrow for what had been as well as what now was. "Please," she said quietly, and after an endless pause where the only sound was his laboured breathing, he finally gave a jerky nod.

Anna exhaled quietly in relief and then reached over to cut the fried egg into neat, bite-sized pieces. She speared one with the fork and then gently took Peter's hand and wrapped his arthritic fingers around its handle, hoping he could guide the fork to his mouth by himself. She wanted to save his dignity as much as possible, but she didn't know what his capabilities were.

Her ex-husband's eyes were full of impotent anger and a deeper grief as, with a huge amount of effort, his hand shaking the entire time, he managed to eat the bite of egg, a bit of yolk dribbling down his chin. It both amazed and saddened her, that this man who had once slung bales of hay and lifted a strapping calf could now barely feed himself. It happened to everyone one way or another, she supposed, yet it was still hard to witness. It had to be all the harder for Peter to endure.

Anna smiled in encouragement as he returned the fork to the tray. "Another?" she asked, and he nodded again.

They managed four good bites before it all went wrong, as Anna had been bracing herself for, because she knew Peter would only be able to take so much of her seeing him as he was—trembling, weak, pathetic in his own eyes.

On the fifth bite, this one of toast, the piece of toast fell marmalade-side down onto his pyjama top.

"Never mind," Anna said quickly, reaching for the bite of toast, but once again Peter batted her hand way, and once again it hurt. She pressed her lips together to keep from saying something sharp as he glared at her, his mouth working as he attempted to get the words out.

"Peter—"

"Go," he finally choked out. "*Go.*" And then he pushed the tray off the lap table, so it fell to the floor in a clatter and splash of dishes and food.

"*Peter*," Anna exclaimed in dismay, and then knelt to clean up the mess. The tea had gone everywhere, and she looked around futilely for something to mop it up with. She was just grabbing a shirt when Harriet and Rachel both hurried into the room.

"What's going on—" Rachel began cautiously just as Harriet burst out, "Why are *you* in here?"

Oh, help. She didn't need this now—both her daughters, accusing her in their different ways, while Peter glared on. "We had a bit of an accident," Anna told them, thankful her voice didn't tremble. She kept mopping up the mess, like her life depended on it. "It will be sorted out shortly—"

"*Go*," Peter shouted again. His gnarled fists were loosely bunched, his weakened frame shaking with aggravation and effort. He looked furiously at Rachel. "Make…make her *go*."

A tense pause tautened the very air of the room, so Anna found it hard to breathe. Harriet was still seeming like she wanted to have a tantrum, and Rachel looked torn.

"Mum," Rachel said quietly—the first time she'd used the term since before Anna had left—"maybe you should go, just for now."

After a second's pause, when she kept mopping up the mess, her eyes blurred with tears, Anna rose from the floor. "All right," she said, and walked out of the bedroom before either of her daughters—or Peter, for that matter—could see how close to crying she was.

What a disaster this morning had been, she thought despondently as, back in the kitchen, she threw the sopping shirt into the washing machine and then washed her hands. Nothing had gone the way she'd hoped it would. Everything seemed only a terrible confirmation that she shouldn't be here, that she wasn't wanted, needed, or helpful.

Anna took a deep breath and let it out slowly. She glanced at Fred, who was still lying by the Rayburn. He lifted his droopy head from his paws as he saw her looking at him, and his tail beat against the floor a few times, like a question.

"All right," Anna said, an answer. "Let's go for a walk, Fred. Clear our heads."

She reached for her boots and coat and found Fred's lead in the hall. The girls were still upstairs, and Anna could hear them conversing in hushed murmurs. Were they deciding what to do about their unwanted mother? Maybe they were thinking about how to ask her to leave.

Well, she'd save them the trouble, she thought, at least for the rest of the morning. Maybe a walk would help her decide what was best to do in the longer term. Slipping the lead around Fred's shaggy head, she headed out into the crisp winter's morning and started walking briskly down the drive, determined not to look back even once.

Chapter Three

THE MORNING MIST had burned off, leaving a fragile blue sky, the wintry sunlight gilding the distant moors in pale gold. Anna's boots crunched on the frost-rimed gravel of the drive as Fred trotted faithfully beside her. She wondered, belatedly, if her daughters would protest her taking him for a walk; maybe they felt as proprietorial over the dog as they did their father. *Well, too bad,* she thought recklessly. *I'm doing it.*

She followed the same path she'd taken years ago, when she'd needed to get away from the farm and clear her head—down the lane, and then a right turn onto the footpath that ran along the sheep meadows and pastures to the River Derwent, before turning left to follow the river into the top of town. Anna didn't think she'd walk that far this morning, but right now, keeping at a good clip, she certainly felt like she needed to burn off some energy as well as some anger—or maybe it was despair. Sometimes, she mused, they felt like two facets of the same emotion.

It took fifteen minutes of steady walking before she felt herself come back into her usual sense of calm. It felt like a comforting cloak, a safety blanket, because heaven knew she didn't like or want all those old emotions bubbling up, taking her over. She'd had enough of that, right after she'd left, not that she wanted to think about those desperate months in any way at all.

By the time Anna reached the Derwent, the water bobbing with chunks of ice, she felt restored, or at least mostly. Enough to contemplate heading back and talking to her daughters directly, asking her what they wanted her to do. There was no point staying, she realised, if it was causing more harm than good to everyone, herself included. The knowledge hurt, but at least she finally recognised it. If they wanted her to go, she'd go, even if she feared it would feel like a second death.

She was just turning to head back when, to her surprise, she heard someone call her name.

"*Anna…*" The voice was female, her name said in a wondering tone. "Anna Mowbray? I knew you'd come back—Ben had said, but…"

The woman let that sentence trail away as Anna turned to see her old neighbour, Diana Mackey, walking towards her, a trio of dogs, two springer spaniels and a black Lab, trotting behind her. She carried their leads in one gloved hand, a waxed jacket buttoned up to her chin, and a fuzzy bobble hat pulled down over her ears.

"It's Diana," she said, and Anna managed the approximation of a light laugh.

"Yes, of course. I remember you, Diana." They'd been neighbours for twenty years, sharing pots of tea and slices of cake around each other's kitchen tables. Did Diana really think she would have forgotten her?

"Goodness." Diana came to stand in front of her as she

shook her head slowly. "I've been meaning to pop round and say hello, but..."

"It's awkward, I know." Anna heard how brittle she sounded.

"It's not that," Diana replied quickly. "I wouldn't care a fig about that, even if it was. I just...I just didn't know if you'd want to see me."

What could she say to that? "I always felt we were friends," Anna replied after a moment, sounding even more brittle.

"Yes, as have I," Diana replied, "but it's been a long time. And I've known Peter since I was born. He's a few years older than me, admittedly, but...we're both born and bred in Mathering. I...didn't know if that would make a difference, to you."

Did that somehow invalidate their own friendship? Anna wondered. She supposed she'd been aware of that relationship, when she had chosen not to stay in touch. "I came back to help with Peter," she told Diana. "Now that his health is starting to fail."

Diana nodded. "That's very good of you."

"Not really," Anna replied, the words wobbling all over the place. She'd been able to hold it together for her daughters, but in the face of someone she'd once counted as a friend, she felt herself starting to fall apart. "At least, it's not *helpful* of me. I'm just making everything worse. Much worse." She blinked back the tears, but there were too many and a few slipped down her cold cheeks. She dashed them away quickly, embarrassed. "Sorry..."

"Oh, you poor love." Diana's voice was warm and full of

empathy, which made Anna want to positively howl. "Why don't you come back to mine for a cup of tea? I've got a banana loaf that needs eating, as well."

"Oh…" Anna felt she should refuse, although she couldn't say why. Some part of her didn't feel she deserved this kindness, especially from a childhood friend of Peter's.

"Come on, then," Diana said, clearly not taking no for an answer. "We can go through the sheep pasture and get there all the quicker."

"All right then," Anna mumbled, still wiping away tears. "Thank you."

They didn't speak as they headed across country towards the Mackey farm; it was enough effort to round up the dogs and navigate the tufty and uneven ground of the sheep pasture. A few heavily pregnant sheep looked at them balefully as they passed, and Anna made sure Fred was securely on the lead even though she doubted he had the energy, never mind the desire, to worry a sheep.

Ten minutes later, they were at the Mackey farmhouse, a long, low, whitewashed building that seemed as if it had sprung right from the earth. The kitchen was exactly as Anna had remembered it—rambling and cluttered, warm from the Aga, with the promised banana loaf cooling on one of its round lids. It all looked so welcoming and homely that she felt as if she could cry again, and just when she'd finally got herself under control.

"There now," Diana said comfortably as she unwrapped herself from her hat, scarf, and coat, leaving her boots by the door. Her hair was liberally streaked with grey, and the years had added a few lines to her face as well as a few inches to her middle, but she looked comfortable in herself, which was more than Anna could say. Diana had lost her husband a few years ago, Anna recalled. Rachel had told her about it recently, as she hadn't kept up with any Mathering news since she'd left.

The dogs had rushed into the kitchen, sniffing for crumbs, only to flop, seemingly exhausted, in various places around the room. As Diana moved about, filling the kettle and cutting thick slices of banana bread, she stepped around them, as nimble as a ballet dancer.

"Take a seat," she told Anna, who slowly unbuttoned her coat. As grateful as she was to be here, she couldn't help but feel apprehensive about whatever conversation was coming next. She hadn't been in touch with Diana since she'd walked out of Embthwaite Farm one morning in December, having no idea where she'd go, only that she had to.

Months later, when she'd finally had the strength and wherewithal to reconnect with people, her daughters had been on the top of the list. When they'd both rebuffed her, she hadn't seen the point of trying to reach out to anyone else in Mathering. It was too painful, and her life there had clearly come to an end. It felt safer and cleaner simply to cut all ties.

Yet here she was, in Diana Mackey's kitchen, just like old times, the kettle starting to whistle as Diana pushed a plate with a slice of banana bread towards her.

"Get that inside you," she said, which made Anna smile, because that was exactly the sort of thing Diana always said, as if banana bread or tiffin or whatever traybake she'd made was some sort of restorative medicine, and maybe it was.

Diana didn't speak again until they were both settled at the table with cups of tea alongside the banana bread, the dogs settled by their feet, the Aga rumbling away.

"Well," she said, and took a sip of tea. "Isn't this a turn-up for the books."

Anna managed a tiny, wry smile. "I suppose it is."

"How did you hear about Peter?"

"Rachel phoned me."

"That was good of her."

Anna tried not to wince at the implication that she hadn't been entirely deserving of being kept in the loop. "Yes, it was," she replied dutifully, and broke off a piece of banana bread only to crumble it between her fingers. As comforting as this kitchen was, and as delicious as she knew Diana's baking to be, she didn't have any appetite.

"Well," Diana said again, and then a lengthy pause ensued that started to feel uncomfortable until Diana put her cup down and leaned forward, one hand outstretched towards Anna. "How are you, Anna love?" she asked, her face wreathed in kindly concern. "Really?"

"Oh…" Anna tried to summon some milquetoast response, only to feel her face crumple. She'd shed a few tears back by the river, but now she feared she might out and out sob. She drew a shuddering breath and willed it all back. She only partially succeeded. "Honestly, I've been better," she managed in a clogged voice.

"Of course you have," Diana murmured and patted her hand. "Of course you have."

"I knew they'd both be angry with me," Anna continued, the words coming in stilted, protracted gasps because she was that close to breaking down. "I thought I was prepared for it. But I've been here two weeks and there's been no change at all." She wiped her eyes and took a calming breath that worked only a little. "Back before Christmas, at the party at the hotel, I thought Harriet was thawing towards me, a bit. She smiled at me, anyway, but she's changed her mind since then because now she's acting like she can't stand me. As usual."

"It's complicated," Diana murmured, taking up her tea again, and Anna shot her a suddenly fierce look.

"Trust me, Diana," she said, her voice turning surprisingly sharp, "I, of all people, know just how complicated it is."

The silence that followed felt heavy with too many unspoken things. Anna didn't actually know how much Diana knew about the difficulties in her and Peter's marriage, or how much she suspected. She thought it must be something, at least, but Diana had never said and neither had Anna. She wasn't about to say now, not after all this time. She'd maintained her silence for a reason—to protect her daughters.

A sigh escaped Diana, long and sorrowful. "Peter was a difficult man to live with, I know," she said at last.

"It wasn't that," Anna replied, although heaven knew he had been difficult, extremely so, to live with. "I mean, that's not why I left."

Diana glanced at her sharply, her kindly eyes narrowing as she leaned forward. "He wasn't…" she began, and then stopped, clearly not wanting to put it into words.

"Abusive?" Anna filled in shrewdly. "No. He never was."

Not like that, anyway. She thought of how he'd batted her hand away earlier that morning. It had been the closest he'd ever come to physically hurting her. Emotionally, however…

That was a very different story.

"I didn't think he would be," Diana said, almost in apology, as she resettled herself in her seat. "I know he's a quiet man, and he's not one to show his emotions, but…"

Anna shook her head, weary now. "It wasn't anything like that," she said, and she hoped her tone did not encourage any more questions. She didn't want Diana asking what was it, then, because she wasn't about to tell her, or anyone. Not, at least, without telling her daughters first, and she hadn't told them because she'd wanted them to be able to have a relationship with their father, although how well that had worked out was debatable in the extreme. Still, underneath all the aggro and tension, she knew they both adored him, in their own ways, and longed for his returned affection. She didn't want to take that from them, especially not now, when Peter's life was coming to its close. Still, she acknowledged ruefully, it was hard to make a self-sacrificing choice and not feel—and, unfortunately, act—like a martyr.

"So, what are you going to do?" Diana asked as she poured them both more tea, even though Anna had barely drunk any of hers.

She looked at her old friend in surprise. "Do…?"

"About your girls?" Diana gave a knowing nod. "You said being here is making things worse, so let's think of a way to make things better. Those girls might be adults, but they still need a mother, and you're here to be one…aren't you?" The last bit was said gently enough, but still clearly a challenge.

"Yes, I am," Anna replied. "I want to be, anyway. But I don't think they do. And I can't force it. I know I can't."

"Girls always need their mothers," Diana replied as she sipped her tea. "And you're here, which shows you care."

"I've always cared," Anna replied quietly, just in case Diana was implying this was some sort of new development. "I know I haven't always tried as much as I should have, because it was so hard, but I've *cared*, Diana—"

"I know you have." Diana reached over to pat her hand, her smile kindly enough although Anna thought she saw confusion or maybe even doubt in her old friend's eyes. *What kind of caring mother abandons her children for twelve years?* Diana might as well have spoken aloud. "It's just that Harriet and Rachel are both angry," she continued as she withdrew her hand. "And sometimes it can feel stronger as well as safer to stay angry. Much easier than actually having to deal with all the other emotions."

"Yes, I understand that," Anna said after a moment. "But they're both adults, and they're behaving like little children in a strop." Until she said the words, she hadn't realised how much she meant them. She'd felt she hadn't had the right to think that way, and yet…maybe she did.

"Adult children often revert to acting like toddlers when they're with their parents," Diana replied bemusedly. "That must be why Ben still leaves his wet towel on the bathroom floor."

Anna smiled faintly in acknowledgement; it wasn't, she thought, remotely the same kind of thing.

"They might be acting like children," Diana continued

more seriously, "but you need to act like their mother. You may feel as if you've forfeited that right, Anna, but you haven't. You're still their mother. You raised them to adulthood—yes, you *did*—and I saw how hard you worked all those long years—cooking, cleaning, ironing their uniforms, baking them birthday cakes, all of it. You did all the hard work, the endless slog, and they can't pretend now as if you hadn't. And you shouldn't have to, either."

Anna blinked, amazed and incredibly gratified by this unexpectedly impassioned response. It was, she realised, exactly how she'd felt, but she'd never given herself permission to acknowledge it, even to herself, never mind to her own daughters. And yet Diana saying it validated it somehow, made her realise she'd been right all along. She just had to explain that to Harriet and Rachel…a thought that filled her with complete dread.

And yet…what if she could? What if she *did*?

"Thank you," she told Diana, meaning it utterly. "I think I needed to hear all that."

"I think you did, as well," Diana replied. "And your daughters do, too." She eyed her beadily. "So, the question is, Anna love, are you going to tell them?"

Anna took a deep breath and let it out slowly. Was she? Did she dare? And yet what was the alternative—tiptoeing around for another few days before she couldn't bear it any longer and slunk back to Stroud? No, she definitely did not want to do that. Confronting Harriet and Rachel would be good for them as well as her. It was something that needed to happen.

"I am going to tell them," she told Diana, managing to

inject a determined note into her voice she wasn't quite yet feeling. "It might all go horribly wrong, but at least I know I'll have tried."

"And it might not go horribly wrong, or wrong at all," Diana replied with a brisk smile. "Let yourself believe that it might actually go *right*!"

Chapter Four

DIANA'S ENCOURAGING WORDS rang in Anna's ears all the way back to Embthwaite Farm. She was going to talk to Rachel and Harriet, she told herself. Today. As soon as she got back, even. They'd all sit down and have it out, and it would lead to…

That was where her pep talk petered out. What would it lead to? Happy families once more? Reconciliation, hugs and happily-ever-after? No, probably not. Like Harriet had said, too much troubled water had flowed under that particular bridge…but it would lead to *something*, Anna told herself. And like she'd said to Diana, at least she would have tried.

Buoyed by this thought, she marched into the farmhouse, Fred trotting behind her, only to find the house feeling depressingly empty. Rachel wasn't at her desk, and Harriet wasn't in the kitchen, baking up a storm as she usually did. When Anna tiptoed upstairs and peeked in Peter's bedroom, she found, to her shock, that he wasn't there, either.

Alarm rippled through her. Had something happened? She'd only been gone for an hour or two. Quickly she typed out a text to Rachel. *I came back and everyone was gone. Is everything okay??*

A few minutes later Rachel's rather terse reply came through: *Took Dad to the GP to see the palliative nurse and get his meds. Be home by lunchtime.*

Okay, then. Anna breathed out, relieved that nothing serious had happened, but also wondering why neither Harriet nor Rachel had thought to tell her this. They seemed almost to delight in keeping her out of the loop.

Well, in the meantime, she decided, she would set the stage for a Conversation, definitely with a capital C. She tidied the breakfast dishes away and started slicing some leeks and potatoes for soup. It felt good, to be in the kitchen doing something useful. The last time she had felt useful was when Harriet had been in a complete tizz about the party, and Anna and Rachel had helped bake the cookies for it. For a short time—a very short time, admittedly—they'd all worked together. It had given Anna hope, as well as a lovely picture of the way things could be…if her daughters would allow it. For some reason, they'd quickly decided after the party that they wouldn't.

But Anna was hoping that would change today.

BY THE TIME Rachel's car pulled up in the drive, the soup was simmering, and a couple of par-baked baguettes were warming in the oven. Anna had set the table, and even gathered a few hellebores from a straggly flower bed and put them in a little blue vase—one she remembered using for flowers from before. All in all, she thought it looked pretty and welcoming, and she hoped her daughters thought so, as well.

"Hello," she called out, stepping into the hallway as they came through the front door. "How was it?"

Peter was walking slowly, flanked by both Harriet and Rachel, who each had an elbow and were helping him along. All three of them looked up as Anna spoke, looking at her as if she had sprouted three heads.

"It was fine," Rachel replied shortly. "The dosage of Dad's Martapan prescription had to be upped."

"I see," Anna replied after a second's pause. "Well, I'm glad it was sorted." They continued to shuffle into the house, heading for the stairs.

"Can you take the stairs, Dad?" Rachel asked gently. "Or do you want to rest in the kitchen for a bit first?"

"I've made lunch," Anna chimed in helpfully. "We could all sit down for a bit—"

"We bought lunch in town," Harriet told her. "Some sausage rolls from the bakery."

Anna blinked. Kept her smile. "Have you eaten them yet?" she asked. "Why don't you bring them to the kitchen, and we can add it to the rest."

"I'll go upstairs," Peter announced, and with a quick, repressive look for their mother, Harriet and Rachel started to help him upstairs.

Well, that was fine, Anna told herself. She hadn't envisioned including Peter in their little chat, anyway. She decided to keep being helpful and she made him some lunch to bring up, slicing the baguette thinly enough for him to manage, and making sure the soup wasn't too hot. She'd just finished putting it all on the tray when Harriet came into the kitchen, taking in all of Anna's work.

"This wasn't necessary," she said in the same flat voice as before.

"Well, I figured you'd all be hungry," Anna replied lightly. "And I feel like I need to earn my keep around here. I haven't been nearly as helpful as I hoped to be."

"Because this is all about you," Harriet retorted, which Anna thought was a rather unjust remark. She'd been tiptoeing around for weeks, and suddenly making lunch was all about her?

"No, it isn't all about me, Harriet," she replied evenly, "but you know what? It isn't all about *you*, either."

Harriet gasped as if Anna had slapped her. Anna felt as if she had; she hadn't spoken to her daughter this way since she'd returned. Maybe not since she'd been a small child in need of disciplining. "Has that occurred to you?" she continued in the same, level voice when Harriet seemed too outraged to respond. "You're so fixated on your hurt that you can't see anyone else's—"

Harriet made a scoffing sound. "Oh, am I supposed to believe you're hurt?" she replied, and Anna let out a rather hard laugh.

"And is that so hard to believe?" she countered, her voice rising. "You and Rachel have made me feel like a positive *pariah* since I've come back. I know there's water under the bridge as you've said, but I came back to try to deal with it, and all I've been getting is a lot of passive-aggressive attitude and hostility."

"Well, you know where the door is," Harriet snapped, colour flaring in her cheeks.

Their friendly little chat, Anna acknowledged wretchedly, was not going as she'd hoped. She wasn't acting like a mother; she was behaving like a wounded harpy, which was basically how she felt.

Briefly she closed her eyes while Harriet gave a snort as if to say *drama queen.*

"Harriet, I don't want to leave," Anna said as she opened her eyes. "I want to stay here and work things out with you. I want to be helpful with your father, and I want to make amends. I know you're hurt, as well as angry. I know my leaving all those years ago is still incomprehensible to you. But does staying angry help either of us in the end? I want us to have a relationship—"

"Really?" Harriet drawled, although her voice was shaking. "Because you haven't seemed to have wanted much of a relationship for the last thirteen years."

"You didn't, either," Anna reminded her quietly. "I did try—"

"A couple of voicemails isn't exactly making much of an effort."

"What would you have liked me to do?" Anna challenged. "Would you have accepted any peace offering? Would you have liked me to show up at your front door like I did two weeks ago? Because I have a feeling I would have received the same sort of reception—"

"*Don't make this my fault!*" The words came out in an ear-splitting shriek, startling them both. Harriet pointed a shaking finger at her. "This is not about me doing the wrong thing," she continued. "I *stayed.* I stayed and took care of *your* husband because you couldn't cut it. You got bored or annoyed or whatever, and you just left without a care in the world—"

"That's not true." Anna's voice caught jaggedly. She understood why Harriet had framed the narrative that way, but it was so far from what had really happened it was laughable…except it utterly wasn't. There was nothing funny about this awful situation at all.

"Well, that's how it looked from here," Harriet tossed back, turning away. "And it still does."

She started to walk out of the kitchen and Anna's fists clenched. "Harriet Emily Mowbray," she snapped out, "do not turn your back on me in the middle of this conversation!"

Slowly Harriet turned around, a stunned look on her face. "*Excuse* me?"

Anna's lips twitched in the most unlikely smile. For the first time in over a decade, she'd sounded like a mother. It had, she realised, felt good. "You heard me," she told her daughter. "It's rude to walk out on someone, as you very well know. *And* I've made you lunch, and it would be both spiteful and stupid to refuse to eat it simply because you're annoyed with me. You're not a child, Harriet, so don't behave like one."

Harriet's mouth opened and closed like a fish as her eyes bulged. Anna moved to the Rayburn and started ladling out soup. While Harriet mutely watched, still gaping, she put a bowl on the table and nodded to it. "Don't let it get cold."

Anna more than half expected her daughter to storm out of the kitchen, but amazingly, Harriet didn't. She walked to the table and pulled out a chair, then sat down. She picked up a spoon, then laid it down again. Anna met her sullen gaze with a cool stare of her own.

"Thank you," Harriet said, not particularly graciously, but still.

Quietly Anna breathed out. "You're welcome," she replied.

Anna was ladling out a second bowl of soup just as Rachel came into the room. She stopped at the door, glancing between the two of them. "What's going on here?" she asked, and Anna realised the tension in the room was palpable, like an electrical storm, a current in the air, sparking and buzzing.

"Mum's just going off on one," Harriet replied, but she sounded so much like a sulky teenager that, improbably, Rachel smiled.

"*Is* she?" she asked with a curious glance for Anna.

"Soup," Anna replied, and handed her a bowl.

Soon they were all three of them sat down at the table, spooning soup into their mouths, the silence so thick it felt like something to saw through. Finally, after several mouthfuls, Anna decided to try.

"I was telling Harriet that I came back to help with your father," she stated, keeping her tone briskly practical. "But also to make amends. I know I can't make up for being mostly absent for the last—"

"*Mostly?*" Harriet cut across her, her tone witheringly incredulous.

"Harriet," Rachel murmured.

"All right, completely," Anna replied, determined to remain unfazed. "Completely absent for the last thirteen years.

I *was*. But I'm here now and having the pair of you treat me like some unwanted stranger barging into your lives is…unhelpful, for all of us." She paused to take a breath, and neither of them so much as twitched an eyebrow. "That might be what you feel I am," she continued, "but this was my home once. I lived here for twenty years, I made all the meals, I mothered you until adulthood…" Anna trailed off at the stony looks on both their faces. Somehow, when it came out of her mouth, it didn't sound the way it had coming out of Diana's. She sounded, Anna realised, as if she were whinging.

"So, what do you want?" Harriet asked dryly. "An award? 'Mother-of-the-Year Until You Turn Eighteen'. Except, you weren't even *that*."

"Harriet," Rachel said again. "Come on."

Anna blinked, absorbing the snark as well as the pain behind it. "Like I said, Harriet," she said quietly. "You weren't the only one who was hurt."

"But you're my *mother*," Harriet burst out. "It's different."

"Is it?" Anna replied with a small, sad smile. It was supposed to be—she got that. Mothers weren't allowed to get hurt, or tired, or have any feelings at all. They had to be patron saints of smiling nobility—always cheerful, always loving, never having any needs or wants at all. It wasn't expressly said, of course, by anyone, but it was felt and shown every single day, all around the world.

Anna had bought into it herself, for years. She still did, on some level, which was why she felt so wretchedly guilty. And yet at the same time, she longed to be heard by her daughters. Accepted and understood, even as they stubbornly refused so much as to attempt either.

"Maybe it isn't different, Hats," Rachel said quietly. "We haven't exactly been making her welcome these last few weeks." She gave Anna an abashed look. "I *mean* to, but then…I don't." She shook her head, grimacing. "A lot of old feelings come rushing back, I suppose."

"I understand that," Anna replied. "I'm the same."

"What old feelings of yours come rushing back, then?" Harriet asked, her voice caught between determined sulk and curiosity.

"Oh, I don't know." Anna wasn't about to level with them how she'd felt in this house—despairing, desperate, driven to a wild sorrow that had felt like grief, although she had never been sure what she'd been mourning. "Not good ones, anyway."

"*Why* were you so unhappy, Mum?" Rachel asked suddenly. She leaned forward, her bowl of soup forgotten. "I have memories…memories I suppressed or forgot or whatever, and they came back when I returned here a couple of months ago. Memories of you crying on the stairs or staring into space like you'd lost your best friend. I remembered you throwing a pan of Yorkshire pudding onto the table, right here." She pointed to a faded scorch mark on the centre of the table while Anna felt herself flush.

"I was unhappy sometimes," she whispered, staring down at the table because she couldn't bear the looks of confused accusation on her daughters' faces. No mother should be that unhappy, she supposed, or at least no mother should let it show as much as she had. She couldn't even remember throwing a hot pan onto the table, but she didn't doubt Rachel's story.

"Was it because of Dad?" Rachel asked.

Now they were getting into dangerous, murky waters. "In part," Anna replied carefully. Her throat felt tight and there was a stinging behind her lids that she was determined to ignore. "But in part it was just me, I think. I had a naïve view of what life on this farm would look like."

"So, you did get bored," Harriet filled in, sounding grimly exultant. Rachel threw her a quelling look.

"Harriet…"

"I wasn't *bored*, Harriet," Anna replied, and now there was a steel in her voice that hadn't been there before. "I didn't get tired of life here or want something new and different and *fun*." Her voice was rising, her hand, lying flat on the table, curling into a fist of its own accord. Emotions were bubbling up, memories threatening to overwhelm her, no matter how hard she tried to suppress them. "If you want to know why I left, it was because—because I didn't think I could stay here and survive. *Live.* If that sounds melodramatic, so be it, but that, back then, was how I felt with every fibre of my being." Her voice choked on a sob, and she swallowed it down. Through her blurred vision, she saw Rachel and Harriet staring at her, stupefied, and despite the wild grief coursing through her, she almost wanted to laugh.

"I meant to wait until you were at university," she continued, gulping again. "That was my plan. But, in the end, for my own…my own safety, I couldn't."

"Your own *safety*?" Harriet repeated after a moment, trying to sound incredulous but coming across as merely uncertain. "What are you saying…that Dad *abused* you?"

Anna let out a shuddery sigh. Was domestic violence the only legitimate reason for a mother to abandon her children? "He never harmed me physically," she told them both. "And if he had, I wouldn't have left you with him. I would have taken you both with *me*."

"But you didn't," Harriet replied flatly. "You didn't even suggest it."

Anna shook her head slowly. "Harriet, please believe me when I tell you, if that had been possible, I would have done it."

"What is *that* supposed to mean?" Harriet burst out.

"Hats, be reasonable," Rachel protested. She was looking at Anna with a thoughtful expression on her face. "You were in the middle of your A levels—"

"Which I failed." Harriet threw Anna an accusing look. "Did you even know that?"

"No," Anna replied quietly. Yet another *mea culpa* moment. Was that why Harriet had stayed all these years? "I didn't. I'm sorry."

Harriet just shook her head. "You're not actually telling us anything, you know," she told her, her voice choking a little, reminding Anna that no matter how angry Harriet seemed, underneath all that fury there was only a little girl's hurt. "Why you left, or even what you did. Did you just go live in a flat somewhere, or a house? Did you go on holiday?" Her voice rang out. "I don't know anything about your life from then till now. Not one thing."

"Harriet, that's on you, at least a little bit," Rachel said gently. "Mum did reach out—"

"*Once—*"

"More than once," Rachel protested. She glanced at Anna. "Didn't you?"

Anna knew what Harriet was referring to—the first time she'd telephoned, a few months after she'd left, desperate to talk to her. Harriet had hung up on her, almost immediately. Anna had been devastated. She'd tried again a few days later, and then a few weeks after that, and Harriet hadn't answered either. Then not for a long while after that, because it had simply been too painful. But somehow, that wasn't a good enough reason. Anna accepted that; she felt it.

"I should have," she told Harriet. "I know I should have."

"Where did you even go," Harriet demanded, "after you left? Were you just laughing it up somewhere—"

Briefly Anna closed her eyes. Opened them. Maybe now it was finally time for some truth. Not all of it, just a little. Enough. "No, Harriet," she said quietly. "I wasn't laughing it up. The truth is, right after I left here…I was…" Deep breath. "I was sectioned," she confessed flatly. The words fell into the stillness, like pebbles thrown into a pond, disappearing under the surface as the water rippled out. She drew another shuddery breath and then made herself continue. "After I left here, I spent three months in a psychiatric facility."

Chapter Five

THE LOOKS ON *their faces…*

A bubble of laughter rose in Anna's throat at a most inconvenient time. And it wasn't genuine laughter, anyway; it was closer to hysteria. She'd just told her daughters she'd been *sectioned.* It was something she didn't like admitting to anyone, chose never to talk about, never even to remember. And yet here she'd just said it, like some sort of trump card. *Beat that.* And that wasn't how she actually felt about it at all.

"What…" Harriet began, looking flummoxed. She shook her head slowly. "What…" she said again, no more than a breath of sound, and then stopped.

"I think this might call for a cup of tea," Rachel said firmly and rose to fill the kettle. Anna glanced down at the table. She had a feeling making tea was a stalling tactic more than a medicinal necessity at this point. She'd really shocked them. She'd shocked *herself,* because she hadn't planned on admitting that painful episode in her life. She really did try not even to think of it, because remembering hurt too much.

She knew there was meant to be no shame around mental health issues, and she was *glad* of that, but…it didn't make it much easier to admit to your children that you'd been so low, so in danger of hurting yourself, that you'd needed to be institutionalised.

No one spoke as Rachel made the tea, the only sound the whistling of the kettle on top of the Rayburn and the clatter of cups. Harriet was looking dazed, her expression vacant as she stared into space. Anna took a deep breath, let it out slowly. She could not think of a single thing to say, or at least that she *wanted* to say, but maybe silence was better. They all needed to absorb the emotional grenade she'd just lobbed into the middle of the kitchen; it still felt as if the smoke was clearing, the rubble all around them.

"Here we are." Rather forcefully, Rachel set a tea tray onto the table then gave them both a firm yet brittle smile as she set about pouring. Harriet still hadn't spoken, hadn't really come to. Oh, dear. This really had been a bombshell.

"Thank you, Rachel," Anna murmured as she handed them all cups before sitting down with her own.

"Well." Rachel shook her head slowly. "I don't really know what to say. Do you… Do you want to talk about it, Mum?"

"It's not a time of my life that I enjoy looking back on," Anna answered carefully, "but I understand that you both will have questions, and I want to be honest with you." She paused to take a sip of tea and steady herself. Already this felt far too painful, like picking at barely healed scabs, revealing the raw and wounded flesh underneath. "Perhaps I should have been honest about it before," she continued.

"Why weren't you?" The words burst out of Harriet like lava from a volcano, startling everyone, Harriet included. She blinked and sat back before blindly reaching for her tea.

"I…don't know exactly," Anna replied after a moment. "I suppose I…I felt ashamed. That I hadn't been able to cope."

"There's no shame in having mental health issues," Rachel protested, her voice gentling. "Especially these days. Maybe years and years ago, it was—"

"I know that," Anna cut across her. "Intellectually. Emotionally is another matter." She smiled sadly. "The difference between head and heart knowledge, I suppose."

They all lapsed into a silence that didn't feel uncomfortable, exactly, but decidedly morose. Anna half-wished she hadn't said anything. Why *had* she mentioned it? She'd kept it quiet for twelve years. Why talk about it now? The answer, of course, was because she'd been so nettled by Harriet's assumptions that she'd been swanning around, having a grand old time. Responding in a fit of pique, Anna acknowledged with a sigh, was not the best way to conduct these matters.

"Still," Harriet finally said, her hands wrapped around her cup as she stared straight ahead. "If you'd explained it before…maybe we would have been more understanding. Accepting."

Now was not the time to remind Harriet that she'd hung up on her when she'd called to do just that. "I suppose I could have written a letter," Anna conceded after a moment. "I think I was afraid it would feel like an excuse…some sort of get-out-of-jail-free card for having left. I know what I did hurt you both, and you especially, Harriet." She gazed at them both, but only Rachel met her eyes, and then only briefly. "I've always been aware of that."

More silence. The air felt thick and heavy, as if it was weighted down with sadness.

"I knew you were unhappy," Rachel finally said quietly. "I guess I just didn't realise how unhappy."

There was nothing, really, that Anna could say to that.

The sound of a chair scraping across the floor upstairs had Rachel rising from her seat. "I should check on Dad," she said. "I haven't even taken him his lunch—it's probably cold by now."

"I'll heat it up," Anna replied quickly. "I can bring it up to you, if you like."

Rachel hesitated and then gave a little nod. "Thank you," she said and left the kitchen. It felt, in a very small way, like progress.

Harriet remained silent as Anna set about reheating the soup. She'd just put it back on the tray when Harriet said abruptly, "I need time to process this. I feel like I can't be angry with you anymore, but I still am. Sort of."

"Okay," Anna answered, keeping her voice neutral. She glanced at her daughter, who was frowning, a deep furrow between her dark brows. She looked so much like Peter in one of his scowls that it *almost* made her smile. She understood Harriet being angry with her, and yet…

"Harriet…" she began hesitantly. "At the Christmas party, at the hotel, you didn't seem so angry. You smiled at me, a few times. It made me wonder if…if maybe you weren't as angry as I'd thought you were."

Harriet let out a long sigh as her gaze flitted towards Anna and then away again. "I didn't want to be angry, I suppose," she admitted. "And at the party, things with

Quinn felt so hopeful—"

"They're still hopeful, aren't they?" Anna asked, a note of anxiety creeping into her voice. Harriet had seemed so loved up, but she hadn't wanted to press about the new relationship, or really, about anything.

"Yes. They're good. Really good." Harriet glanced down at her tea, tracing the rim of her cup with one finger. "But you can't just turn feelings off like a tap," she continued slowly. "And as much as I want to let go of the anger—well, part of me does—I can't." She glanced at her, a miserable look on her face. "And the truth is, having you here…it stirs everything up, in me. Every time I come into the kitchen and see you've, I don't know, washed a dish or just *been* here…I feel angry." She held up a hand to stop Anna from speaking, although in truth she wasn't sure what she would say. "I know that sounds awful. It *is* awful, and I'm sorry. I don't want to feel that way, I'm trying not to…" She trailed off, shaking her head. "It's just hard."

And it was made harder by her being here, Anna realised. She *had* been right; she was making things more difficult, even when she was trying to be as unassuming and innocuous as possible. She was still *here.* But, Anna knew, she still didn't want to just leave, slink back to Stroud as a failure of a mother…

So, what was the solution?

"You need some space," she stated slowly, and Harriet gave her a suspicious look.

"Well…I guess?" she answered cautiously. "But I don't want you to have to go all the way back home. That's not…" She blew out a breath. "I know that wouldn't actually be helpful for anyone. I know we need to work through this, if we want to have any semblance of a mother-daughter relationship." She managed a wry smile that made Anna's heart ache. "I do know that, even if it doesn't seem like I do." She grimaced. "Even if I don't act like I do."

"I understand, Harriet," Anna said softly, grateful for her daughter's honesty. "Really, I do."

They were both silent, and then Anna hefted the tray. "I'd better bring this upstairs before the soup gets cold a second time."

Harriet gave a small smile. "Okay. Thanks."

Anna's mind was whirling as she headed upstairs with the tray, without being able to settle on any specific thought or idea. She just…*felt.* It was a messy, complicated tangle of emotions, but in there somewhere was a seedling of hope, just like the snapdragon seedling she'd planted this morning, tiny and miraculous, pushing determinedly upwards, seeking the light.

She tapped on Peter's bedroom door and Rachel came to it quickly, giving her a brief smile of thanks before murmuring that she'd be down soon. Accepting it as the dismissal it undoubtedly was—and not being mad about it—Anna headed back downstairs.

Harriet was tidying up their lunch dishes, and Anna went to help her without either of them speaking, simply working in harmony, which was certainly better than it had been. And still Anna was thinking, trying to figure out a way forward.

Harriet needed space. And maybe Rachel too, and maybe even Anna herself. She would, she realised, appreciate not feeling like she had to tiptoe around everyone, apologising for her presence, her very existence.

Her thoughts continued to buzz around in her brain as they finished tidying up and then Harriet excused herself to go meet Quinn at the hotel. Rachel had ensconced herself in her office again and so Anna was left on her own, kicking around her old home like a stranger. It was, even after two weeks of it, an odd feeling. And not a particularly nice odd feeling. Yes, she mused, she really would like her own space.

IT TOOK ANNA three more days before she settled on a solution, and one that came entirely unexpectedly. She, Rachel, and Harriet had managed to come to a sort of silent accommodation, something slightly better than a truce, although perhaps not by that much.

Anna didn't help directly with Peter, but she was able to be helpful with laundry and housework, making meals and generally being useful. Her daughters still didn't talk much to her beyond the pleasantries and practicalities, and no one prodded the hornets' nest Anna had unleashed when she'd mentioned being sectioned. No one, herself included, seemed to want to discuss that again, or at least not anytime soon.

Anna spent a lot of time out in the greenhouse or garden, planting up seedlings or tidying the raggedy winter flower beds, remembering when this garden had been not just her pride and joy, but her much-needed sanctuary. She hadn't even known gardening was a *thing* until she'd married Peter and moved to Embthwaite Farm, with its veg patch and orchard, and then she'd found a joy and a comfort in the sowing and growing.

Her thumb had turned greener with the years, so that when she'd moved to Stroud after being released from hospital, feeling as if she had been in some sort of mental and physical hibernation, now blinking and reeling in the light, and still so very raw and wounded, she'd found work in a garden centre, and stayed there for the next twelve years. Her boss, a woman in her thirties called Maisy, had been very understanding of her taking an unspecified amount of time off to come up here.

And yet in the midst of generally trying to keep busy, she'd felt restless. She didn't think any of them were going to make any progress if they kept to this uneasy status quo. Then, when she ventured into Mathering one morning, having avoided the town since her arrival, she paused in front of a flyer tacked onto the noticeboard outside the post office. *Two-bedroom furnished terraced cottage for rent, available immediately, short- or long-term lets.* The photo was of the front of a lovely little cottage on one of Mathering's side streets, and the weekly rate was certainly reasonable. What if she took it?

It was a novel thought, and one that she needed to let sink in for a bit. Would Harriet or Rachel be offended if she left—or relieved? It was so hard to know what might set them off, what they would take to heart. And yet…if she did move out, it would give them—and her—the space they all needed, without her being very far away. She could still come over to help with things, still be available…

Slowly Anna walked down the street, not really paying attention to where she was going. Since her return, she hadn't wanted to come into Mathering in case people recognised her, but somewhat to her surprise, she felt fairly anonymous as she wandered its few narrow streets. Maybe even in places like Mathering, in the deepest part of North Yorkshire, people moved on, in and out. Life kept going, rolling on without taking any notice of those who had left.

"Anna Mowbray, as I live and breathe!"

Or maybe not.

The voice, strident and booming, was followed by a positive cackle of laughter that had the hairs rising up on the back of Anna's neck. She blinked at the wizened woman in front of her, hands planted on bony hips, her white hair crimpled in a tight perm as she gave Anna a decidedly beady stare.

"Agatha…" Anna replied faintly. She recalled the woman who had run one of Mathering's two tea rooms from her front parlour and seemed to know everyone's business without even trying; it was as if she absorbed the news, inhaled it like oxygen and then breathed it out again.

"I wondered if you'd come back," Agatha stated matter-of-factly, and Anna couldn't keep from wincing. This kind of scenario was exactly the reason she hadn't ventured into Mathering until now. What had emboldened her to finally brave it? Clearly it had been foolhardy.

"Well, I did," she replied, trying to sound cheerful. "Needs must."

Agatha clucked her tongue. "You look like you need a cup of tea and a cream bun," she pronounced, like she was giving out a prescription. "Come with me."

"Oh, I—"

But Agatha had already turned and started walking down the street, so Anna felt as if she had no choice but to follow her, and truth be told, she *would* like a cup of tea and a cream bun, if not the interrogation that inevitably would come along with it.

Five minutes later, she was settled as the only customer in Agatha's tea room, which was exactly as she remembered—patterned carpet, patterned curtains, patterned drapes, and all different patterns. Somehow, in a crazy way, it worked. And Agatha's baking, she recalled, was absolutely wonderful.

"Make yourself comfortable," Agatha called as she bustled back to the kitchen. "I'll put the fire on."

The fire was a three-bar electric fire of the kind Anna remembered from her childhood. She recalled there had been something oddly comforting about its orange glow, but it had produced very little warmth. Still, she appreciated the effort, along with the friendliness. She'd been lonely since coming back to Embthwaite Farm, she realised. She didn't have dozens of friends back in Stroud, and she tended to be quite a reserved person anyway, but she'd made a few and she missed the chats at the garden centre, the occasional night out for a glass of wine.

"So." Agatha came back into the room and plonked a tray onto Anna's table. "Let that steep for a bit," she said, nodding towards the teapot-for-one. "I'll put the fire on." She flicked a switch by the hearth and with a buzzing sound, the electric fire started to turn a pale orange. Anna smiled.

"Thank you, Agatha," she said. "This is lovely."

"You used to come here quite a bit, as I recall, with your wee one."

"Harriet," Anna confirmed, feeling a pang of sorrow at the memory. "It was a treat after dentist appointments, although I don't know if a cream bun was the right choice, considering she usually got a lecture from the dentist about avoiding sweets." A sigh escaped her, the sound more accepting than melancholy. Those days felt like a very a long time ago.

"She was such an affectionate thing, your Harriet," Agatha continued as she moved around the room, tweaking a napkin or straightening a spoon on the already laid tables, as if she was expecting a dozen customers to stampede the doors. "Thought the world of you, it seemed to me. Hanging on your every word."

For a second, Anna could picture it perfectly—Harriet with her dark button eyes and head of glossy black curls, grinning up at her with a whorl of whipped cream on her chin. Anna laughing, touching her finger to the cream before Harriet grabbed her finger and with eyes sparkling with mischief, licked it off. Anna's laugh, as clear as a bell, as she shook her head, too amused actually to scold her.

Rachel would have never shared a moment like that, Anna reflected. She'd been so serious as a child, so anxious to always get it right, to please her father. Harriet had been the mummy's girl, and Anna had adored her for it. Her lonely, battered soul had craved the connection, the comfort.

Of course, as Harriet had grown older, that connection had lessened, or at least changed. In secondary school,

Harriet had made a boisterous gang of friends who often came to the house, sprawled in the living room or around the kitchen table with crisps and fizzy drinks while Anna had retreated upstairs. By that time, her depression had started in earnest, a black cloud of dark thoughts that followed her wherever she went. It hadn't helped that she'd felt, in some way, as if she'd lost Harriet; even then she'd known it wasn't really a fair or healthy way to think. Being a mother was, at its essence, a continual process of letting go. Children needed to find their way in the world, away from their parents.

But maybe not quite as far away as Harriet had ended up going.

"Well," Anna told Agatha, with a small, bittersweet smile. "She did, once."

Agatha cocked her head. "That doesn't change," she said quietly. "Even if it looks like it does. Inside." She pressed two bony fingers to her heart. "They don't change."

Anna stared at her, hope warring with a deep-seated scepticism. Was *that* why Harriet was holding on to her anger? The other side of love, as it were?

"Now," Agatha stated briskly, all traces of sentiment gone, "eat your cream bun!"

Chapter Six

IT TURNED OUT to be remarkably, ridiculously easy to rent a house. After her tea at Agatha's—the cream bun was just as delicious as she'd hoped—Anna decided, rather recklessly and on the spur of the moment, to call the number that had been on the flyer outside the post office.

She wasn't even sure what she was going to say; she just felt the need to do something. Talking to Agatha, recalling how she and Harriet had tea in the cosy little tea room, had stirred up far too many memories. Good memories, ones she'd repressed because she hadn't felt she deserved to remember them, somehow. To recall the happy times she'd once had with her daughters.

It made Anna wonder if she was the one who had subconsciously negated everything she'd ever done in light of her abandonment. No, she decided, her daughters had done that, too. But she'd let them. She'd believed they were right, and truth be told, she still wasn't sure that they were wrong.

But those memories were in the past, and she wanted to think about a future. A future for herself, as well as for Harriet and Rachel…a future in which they could all be together, which, she was coming to conclude, necessarily involved some kind of *space*. Hence, the house.

A cheerful but slightly hassled-sounding young woman answered the mobile number Anna dialled after a couple of rings, and Anna haltingly explained her interest.

"The rental?" the woman exclaimed distractedly. "Oh, yes, it's free. Do you want to come and have a look round? I'm home now and the baby's not too grumpy so now is as good a time as any, if you're nearby."

"All right," Anna replied, startled by the seeming simplicity of the thing. The woman, Jane, gave her directions while a baby began to grizzle in the background, and it turned out the rental house was only two streets away from Agatha's, on a quaint, narrow little street of similar houses, all with doors painted in different colours, like a rainbow. The door of the rental was lavender, and the house next door, where Jane lived, was a deep cobalt blue.

As Anna knocked, she could hear wailing and surmised the baby in question had decided to be well and truly grumpy, after all.

"Coming…coming!" a woman called breathlessly, and then she flung open the door, blowing a strand of strawberry-blonde hair out of her freckled face, a large, chubby baby balanced on one hip. The baby's face was screwed up and red from crying, but as he (or she? Anna wasn't sure) caught sight of her, a lively interest came over the chubby, dimpled face and then the baby let out a squeal of what sounded like delight before starting to gummily gnaw one fist.

"Oh, he likes you," the woman, who had to be Jane, exclaimed in approval. "He doesn't take to everyone. He particularly doesn't like my mother-in-law, which, I have to say, is *very* unfortunate."

"I think that's a fairly standard reaction to mothers-in-law," Anna replied with a smile, and Jane let out a positive hoot of laughter.

"Oh, I'm going to *like* you," she exclaimed. "Do you like gin?"

Anna let out a surprised laugh. "Definitely."

"Excellent." Jane let out another hoot. "This is Henry." She hoisted the baby a little higher on her hip. "He's six months old and he's teething terribly. Shall I show you next door?"

"Yes, please." Anna smiled, liking the innate and easy friendliness of this woman. She felt as if they were friends already, and it certainly, she acknowledged ruefully, made for a change.

"I'll just get the key," Jane said and ducked down the hallway, returning within seconds with a large brass key that looked like something out of a costume drama or a murder mystery. "Here we are," she said cheerfully and headed out her neat front garden to the one next door which looked, Anna noticed, a bit straggly and woebegone.

"Dad's not much of a gardener," Jane told her as she unlocked the door, trying to balance Henry as she did so, while the baby lurched to the side like a listing ship.

"Do you want me to unlock the door?" Anna asked. "Or I could hold Henry, if you'd rather?" Belatedly she wondered if that was a bit forward, asking to manhandle another mother's child.

"Oh, *would* you?" Jane asked gratefully, thrusting the baby towards her so quickly that Anna practically had to lunge forward to grab him. It had been a long time since she'd held a baby, and for a second, she grappled with his chubby, flailing limbs, wincing as he smacked her in the face before patting her cheeks with both hands in a more experimental manner.

"I've been holding him all day," Jane explained with a grateful sigh as she unlocked the door, "and he's so heavy, the monster. A few minutes without him in my arms is *heaven.*" She glanced back approvingly as Anna adjusted Henry onto her hip and he continued to pat both her cheeks, making breathy noises as he did so. "He obviously likes you. Do you have children?"

Anna swallowed, discomfited by what was clearly meant to be an innocuous question. "Yes, two daughters. They live locally, actually, which is why I'm interested in renting here in Mathering."

"Oh, do they?" Jane asked in interest. "I wonder if I know them." She pushed open the door and ushered Anna into a narrow hallway painted in dove grey. "What are their names? Not that I've met many people yet. I've only been living here for nine months, and it's been all baby, baby, baby for most of that time." She rolled her eyes, making Anna smile. She remembered that *baby, baby, baby* stage all too well.

"They're Harriet and Rachel Mowbray," she told her as she stepped into the hallway. "Rachel just moved here from London in September, and Harriet's lived here all along, but she's started a bakery business recently." She stopped abruptly, not really wanting to go into her daughters' complicated lives—or really, her complicated presence in them—any more than that.

"Sounds lush," Jane replied easily. She flicked on the lights before glancing at Anna in query. "Do you want me to take him back so you can have a proper look round?"

Anna sensed that the young woman would happily have her keep holding the baby, and so she smiled as she gave Henry a little jiggle, which elicited another delighted squeal as well as a rather firm pat of both her cheeks. "I don't mind holding him a bit longer," she told her. "If he's happy. I haven't held a baby in a long time. I forgot how lovely it was." And it was lovely, this warm armful of wriggling and curious humanity.

"Lovely until you feel like your arms are going to fall off and your shirt is covered in dribbled milk, and let's be real, sick," Jane returned with a laugh. "But please, by all means, go ahead. He's gorgeous, I'll be the first to say so, but you know what? The days can feel long."

Anna remembered all too well just how long the days had felt. When she'd had Harriet, Rachel had only been fifteen months old. Those first few years had passed in a dreary haze of exhaustion, a sleep-deprived trudge through the hours. She'd thought there was something wrong with her, for dreading each day the way she had, but maybe all new mothers felt that way, to one extent or another. It was *hard.*

"Now, the kitchen is here in the back," Jane said as she led Anna down the narrow hallway to an open space in the back. "It's been completely renovated, as you can see."

"Oh, it's gorgeous," Anna exclaimed in surprised delight. The space was far better—and bigger—than she'd been anticipating from the exterior. The original, poky rooms had been knocked together, with a massive, vaulted skylight put in to let in loads of light. French doors opened to the postage-stamp-sized garden, which was as bedraggled as the front.

"Dad thought he'd wait until spring to get the garden in order," Jane explained. "Although, let's be honest, he hasn't much of a green thumb."

"So, your dad did this place up?" Anna asked as she wandered around the kitchen. It had all new appliances, including a cheerful, cream-coloured cooker and a built-in fridge. A tiny utility room, more of a cupboard really, housed the washer and dryer. On the other side of the kitchen, there was a table for two as well as a wood burner, flanked by a pair of squashy leather armchairs.

"Yes, he bought it when Eric—that's my husband—and I moved here. He's just retired, and he wanted a project."

"But he didn't want to live here himself?" Anna asked in surprise.

"He thought about it," Jane conceded, "but he decided he needed a little more space. And we probably did, too, to be fair. He can be a bit protective, my dad, and Eric and I have only been married eighteen months. We're still finding our feet, and I think we both appreciate having Dad nearby, but not *too* close. He bought a barn conversion just outside Mathering. It's nice and big, and it's got a lovely garden for Henry, when he starts to toddle."

"Makes sense," Anna murmured. She was intrigued by this man who had upended his whole life to follow his daughter yet had the sense to stay that little bit away…kind of like she was.

"Do you want to see the rest?" she asked, and Anna nodded with firm decision.

"Yes, please."

They walked through the rest of the cottage—a small sitting room facing the front, with a two-seater sofa, coffee table, TV, and armchair by the small open fireplace with a prettily painted Victorian tiled surround. Upstairs there were two bedrooms, one clearly the master, with a built-in wardrobe, the other with two twin beds. Both were tastefully decorated in a palette of blues and greys, and the bathroom between them had a deep, claw-foot tub as well as a separate, stand-in shower and a pedestal sink. Everything was top-notch, elegant and understated, and exactly Anna's sort of style. She couldn't believe the place hadn't been rented before, and she already knew she wanted to take it.

"So have you had much interest in this place?" she asked Jane as they headed back downstairs.

"No, not a bit," the younger woman replied with a laugh. "Dad's sceptical about putting it on Airbnb, and in any case, he only put it on the market a couple of days ago. Where did you happen to see it, by the way?"

"A flyer outside the post office."

Jane nodded. "Yes, he put up a poster there, and another one by the village hall. I'm not sure how many takers he thought he was going to get just from those, but I'm glad you're interested. That is…" She glanced at her with a flicker of apprehension. "Are you?"

"Yes," Anna said firmly. "I am." Henry chose that moment to decide he wanted his mother back, and he suddenly lunged from Anna's arms towards Jane, about to do a nosedive right onto the floor until his mother neatly scooped him up, blowing a raspberry on his tummy before she settled him on her hip.

"Sorry," Anna said a bit breathlessly. Her heart was racing from how close she'd come to dropping him right on the floor, and she wondered if Jane would be annoyed.

"Oh, he does that all the time," Jane replied breezily. "Eric calls it his rugby tackle move. Anyway. Shall we head back to mine? We can have a cuppa and sort out all the details."

The prospect filled Anna with a rush of gladness, as well as relief. She'd become so used to bracing herself for being an irritation, for always apologising, bowing and cringing. It was nice to have a normal conversation. To feel completely accepted, even by a stranger. "That sounds wonderful," she told Jane, a thrum of sincerity in her voice that embarrassed her, but Jane just grinned and locked up.

Jane's house was identical to the rental in layout, but utterly different in every other way. It was a happy clutter of colourful dishes and curtains—a patchwork blanket in a rainbow of colours thrown over a chair, wildly striped curtains fluttering at the windows. And everywhere Anna looked was the paraphernalia of babyhood—high chair, nursing pillow, changing table, bouncy seat, burp cloths and plenty of toys.

"Sorry," Jane said, not sounding remotely abashed by the mess as she led her back to the kitchen. "I'd like to tell you the house is a mess because I have a six-month-old baby, but the truth is, I've never been the neatest person. Not like Dad."

The way Jane talked about her father, Anna reflected, suggested a close-knit relationship, and one without anyone else involved. What about her mum? Jane hadn't mentioned her once, but Anna didn't feel she could ask—not yet anyway—even though she was curious.

"So, you really think you want to rent the house?" Jane asked directly as she plonked Henry into his high chair and handed him a teething rusk, which he promptly hurled onto the floor with gleeful abandon. Jane glanced at Anna in inquiry as she went to switch on a bright red electric kettle.

"I'd love to, but I should let you know that I don't know how long I'll be here," Anna replied, feeling compelled to be honest. "I actually live down in Gloucestershire, but I'm in Mathering to help my daughters out for a bit."

"Oh?" Jane's tone was friendly, her eyes bright with curiosity, but she was too polite to press. Still, Anna felt she had to explain, at least a little. Henry, meanwhile, had twigged that his rusk was gone, and let out an ear-splitting shriek of despair. Without missing a beat, Jane took the rusk from the floor, dusted it off, and then broke it into pieces and handed them one by one to Henry, who stuffed each piece gleefully into his mouth.

"My ex-husband lives just outside Mathering," Anna explained hesitantly as Henry smacked his lips, delighted with his rusk. "He has a terminal brain tumour, and my daughters have been nursing him. I came to help."

Jane's eyes widened as she instinctively glanced at Henry, as if she needed to protect him from such a fate. "I'm so sorry," she told Anna sombrely. "That sounds incredibly difficult."

"Yes, well." Anna gave an uncertain little shrug. She hadn't even let herself think about how she felt about the possibility of Peter, the only man she'd ever loved, dying, and soon; there had been too much else going on to dwell on it, and in any case, she wasn't sure she had the emotional energy to. "I suppose it is."

The kettle switched off, which was something of a relief, as it kept Jane busy, so Anna didn't have to struggle to say anything else or brace herself for more of Jane's sympathy. By the time she'd taken their two cups of tea to the table, it felt as if the conversation had moved on without anyone having said anything more.

"So, in terms of the house," Jane said, once they were seated at the table by the French windows, Henry still munching his pieces of rusk, "you could rent it on a week-by-week basis, if you liked? That way you could have some flexibility."

"But wouldn't that put you out?"

Jane shrugged as she took a sip of tea. "I don't see a big queue of interested parties, especially not this time of year. If something changes, I can let you know, but I think I'll like having you as a neighbour."

"I think I'll like having you as a neighbour, as well," Anna answered honestly. "And Henry too," she added, giving the baby a smile. Jane's easy friendliness, so generous and without reserve, was—she realised—a much-needed balm after her own daughters' prickliness. Jane was about their age, and it had been a long time since Anna had been able to befriend someone so young. Everybody at the garden centre where she worked was on the older side, apart from Maisy, and she hadn't met many people outside of it, in all the thirteen years she'd been on her own. It made her a little sad, how small her life seemed, now that she was on the outside, looking in, but she'd been content, and in truth she hadn't dared to try for anything more.

"So, it sounds like it's sorted," Jane pronounced. "When do you want to move in?"

Anna gave a little laugh. "It doesn't feel like it should be that easy. Shouldn't I be giving you personal references, or a month's deposit, or something like that?"

Jane wrinkled her nose. "Probably, now that I think about it. I'm sure Dad would want something. But since you're only renting by the week, how about a week's deposit? Say, one hundred and fifty pounds?"

That seemed a negligible amount, and Anna agreed with alacrity.

"As for personal references," Jane continued, "the fact that you're here to help your daughters is reference enough to me." She smiled kindly at Anna. "Not every mum would do something like that."

The tea that Anna had just taken a sip of suddenly tasted bitter in her mouth. She doubted either Rachel or Harriet would agree with Jane's benevolent assessment, but she was hardly going to make that point now—or ever. "Thank you," she managed after swallowing the tea. "That's very kind. But really, I probably should have come back sooner."

Twelve years sooner, she acknowledged darkly. Something else she wasn't about to tell her new landlady. As much as she liked Jane, Anna knew there would always be some secrets she had to keep.

Chapter Seven

"YOU'RE WHAT?"

Rachel stared at Anna blankly, her cup of tea raised halfway to her lips. "You're *moving*?"

"Just into Mathering," Anna replied patiently. Somehow, she'd known this conversation wouldn't go according to plan. Nothing, when it came to her daughters, seemed either straightforward or easy. It had been three days since she'd read the flyer advertising the house for rent, and now the contract was signed, everything sorted. All she had to do was tell Rachel and Harriet her intentions. "I thought we could all use a bit of space."

Rachel's eyebrows rose. "I thought you were here to help."

"I am," Anna replied, determined to stay even-tempered despite the implied accusation in Rachel's words. Admittedly, she was absolutely champing at the bit to get settled in her new place, but she appreciated her daughter's surprise at this development. "I can come over every day to help with housework, cooking, whatever it is you'd like," she added. "It's just...we've been on top of each other, Rachel, and sometimes it's felt a bit...fraught. I thought we could all use a little space to...process things."

She'd meant to have this conversation with both Harriet and Rachel at the same time, but somehow that hadn't happened. Harriet was out delivering orders of cookies and had been running between kitchen and car like the proverbial headless chicken. And meanwhile Anna wanted to move into her new place today.

"Okay," Rachel said after a moment as she put her mug down. "I can see how that makes sense."

Anna let out a long, low breath of relief. Maybe they were making progress after all, and this would be less complicated than Anna had feared. "I'll be over here as much or as little as you want me," she promised. "I really am here to help, but sometimes I've felt like I'm in the way." She held up a hand to forestall Rachel's protest, which she could see forming on her daughter's lips. "That's not a criticism, or a woe-is-me moment. It's just a fact. And," she continued, determined to be honest, "I think I could probably use a bit of space, as well." She glanced around the kitchen, her lips twisting. "This place brings back a lot of memories."

"Bad ones?" Rachel asked in a low voice.

"Painful ones, some of them," Anna replied carefully. "Happy ones too, with you girls." She had a sudden, piercing memory of baking with both Rachel and Harriet when they were just toddlers—chubby hands covered in flour, licking wooden spoons and giggling. "But it's just…a lot," she finished, "to have smacking me in the face every moment of the day."

"Did you love Dad, Mum?" Rachel asked abruptly. "I mean, at all?"

Anna let out a surprised, and rather disconcerted, laugh.

What had Rachel been thinking—that she'd hated him, all the years of her marriage? "Of course I loved him. Why do you think I married him? I was wildly, passionately in love with him at the start, and for a long time after." Which had been all part of the problem. How could you love someone who could hurt you so much, knowingly if not quite deliberately?

Rachel made an 'ew' face and Anna laughed again, this time with genuine amusement. "Sorry if that grosses you out, but it's true."

"It does a bit," Rachel admitted wryly, "but I'm glad you weren't unhappy the whole time."

"Well…" Anna felt uncomfortably compelled to honesty. "To be fair, things unravelled pretty quickly."

Rachel frowned. "Before I was born?"

This was starting to become dangerous, Anna acknowledged. There were a lot of truths out there that she was reluctant to impart to her daughter. "Right after, I think," she answered. "But that was still quite early on. You were more or less a honeymoon baby, remember." Not that they'd actually *had* a honeymoon; Peter, in typical farmer fashion, had neither been able to spare the time nor see the point. They'd spent their wedding night in the bedroom upstairs.

"I really don't need to hear about that," Rachel replied quickly. "Just…ew."

"I know, I know," Anna assured her. She didn't particularly want to remember it; that had been such a painful time of bittersweet joy and naïve confusion. Quite quickly, Peter had not turned out to be the man she'd made him out to be in the romantic fairyland of her twenty-one-year-old mind—

and heart. But that wasn't necessarily his fault. "I won't say another word about it," she promised.

"And when Harriet came along?" Rachel asked slowly, her forehead furrowed. "It must have been a crazy time, with us so close in age."

"It's all a blur now, to be honest," Anna replied. "As I think it is for most new mothers." She paused and then dared to add teasingly, thinking of how close Rachel and Ben had become, "As you might find out one day…who knows, one day rather soon?"

Happily, Rachel blushed at this rather than turning prickly. "Not one day soon," she answered. "But yes, maybe. Hopefully. One day."

Anna reached for her tea, relieved that they'd moved on from the past. They seemed to spend so much time stepping over it and *not* talking about it in helpful ways that they hardly ever spoke about the present, and all of its exciting developments. "So, things with Ben—they're going well?" she asked.

"Yes, really well," Rachel replied, her cheeks pinkening all the more. "Although I think I'm surer about me than Ben is."

Anna frowned. "What do you mean by that, exactly?"

"Well…he's sure about how *he* feels," Rachel replied with a shrug. "But he's worried I'm going to change my mind one day and hare back to London." She paused and then confessed, "I can understand why he feels that way. I left once, after all."

It didn't sound like a dig at Anna for having done the same thing, but rather a bit of self-recrimination Anna had never known about. "Do you feel guilty, Rachel?" she asked in surprise. "For going to university?" Was that why she'd become so prickly, when Anna had pointed it out a few days ago? Things were starting to make sense.

Rachel let out a breath. "No, not *exactly*. I mean...why should I feel guilty about that? But...I didn't really ever come back, did I?" She bit her lip, looking guilty indeed. "Only here and there, for a few holidays and flying visits. But I never stayed, and I didn't realise how Harriet felt...abandoned."

Harriet would have felt abandoned if Rachel had gone out to empty the bins, Anna thought ruefully, but that was Anna's fault, not her daughter's. "Point taken," she answered, "but what does any of that have to do with Ben?"

"We rowed, before I left," Rachel explained. "We were dating back then—do you remember?"

"Of course I remember." Rachel had seemed as if she were walking on air, a silly smile on her face every time Anna had looked at her. Young love. It had made her feel happy and nostalgic and just the teeniest bit sad, all at once.

"A few months before the end of the year," Rachel continued, "we had a conversation. Or really, we *didn't* have a conversation, and that was the problem. I think I wanted Ben to suggest a long-distance relationship when I was at uni, and he didn't. He just let me go, didn't say a word about anything. We both felt rejected by the other and then we never spoke about it. Not that it was a simple case of misunderstanding," Rachel added on a sigh. "More...choosing not to understand, I suppose. Not being brave enough to speak out." She squared her shoulders, managing a smile. "We've worked through it now, and I'm happy here, so that's all good…but sometimes it feels like Ben doubts me. Like he doesn't believe I'm happy with the choice I've made, or that I will be, later."

Anna had had no idea about any of that, either years ago or more recently. It saddened her, to realise how much she'd missed out on, but she pushed that unhelpful emotion away to focus on practically helping her daughter now. She was here now, and Rachel was opening up to her. That was wonderful, and that was what mattered.

"It might take a little time," she offered. "A few more weeks or months of you staying here, showing up day after day. Your relationship is still quite new."

"Yes, it is, but in some ways, it feels old, because we never stopped caring for each other, from all those years ago. But you're right. I'm probably rushing things without even realising." Rachel gave her a sudden, wry smile that lit up her whole face and lightened Anna's burdened heart. "Thanks, Mum. It's been good talking to you about all this."

When had she last heard *that*? Had a conversation like this? "My pleasure," she replied lightly. "I'm always happy to listen."

"So, where is this place you're going to move to?" Rachel asked. "In Mathering itself?"

"Yes, on Jubilee Street," she replied. "Behind Agatha's tea rooms. Do you know it?"

"I think so," Rachel replied, wrinkling her nose. "It's not as if Mathering is all that big, is it? Is it the one with all the painted doors?"

Anna smiled and nodded. "Yes, that's right, like a rainbow."

"I think all the residents agreed to do it together or something, a few years ago," Rachel recalled. "It made the front page of the *Mathering Beacon*."

"As it would," Anna replied with a laugh. "That's what passes for big news in this town." She spoke without any rancour, but Rachel still frowned.

"Does it feel very small and provincial to you, coming back here?"

"No, not really," Anna answered thoughtfully. "A bit more than Stroud, maybe, but I live in a small market town. I'm used to it." She paused. "Does it to you, coming from London?" Anna was starting to realise that some of her daughter's comments weren't the passive-aggressive criticisms she sometimes feared they were, but rather were directed inward.

"Sometimes," Rachel admitted. "Not in a bad way, at least not entirely, but…everybody knows your business. You can't go to the post office without someone later asking you who you've been writing to."

"That definitely has its up and down sides," Anna agreed. If she lived right in Mathering, would people poke their noses into her business? Maybe half the town was already talking about how Anna Mowbray had finally come back, just as Agatha had said. Did she care? Anna asked herself, and was surprised to realise she didn't, at least not as much as she once might have.

"Well, I think it's great," Rachel suddenly pronounced. "You're right—we could all do with a bit more space, and I imagine you'd prefer not to be stuck in the back bedroom and tiptoeing around us."

"Well..." Anna gave a good-natured grimace and Rachel laughed.

"Do you need any help with your stuff?"

"No, I've just got the one suitcase. I'll be fine." She hesitated and then added, "Thank you, Rachel, for understanding. I'll come back after I've unpacked and talk to Harriet about it all."

Rachel nodded. "I think she'll understand." She paused. "We are getting there, Mum. I think."

Anna felt a warm rush of love not just for Rachel, but for Harriet, too, for the three of them, bumbling towards a new beginning. "Yes," she agreed, smiling. "We are. Definitely."

IT WAS WITH a lighter heart that she packed her one suitcase and headed out to her car for the move to Mathering. If she was going to stay for an extended period, Anna reflected, it might be worth going back to her place in Stroud to get a few more things. It was four hours by car, which meant she'd most likely have to go overnight, but she found she liked the idea of having a few of her own things about her. If Rachel and Harriet could spare her—and Anna suspected they probably could—perhaps she'd head down there one weekend soon.

It gave her time in Mathering a certain longevity that she hadn't entirely anticipated when she'd first made the admittedly spur-of-the-moment decision to come up here after Rachel's text. She hadn't thought it through properly at all, simply got in the car and gone. It had felt like the last chance for her to make amends for the past, or at least to make peace with it. With Peter, even, although that seemed unlikely at this point, since he couldn't seem to stand the sight of her. But who knew, Anna told herself, determined to stay optimistic. Stranger things had happened.

As she pulled up in front of 32 Jubilee Street, with its friendly, lavender door, Jane came out of Number 30, almost as if she'd been waiting by the window for Anna's arrival, although she hadn't said when she was coming, only that it would be sometime in the morning.

"I've put the kettle on," Jane cried as she bounded toward the car. "And Henry's asleep, so I can help you with your things."

"I'm afraid I've only got this one suitcase," Anna told her as she got out of the car, gratified but also slightly taken aback by Jane's unbridled enthusiasm. "I travel light."

"Oh, so you do!" Jane looked a bit disappointed by this news. "Well, I'll show you in, anyway."

With a flash of insight, Anna realised that this was probably the highlight of Jane's day. She'd forgotten how isolating having a baby could be, when you were positively starved for adult interaction.

"That would be wonderful," she told Jane. "And you said you'd switched on the kettle…?"

She was gratified to see her new neighbour perk up. "Yes, I did, if you fancy a cuppa…?"

"Always," Anna assured her.

AN HOUR LATER, after a friendly chat and a cup of tea with Jane, Anna was back in her own place, her things unpacked—she really hadn't had that much—pootling about with not much to do. She considered going back to Embthwaite Farm to check on things there, but she decided instead simply to savour the peace and quiet of her own place for a good fifteen minutes before she headed back into the fray.

She curled up in the armchair by the wood burner, imagining sipping her morning coffee and watching the sunrise over the frost-tipped garden while the wood burner blazed merrily away. It was a lovely thought, although also, Anna admitted, a slightly lonely one.

She was used to being on her own, heaven knew, and she'd always liked her own company, but she had to admit that being around her daughters again, as prickly as they could be, had opened up something inside her. A longing for more—more relationship, affection, intimacy even.

The thought was surprising. Beyond renewing her relationship with her daughters, she had not considered any other possibilities. For thirteen years, there had been no other possibilities, not even the of the remote kind. She'd gone on a few cringeworthy blind dates, urged on by a friend, but they had been lessons in endurance more than evenings of enjoyment, and she'd been glad to see the last of them.

Maybe it was Rachel asking about her marriage earlier or remembering the heady whirlwind of her and Peter's first romance…but for the first time in donkey's years, Anna found herself missing that connection with another person.

With a man.

She was fifty-three years old, she told herself, as something of a warning, but then she thought—what of it? Fifty-three wasn't *dead*. Why shouldn't she meet someone, find love again? Yet the likelihood of finding that person—should he even exist—in *Mathering* seemed minimal, indeed. If she hadn't met someone in Stroud in all these years, not even so much as a wistful what-if, she was hardly likely to meet someone here, in a place even more rural and remote than Gloucestershire, and with so many difficult memories attached to it.

A knock on the door had her startling from her thoughts. Had Jane forgotten to tell her something? But when Anna went to open the door, it wasn't her new neighbour standing there beady-eyed and determined, but her old one.

"Diana!" she exclaimed in surprise.

"Barbara, who runs the post office, told me you'd moved here," Diana announced by way of explanation. "And I was in town, so I thought I'd stop by. Such a dear little place—it looks as cute as a button! Do you mind if I come in? It's cold as the dickens outside."

"Of course," Anna said, still stunned by her arrival, as she stepped aside. "How did Barbara know I was moving here?"

"She had to take down the flyer, didn't she?" Diana replied reasonably as she headed back to the kitchen. "Oh, isn't this space amazing! No wonder you snapped it up. Jane told her all about you—she put two and two together. It wasn't hard."

"No," Anna replied faintly. So, this was how people poked their noses into her business! Well, so be it. It wasn't that terrible, really. "I don't suppose it was," she conceded with a smile. "I'd offer you a cup of tea, but I haven't brought anything in yet."

"Oh, don't mind me, I just wanted a nose round," Diana told her with a smile and a wave of her hand. "And I wanted to invite you to the quiz night at the village hall next Thursday. It's for the Rotary Club and I'm not taking no for an answer! We need teams of six and I'm the fifth, with Ben and Rachel and Harriet and Quinn. You're a natural sixth."

"Oh…" Anna was startled. She hadn't done anything social since she'd arrived in Mathering. "What about Peter? Who will look after him?"

"That's all sorted. Tilly Wiggins, who does my hair, used to be a carer in a nursing home. She hates quizzes and so she said she'd sit with him for the evening."

"I don't know if Peter—"

"Peter can manage," Diana cut her off briskly. "And everyone could use a night out, don't you think? It will be fun."

It *would* be fun, Anna thought suddenly. She'd like to get to know Quinn and Ben better, and to spend time with her daughters that wasn't endlessly raking over the past or attempting to navigate the future. She wanted to have fun—good, old-fashioned fun, with no strings attached.

"Well, then?" Diana asked, looking as if she was about to launch into all the reasons why Anna should attend.

"Sounds wonderful," Anna replied breezily, surprising her neighbour as well as herself. "I can't wait."

Chapter Eight

MATHERING'S VILLAGE HALL was positively heaving with people as Anna stepped inside, behind Rachel and Ben, Harriet and Quinn. Diana had arrived an hour ago to help set up, as she was on the organisational committee for the quiz, and Anna glimpsed her bustling from table to table.

"Looks more popular than the ceilidhs, at least," Rachel muttered, rolling her eyes at Harriet, who grinned back. Apparently, they'd gone to some ceilidh back when Rachel had first returned that had been...interesting. Anna hadn't heard the whole story, but she hoped to.

Tonight, everyone thankfully seemed to have received the memo that this evening was about *fun*, not dwelling on any old scores that still needed to be settled. Rachel and Harriet had both been more than amenable to the idea of them all going to the quiz together, which had gratified Anna, as had her conversation with Harriet the day before, when she'd finally had a chance to explain about her move into town.

"I think that's wise," Harriet had told her with a decisive nod, clearly choosing her words with care. "You're right, we could all use the space, and I'm pretty busy with the baking business now, as it is."

"You were the one who mentioned it first," Anna had reminded her with a smile, "so I think you're the wise one! I just took you up on the good idea you had."

Harriet had smiled rather shyly at that, and Anna had felt something in her heart loosen and expand. These little interactions were still challenging, but they were getting so much easier. So much less fraught.

It really was such a relief, she thought now, not to feel quite so much as if she were tiptoeing around everyone and everything. Yes, things were still a bit tense sometimes, as they were bound to be, especially with Peter's condition looming over them all. The GP hadn't been able to predict his life expectancy, but he had suggested months and maybe even weeks would be generous, and a palliative nurse had been assigned to him, to come to the house twice a week to manage his pain relief. It saddened Anna, mainly for her daughters, whom she knew would miss their father—both the man he'd been, and the man they'd longed for him to be and now never would be.

And yet, despite all that, things overall did feel more positive. Yesterday morning she'd had coffee in the armchair by the wood burner just as she'd imagined, and it had been *lovely*, watching the sky turn lavender and then rose as sunlight stole over the world. She'd done a big food shop and made herself an elaborate and creamy pasta dish, eating it all by herself in front of the television, feeling positively decadent for doing so.

She'd also spent a lot of time at the farm—tidying up, doing laundry, and making meals. She'd avoided Peter, mainly for Harriet and Rachel's sakes, since his reactions to her were so stressful, but she'd done her best to be helpful and she felt, for the first time, that her efforts were genuinely appreciated, with murmured thanks and a few warm smiles. It was, Anna acknowledged, a good feeling.

And it was a good feeling tonight, to be going out all together. Ben had come to the farmhouse to pick them up in his battered Rover; Anna had answered the door since Harriet and Rachel were still getting ready upstairs.

"Looking good, Mrs M," he'd told her with a quirk of a smile, which had made her laugh.

"I'd forgotten how you used to call me that, Ben," she'd replied. "It's good to see you." And his flattery had been nice, as well; she'd made an effort with her outfit, a blue corduroy miniskirt and wool tights paired with a cranberry-coloured cashmere jumper, her usually silvery bob tucked behind her ears and a bit of mascara and lipstick to show she wasn't past it.

"I'm sorry we didn't really run into each other before now," he'd told her. "At least not properly." They'd exchanged hellos at the Christmas party at the hotel, but beyond that Anna had only seen him in passing. She'd supposed she'd been keeping out of the way as much as possible, unsure what her reception was likely to be. She'd been glad she'd felt on firmer footing now, and that Ben had seemed to feel the same.

Now everyone looked around for a free table in the hall before Diana caught sight of them and waved them over. "I've saved you this one," she told them, pointing to a table in the corner with a large 'reserved' sign propped on it. "Get yourselves settled. There should be time to get drinks, as we won't start on time." She tutted with good-natured exasperation. "We never do."

Anna shed her coat as Quinn offered, with his usual smiling alacrity, to get drinks for everyone at the bar in the corner.

"They don't take debit cards," Rachel warned him. "I learned that the hard way."

"Oh, they do now," Diana assured her. "We've got a brand-new card reader, although to be fair it doesn't always get signal."

Quinn dramatically took out a twenty-pound note and held it in the air, whimsical as ever, making Anna smile. His humour was good for Harriet, she thought, who could sometimes see the world a bit too seriously. "I think I'm sorted," he pronounced. "What'll it be, everyone?"

As everyone went round with their drink orders, Anna let her gaze move around the room, wondering if there was anyone she knew among the crowd. There should be, considering she'd lived in Mathering for twenty years, but the motley group of faces seemed unfamiliar. It had, she acknowledged, been a long time since she'd last been here, interacting in any meaningful way.

"Anna?" Quinn asked genially. "What would you like?"

"A gin and tonic, please," she answered with a smile, feeling a little reckless. She didn't normally drink beyond a glass of wine or two, but she felt like being just that little bit more extravagant tonight. Her gaze caught on someone sitting at a table nearby, and it took her a few seconds to recall who it was—the woman who used to run the toddler group, Mary someone. She had to be in her seventies now, with a neat white bob and blue eyes glinting amid her many wrinkles. She caught Anna's eye and gave a small smile of acknowledgement, which made Anna feel both gratified and strangely exposed. She would be glad of that gin and tonic, she thought wryly. She was starting to realise that she might need a little social lubricant tonight.

While Quinn went to get drinks and Diana bustled away to see to the last preparations for the evening, Rachel took the piece of paper from the centre of the table and scanned it critically. "We need to come up with a team name," she told everyone. "Any ideas?"

"Well, we're Mowbray, Mackey and Taylor..." Ben suggested, and Rachel tutted.

"That's not very creative. We need something clever and witty."

"No pressure, then," Ben replied dryly. He glanced at Anna. "Any thoughts?"

"To come up with something clever and witty?" she replied on a laugh, wanting that gin and tonic more than ever. "Absolutely not, I'm afraid."

"Mowbray, Mackey, and Tyler..." Harriet mused. "MMT. How about Mostly Mediocre Trivia?"

"Hey," Ben returned mildly, "the Rotary Club quiz night isn't *that* bad."

Harriet rolled her eyes as she blushed. "I meant Mostly Mediocre *at* Trivia," she amended. "I'm rubbish at these things. I always have been."

"How about the Motley Mathering Team?" Anna suggested, then blushed just like her daughter. That wasn't very clever or witty, really. What had she been thinking?

"I like it," Ben told her warmly. "We are a motley crew, after all!" He glanced round them all with a grin while Rachel rolled her eyes good-naturedly.

"I suppose we are," she agreed. "All right, then." She wrote the name down in neat letters at the top of their answer sheet, just as Quinn came back with a tray of drinks.

"Twenty quid goes a lot farther here than in London," he remarked as he handed them round. "I even got you a double," he told Anna with a wink, handing her the G&T.

"Oh…" Anna felt like she shouldn't protest that she didn't need a double gin, but the truth was, she was already taking a much-needed sip. As Diana joined them and the group continued to sip their drinks and chat around her, she glanced around the room again, and this time she recognised at least half a dozen people, from one place or another—Barbara from the post office, John, the vet they'd taken Fred to, and a few others who she couldn't entirely place but definitely knew from her years in this place.

She hadn't had many friends in Mathering, it was true—her life on a farm with two little children, as well as her naturally reserved nature, had made for a limited social circle—but she'd known people whom she'd seen in a variety of circumstances—the supermarket, the library, the GP. And a lot of them appeared to be here tonight.

"All right, let's get started," the emcee of the evening, a jolly-faced man with hair like cotton wool named Tobias, announced. "First, a shout-out to all the teams." Table by table, he went through all the team names—the Mathering Mavens, the Trivia Terrors, Let's Get Quizzical, and a few others besides. When it came to their turn, everyone shouted out their name, Anna included. Three sips into her gin and she was definitely feeling more relaxed.

"Are you having a nice time?" Diana asked in a motherly sort of way, and Anna smiled.

"Yes, I am. I recognise quite a few people, actually. I don't know why I didn't think I would."

"You did live here a long time," Diana agreed. "You were part of this community, Anna." She said it as a statement of fact rather than one of recrimination, and Anna let the words roll around in her mind. *Had* she been part of this community? She supposed she had, in myriad ways—taking the girls to school, always bringing a traybake to the community bake sales, showing up to toddler mornings and coffee afternoons, chipping in when there was a town-wide effort to clean the church yard or tidy up the school grounds. But despite all that, she wasn't sure that she ever felt truly involved or included; it was generally accepted that if you weren't born in Mathering or at least North Yorkshire, you would always be an outsider, or offcomer, as they were called.

But more than that, Anna reflected, her relationship with Peter—the vacuum at its very centre—had made her feel excluded from normal life in a way she wasn't sure she could explain to anyone. She'd felt, for most of her marriage, as if she'd been the outside looking in on almost everything, including her relationship with her husband. That lack had affected every other relationship, in its own way, although she was doing her best to correct it now.

Still, it made for food for somewhat uncomfortable thought. She didn't want to be like that anymore, she realised, a spectator to her own self.

"All right, first question!" Tobias called, and Anna was glad to be yanked out of her melancholy reflections. "Who wrote," Tobias asked the now silent room, "the children's novel *Chitty-Chitty-Bang-Bang: The Magical Car*?"

Anna watched as groups at other tables brought their heads together, whispering furiously. She glanced around her table and saw everyone looking rather blank.

"Er…Enid Blyton?" Rachel ventured, and Diana shook her head.

"I don't think so. I used to love Enid Blyton as a child myself, and I don't recall that one."

A beat of silence passed as they all tried to think of another children's author. "Arthur Ransome?" Ben wondered aloud. "Didn't I read one of his, Mum?"

"Only under duress," Diana replied with a smile. "He could have written it, I suppose, although I think he was from an earlier time."

All the other teams were madly scribbling away, Anna noticed. It seemed they really were mediocre at trivia.

"Mum, do you know anyone?" Harriet asked. "You used to read us loads of stories."

While it was nice that Harriet remembered that, this particular title still didn't ring a bell. "Yes, but I'm afraid I don't remember that one," Anna replied apologetically. "There was a film of it, though, wasn't there, back in the sixties?"

"Yes, I remember that," Diana exclaimed. "Kind of creepy, as I recall. Wasn't there a child catcher or something?"

"All right," Tobias called. "Second question!"

"I suppose I'll write in Enid Blyton," Rachel said dubiously as she began to write on their paper. "I don't want to leave it blank."

"Second question! In which part of your body," Tobias declared in a booming voice, "would you find the cruciate ligament?"

More blank looks from around the table. Anna fought the sudden urge to giggle. Did they not know *anything*?

"Sounds painful," Quinn remarked, taking a sip of his cider. "Or like something out of Harry Potter…cruciate. The ankle, maybe?"

"Or the elbow?" Harriet suggested.

"Maybe the knee," Ben supplied.

"Or the hip," Diana chimed in.

"You've suggested basically everywhere there's a ligament," Rachel declared in exasperation. "Which is it?"

Just then, Anna's meandering gaze was caught by the piercing blue eyes of a man seated a few tables away. He was tall and rangy, with a lean but muscular build and a shock of thick, wavy white hair, and he was sitting in a relaxed pose, one arm slung over the back of his chair. He was handsome, Anna acknowledged, in a rugged and assured sort of way, in his pressed jeans and a V-neck jumper with a checked button-down shirt underneath. He looked to be in his late fifties, maybe a few years older than her. And, she realised, he was laughing at her.

She bristled with instinctive affront, about to look away, before she realised he was actually *mouthing* something at her. What on earth…? Instead of looking away, she leaned closer, squinting to try to make out what he was saying.

"It's…it's…the *knee*!" Her voice rang out excitedly as she turned back to her table. "It's the ligament in the knee." The man had given her the right answer to the question. They must have been looking particularly gormless, Anna reflected ruefully, for him to feel the need to help her out, all the way from across the room. She glanced back at him, and saw he was still looking at her. He flashed her a cheeky grin and, emboldened by her double gin, she gave him a mock salute in return. His grin widened, his eyes sparkling, even from all the way across the room, making Anna feel…sort of warm inside.

Or maybe it was just the gin.

"All right, question three," Tobias boomed out, and Anna tore her gaze away from the man's, conscious she'd been staring at him for far too long. As she returned her attention to the table, Rachel gave her a thoughtful and rather assessing look. How much had she seen, Anna wondered with something like panic, only to remind herself that there hadn't been anything *to* see. She'd smiled at a man from across the room. Oh, and she'd given him a mock salute.

Why on earth did she feel like she was *blushing*?

It was definitely the gin.

Anna completely missed question three, although she gathered it was something about Shakespeare, and Harriet thought she knew the answer. She caught Diana's eye and saw her old friend was giving her the same sort of appraising look her daughter had been. Why was it suddenly seeming to take a lot of effort not to look at that man again?

He was probably married, Anna told herself, honest enough to acknowledge that the reason she felt as if she were fizzing inside was because of that brief yet immediate flare of attraction when she'd caught sight of that man with the bright blue eyes and wavy, white hair, something she hadn't felt in a very long time. What was it about today, she wondered, that was making all these feelings bubble up inside her after so long? Or was it just after what felt like a very long sleep, she was finally waking up, at least a little?

"Question four," Tobias announced, and Anna leaned forward, determined to be extra attentive. "What is the capital of Finland?"

"Helsinki," Rachel said immediately, and started writing. She'd gone through a phase when she'd been a child of memorising capitals, begging Anna to quiz her all the time. Unable to help herself, Anna glanced back at the man's table again, but he was leaning across it, talking to someone else, and he didn't notice. Foolishly, she felt disappointed.

"Question five!" Tobias called out, and Anna turned back. "What is the Japanese name for cherry blossom?"

"Sakura," she answered automatically, and five faces around the table looked suitably impressed.

"How did you know that, Mum?" Rachel asked as she wrote it down.

"Well, I have been working at a garden centre for the last twelve years," Anna replied teasingly, only to have Harriet give her a funny look.

"Have you? I didn't know," she said, which had the effect of pouring cold water over the entire conversation. Diana murmured something and Anna reached for her drink, only to find it was empty.

"I'll get you another one," Quinn said, rising from the

table. He glanced around at everyone. "Anyone else for another?"

A few people murmured their orders while Harriet looked rather wretched. "Sorry," she said when Quinn had left. "I didn't mean anything by it, I just genuinely didn't..."

"It's fine," Anna replied quickly. "Absolutely fine. I'm sure we have lots to discover about one another." She gave her daughter a firmly reassuring smile as Tobias went on to question six. It wasn't Harriet's fault that she hadn't known that, even if it had been uncomfortable to have her point it out during an evening like this one.

Fortunately, they managed to recover their equilibrium and even their cheer throughout the evening and placed a very respectable fifth out of twelve at the end of the quiz. The man's table, the Smarty Pints, had placed third. As they gathered up their coats, everyone exclaiming, to various degrees of surprise or bemusement, what a lovely time they'd had, Anna looked around for the man. She knew she wasn't bold enough to say hello to him, but she thought she might like to smile at him again.

Unfortunately, as she slipped on her coat and the hall emptied out, she found she couldn't see him anywhere. Well, she told herself, it wasn't as if anything had been going to happen there. Far from it, for a whole lot of reasons.

As they headed out into the frosty night, Harriet slung her arm around Anna's shoulders, much to her gratification and surprise.

"That was really fun, Mum," Harriet said. "I'm glad we all went together."

"Yes," Anna agreed, clumsily putting her arm around her

daughter for a quick, non-threatening squeeze.

This was the takeaway of the evening, she knew, not some shared smile with a stranger she'd never see again across a crowded room. This—her daughters with her, learning to rebuild their relationship all over again.

Chapter Nine

OUTSIDE THE KITCHEN window, the garden was carpeted with snowdrops, bright white clusters sparkling in the winter sunshine, as Anna finished washing up the lunch dishes. She smiled at the sight as she hung the damp tea towel on the railing of the Rayburn. The kitchen felt peaceful in the quiet of the afternoon; Rachel was giving lunch to Peter upstairs and Harriet had gone over to the hotel to work in the kitchen there.

Anna had been in her new place on Jubilee Street for two weeks now, and life had fallen into a fairly pleasing rhythm. She came over to Embthwaite Farm most days to help out with the cooking and housework, to walk Fred among the hills, and just be a general support to her daughters as they—and in particular, Rachel—cared for Peter. Anna had taken care not to go in his room again, but she knew from Rachel that he was sleeping a lot more, and his speech had become more garbled. The palliative nurse, a kindly woman in her early sixties, had come twice a week to check on Peter, tweak his medication, and provide general reassurance that they were all holding up wonderfully.

When Anna wasn't at the farm, she was enjoying life in her little house, and she'd had a fair few coffees with Jane, who was insistent that she come for dinner and meet her father as well as her husband one evening, although nothing had been planned yet. She'd also gone over to the Mackey farm for coffee with Diana on several occasions, and overall, Anna felt as if she'd found a balance, a certain equilibrium, in this strange little life she'd made for herself back here in Mathering.

It worked, she reflected, as long as they didn't talk about anything too serious. There had been no more deep dives into the past, which seemed to suit everyone fine. After all, they certainly had enough trauma to be going on with, including Peter's imminent death. The thought caused a funny little pang to go through Anna, because she wasn't really sure how to feel about that approaching reality.

When she'd walked out of this place thirteen years ago, she'd been in a complete stupor of shock and sorrow. Then, a little while later, she'd started to feel the overwhelming grief, for all she'd lost. After processing that, or trying to, she'd felt relief, that she no longer had to endure what she had.

But it had been a long time since she'd felt any of those emotions. In the last five years or so, she had, at the advice of her therapist, done her best to let go of past hurts and regrets and try to exist in the present. It had worked, sort of…until she'd come here.

Rachel came back into the kitchen with Peter's lunch tray, which looked mostly untouched.

"The lamb casserole was delicious," she assured Anna, "but he wasn't very hungry." Her expression clouded as she nibbled her lip. "It's like he's wasting away before our very eyes. I can *see* it, in real time."

Anna took the tray from her with a sympathetic smile. That was exactly what was happening, she thought sadly. She ached for both Rachel and Harriet, to have to see it.

"I suppose," Rachel said as Anna scraped the casserole into the compost bin, "it's just going to get harder from here on out."

"Harder in some ways," Anna replied, "but maybe easier in others." She paused, feeling for the right words. "Grieving is a process. A journey, even. You can take encouragement, or at least strength, from knowing you've made some of it already." Rachel cocked her head thoughtfully, considering the matter as Anna continued, "I used to console myself, when I felt sad about my parents dying, that every moment of grief I felt was one I wouldn't have to feel again. I know I would feel grief generally, and in some ways that never goes away. But every hard moment felt like a deposit in, I don't know, the grief bank." She gave a self-conscious laugh. "That probably sounds mad."

"No, it doesn't, actually," Rachel replied quietly. "It makes a lot of sense." She fell silent as Anna continued to tidy up the lunch dishes. "I don't really remember your parents dying," she remarked after a moment. "Grandad died when we were little, didn't he?"

"Yes, he had a stroke when you were four," Anna replied. "He died just a few days later."

"That must have been hard."

"Yes, it was. You both were so little, and your father couldn't really take time off the farm, which was understandable." She'd taken both Harriet and Rachel to the funeral on her own, aching with grief and exhaustion. She'd been only twenty-five years old, which seemed like a child now, but she'd felt rather miserably grown-up at the time—burying her father with two small children in tow.

"And Granny?" Rachel asked after a moment. "She got cancer when we were in our teens… I remember you travelling there quite a bit."

"She did," Anna confirmed. "She had a carer who came in, but I'd go down to Reading to help out as often as I could."

"Why didn't we see them more?" Rachel asked abruptly. "Granny, especially, when she was on her own? I feel like we visited her once a year, if that."

"Well." Anna gave a small sigh as she recalled that fraught relationship. "The truth is, I didn't get along very well with either of my parents, and even less after I married your father, although I still loved them and missed them when they were gone."

Rachel's eyebrows rose. "I feel like this needs a cup of tea."

"Maybe," Anna allowed with a small smile. A cup of tea—Britain's great answer to everything.

"That is, if you want to talk about it?" Rachel ventured. "I know we're doing that whole give-each-other-space thing…"

"Emotional as well as physical space?" Anna surmised. "No, I don't mind, Rachel. If you have questions, I want to provide answers." Within reason.

"All right, then." Rachel went to fill the kettle. "Then, question number one. Why didn't you get along with your parents?"

"That's not an easy one to answer," Anna replied as she settled herself at the table while Rachel set about making them both tea. "They were both academics at the University of Reading—"

"I think I knew that," Rachel confirmed. "Grandad was a biology lecturer, right?"

"Yes, and your grandmother taught French. They were both very driven in their careers, very intelligent and intellectual, and they had me late in life, something, I think, of an afterthought."

Rachel's mouth dropped open. "You mean an accident?"

"They never said," Anna replied. "But I suppose it felt that way sometimes. Like I was in the way of all their aspirations. So, for most of my years growing up, I was determined to live completely differently than they did—and I suppose, in a convoluted way, I succeeded."

The kettle began to whistle, and Rachel poured the boiled water into the pot. "You mean by marrying Dad and living on a farm, having kids early…?" she surmised.

"Yes, all of that. My parents weren't pleased that I was marrying a man I barely knew—your dad and I only dated for two months before we got married—and he was twenty years older than me, to boot. Looking back, I suppose they had a right to be concerned."

"I never thought about that," Rachel said slowly as she brought the tea things to the table. "I think if I'd been them, I would have had a right barney about it."

Anna laughed. "Well, they did, in their own way. It was all *very* frosty. 'If you're really sure you want to do this,

Anna' kind of thing. But it created even more of a strain between us, which led to the decrease in visits. Not," she amended, sinking her chin into her hand, "that I think there would have been loads of visits otherwise. My parents were very busy people, even in their retirement, and they weren't all that keen on children, although I think they loved you and Harriet in their own way. It was more that they just didn't know what to do with children. They were like an alien species to them." Which hadn't helped Anna herself figure out what to do with children, when she'd been a mother. Very little had come naturally, but then maybe very little did, generally.

"They sound like real gems," Rachel replied with a wry twist of her lips.

"They had their faults," Anna acknowledged, "but I loved them. But like you, perhaps, with your father, I missed the idea of what they could have been to me—and I to them—if things had been different. If they had, or I had, or maybe we all had." She lapsed into silence, afraid she'd presumed too much, to draw such comparisons.

To her surprise, Rachel's eyes filled with tears which she quickly blinked away. "Yes," she admitted thickly. "That's exactly how I feel sometimes."

"Oh, darling." It felt entirely natural—almost—to pull Rachel into a quick hug, which she did. When had she last touched one of her daughters like this? It made her ache, to realise just how long it had been. "I'm so sorry for what you're going through."

"It sounds like you went through the same thing," Rachel replied, sniffing, briefly hugging Anna back before she pulled away. "And more besides."

Anna gave a little shrug as she picked up her teacup, a smile twitching her lips. "'Life is pain, princess.'"

"'And anyone telling you different is selling you something,'" Rachel finished the quote with a smile. "We must have watched *The Princess Bride* a hundred times."

"It's a good film." She could picture Rachel and Harriet piled onto the sofa, watching the TV, while she'd made the popcorn. There had been happy times, she acknowledged, amidst the many sorrows. Sometimes all she remembered was the hardship and the pain—that annoying negativity bias of memory—but it hadn't been like that.

Rachel hesitated and then asked very quietly, "Why…why were you sectioned, Mum? I mean…what was going on, that had driven you to that point? If you don't want to talk about it," she added hurriedly, "I understand. But it feels like such a big thing, and I mean, I knew you were sad growing up, I remember things, but…I guess I didn't realise just how hard things had been for you."

Anna let out a heavy sigh. No, she didn't want to talk about it, but she'd spent the last thirteen years ducking this question in one way or another. It felt like a particularly bad moment, to talk about it now, when Peter was, quite literally, on death's door. And yet maybe it was the living she needed to focus on. Keeping these secrets wasn't helping anyone, even if she once thought they might have…or maybe she just hadn't wanted to admit the truth. In any case, they would surely have to come out into the light at some point. At least now she could choose the time.

"It was a complicated situation," she told her daughter

carefully. "And I'm prone to depression anyway, I've come to realise. But…your father's and my marriage was difficult. Very difficult. Not just because he could be a stubborn sort of man, as you very well know, but because…" She blew out a breath. *Should she do this?* "Because he loved someone else," she finished. "And I think that's all I'll say about it now, because this is probably a conversation we should have with Harriet here." And Rachel was already looking blindsided, without Anna having told her the half of it.

"Someone else…" she repeated wonderingly. "*Who?*"

"No one you knew," Anna replied swiftly. "And no one I knew, either. No one from Mathering."

"*Who* then…"

"It doesn't matter, and that's not even the point." Anna was starting to regret having been this honest. "Let's talk about this with Harriet, Rachel, please. I wanted to give you an answer, but it's not fair on your sister to go through all this without her."

"Okay," Rachel conceded, very much sounding like she wanted to press. "Okay. But…are you sure? That he did, I mean? Love someone else?"

For a second, Anna pictured the obdurate look on Peter's face when she'd found out about his other woman, just after Rachel had been born. And much later, the icy shock that had trickled through her, when she realised the affair had never stopped. And later still, when Peter had admitted, truculently, just how far it had gone. "Yes," she told Rachel wearily. "I'm sure."

HALF AN HOUR later, Rachel was back at work in the dining room and Anna was driving back to her rental house, feeling all churned up inside from the conversation. She still didn't know whether she should have said anything, if it was fair on Peter. Would the girls view him differently now? Should that even be her concern? And did his affair, long as it had lasted, even justify her own behaviour—walking out on her children the way she had? Admittedly her adult, or at least almost adult, children, but still…

A groan escaped her as she swung into the car park of the Tesco on the outside of Mathering. She was tired of thinking about these things, the thoughts going round and round in her head, achieving nothing. She was going to stop the endless circling, buy something delicious to make for dinner, and watch something absolutely brainless on TV tonight.

She took a basket from the entrance of the shop and started perusing the aisles, chucking things in at random, depending on what she fancied. Despite her determination not to think about all those past things, the memories were still there, looming like a dark cloud on the horizon.

What she really needed, Anna decided, was chocolate. A positive slab of it. She made her way to the confectionary aisle and surveyed the offerings, taking her time to decide between salted caramel and hazelnut.

A movement out of the corner of her eye, as well as some sort of sixth spidey sense, had her turning her head. She saw a flash of white hair before a man passed the aisle, and a ripple of awareness went through her. Was it the guy from the quiz evening? How could she find out?

Recklessly she grabbed a bar of salted caramel and

chucked it into her basket before walking, rather quickly, down the aisle and around the corner, where she'd seen the flash of white hair. It was probably some octogenarian pensioner she'd never seen before, she told herself crossly. She was behaving in a rather ridiculous manner, chasing after him.

She'd just rounded the corner of the next aisle when she saw him again—this time a flash of checked shirt and navy gilet before he rounded the corner at the far end of the aisle. It *was* him…wasn't it? She sped up, practically trotting down the aisle even as she told herself she was acting as if she were positively unhinged. What would she even say to the man if she caught up with him? And what if he saw her running after him like a madwoman?

Anna took a stumbling step back as she rounded the corner of the next aisle, for she was in the produce section now, and the low bins made her feel like she'd just stumbled on a battlefield, totally exposed, no towering shelves of cereal boxes to hide behind. And there he was, browsing by the bananas. *What should she do?*

Slink away was the obvious answer, yet Anna found herself dithering. He'd moved past the bananas in a relaxed stroll before taking a pack of fresh basil from the herbs section and putting it into his trolley. He must cook, Anna thought, to be picking up fresh basil. Or was he shopping for his wife? She could picture the woman already—elegantly coiffed, understated make-up, tailored trousers with an expensive fleece, a faint smile, glasses perched on her nose…

Ugh, what was she *doing*? Suddenly sickened by herself—and she was self-aware enough to acknowledge that the memories of Peter's affair probably had something to do with all this—she turned away from the man and went to finish her shopping.

Resolutely Anna chucked a dozen different things into her basket, barely aware of what she was selecting, although she *did* include quite a large bottle of gin. Why not? Then she moved to the check-out, unloading her stuff, and paying for it without seeing so much as another glimpse of the man. Just as well, really.

Back at the rental, she was just fumbling with her keys at the door when she heard Henry next door, wailing like his life depended on it. She hesitated, concerned because she'd never heard him cry quite that much. Was something wrong? She glanced down at her two carrier bags, the bottle of gin clinking against a jar of spaghetti sauce. Henry's screams ratcheted up a notch.

Anna put the bags down and headed next door. She tapped twice on the door with no answer, save for Henry's continued cries. Deliberating only for a second, Anna turned the knob—the door was unlocked—and then pushed it open.

"Jane?" she called. "Hello? Is everything all right?"

No answer, but she found Henry strapped into his high chair, his face red and snot-smeared from crying.

"Sweetheart…" Anna murmured as she went to him and wiped his blotched face with a cloth. He snuffled, taking a few gulping breaths, but he calmed down as Anna unstrapped him and hoisted him onto her hip. Where on earth was Jane? She glanced around the kitchen—the sink was piled with dirty dishes, there were crumbs all over the floor, and a pile of dirty washing by the machine that stank of dirty nappies. Oh, dear. What should she do?

In her arms, Henry snuffled again and then buried his face in her shoulder. Anna patted his back. She was reluctant to go through the house looking for Jane, as it felt invasive, but what if she'd done something to herself? Slipped in the shower, or…but, Anna thought reasonably, she wouldn't be in the shower, with Henry down here, surely?

Just then the French doors opened, and Jane stepped into the kitchen, a look of surprise flashing across her face before it was replaced by one of guilt.

"*Anna*…oh, no. Sorry." She bit her lip. "You must think I'm the worst mother in the world."

"No, of course not," Anna assured her quickly. She could understand the sentiment all too well, though. "But, Jane," she asked, taking in the other woman's dishevelled clothes and greasy hair, "what's going on?"

Chapter Ten

JANE OPENED HER mouth to reply, stood there completely still for a second, and then, to seeming both her and Anna's shock, burst into noisy tears.

"Oh, Jane—"

"Sorry, *sorry*," Jane moaned, taking a crumpled tissue from her pocket and trying her best to wipe her face. "Sorry. It's just been such a day. And night. And week. And month." She let out a ragged laugh that turned into a sob.

"Let's go back to the beginning," Anna replied. She switched Henry to her other hip as she guided Jane to a seat at the table. "And let me get you a cup of tea. Have you eaten?" The poor woman looked as if she hadn't showered or slept in some time.

"I made some toast," Jane replied vaguely, casting her gaze around the kitchen before it rested on the toaster, where a single piece of toast had popped up what looked like hours ago. Anna went to touch it, and it was stone cold and stale. Poor, poor Jane.

"Tea," she said firmly, and she managed to fill the kettle while Henry clawed at her, tugging experimentally on her hair and making her wince. Never mind.

"You must think I'm a terrible mother," Jane murmured

wretchedly as she sat slumped at the table, her head bowed against her arms. "How could I leave my baby alone like that?"

"I don't think you're a terrible mother," Anna replied, deliberately keeping her tone brisk. "I think you're a very normal, and I suspect, a very tired one, at the moment. Were you in the garden?" Miserably Jane nodded. "That's hardly leaving him alone, then. In my mother's day, you left the baby in the pram at the bottom of the garden for at *least* two hours every day. For the fresh air, apparently."

Jane lifted her head to gaze blearily at Anna, and the ghost of a smile flickered across her face and then died. "Did they really do that?" she murmured doubtfully.

"They did," Anna affirmed. "My own mother swore by it. Anyway," she finished as she put a cup of tea in front of Jane, "I imagine you just needed a bit of a break. Has Henry been rather whingy today?"

"He's been a *monster*," Jane confirmed, murmuring her thanks for the tea. "Not that you'd know it to look at him now." As if to prove his mother wrong, Henry gave a little gurgle of delight and pulled Anna's hair again. Anna wrapped her hand around the baby's and gently but firmly pulled his chubby fingers away from her hair.

"Well, then," she said, as if Jane's confirmation had proved her point, which it more or less had. "You've done what a million or more mothers have done before you and stepped out for a moment to pull yourself together. There's no shame in it, Jane."

"Did *you* ever do that?" Jane asked in challenge, and Anna almost smiled. She'd stepped out for twelve years!

Somehow, Jane had got into her head that Anna had been some sort of paragon of a mother, and she needed to disabuse her of that very erroneous notion.

"Yes, most certainly," she replied. "Once I locked my two out of the house so I could have a moment's peace from their bickering." She smiled faintly. "Why should I be the one to have to go outside?"

"I don't believe it," Jane replied, but she was smiling, at least for a moment, before she once again had to blink back tears. "I'm just so *tired*," she told Anna with a catch in her voice. "Henry hasn't been sleeping because of his teeth, and Eric has been working *all* the time—some pressure at the office. Last night he didn't come home until nine. And Dad tries to help, but to be honest, he's a bit useless with babies. Maybe all men are," she added with a grimace. "Sometimes it feels that way."

"It's hard," Anna murmured. She wished she'd realised just how much Jane was struggling; she could have helped earlier. But at least, she told herself, she could help now. "Look," she told Jane once she'd finished her tea, "why don't you have a shower or a bath and get some fresh clothes on? It can do wonders for your mood, especially when some days you don't even have time to brush your teeth."

Jane put her hand up to her mouth. "Oh, my goodness," she exclaimed, "how did you *know*? Can you tell?"

"No, no," Anna assured her with a laugh. "I'm only saying that's how I was. Henry's happy here with me. Take half an hour, or an hour even, for yourself."

Jane stared at her in incredulity, as if Anna had just offered her the moon. "Do you really mean that?" she breathed, and again Anna felt a rush of reproach. She should have offered more, and sooner.

"Yes, I absolutely do."

Slowly Jane shook her head. "I haven't had anyone to help since we moved here," she told Anna. "Dad tries, I know, and he's very good at the practical things, or doing a bit of shopping for me, or what have you. But *I* want to do the shopping sometimes, you know? I want *him* to be the one to hold the baby."

"Have you told him that?" Anna asked seriously, and Jane shrugged.

"Maybe not in so many words, but…he should take the hint, surely!"

"Men can be a bit dim when it comes to that sort of thing," Anna told her with a smile. "You might need to take a more direct approach."

Jane grimaced. "Maybe, although…I don't want to hurt his feelings." At Anna's raised eyebrows, she continued haltingly, "I suppose I feel a bit protective of him. My mum died when I was seventeen and he's been on his own that whole time."

And so then must have Jane, Anna surmised with a rush of sympathy. Having a baby when you were motherless yourself was hard; Anna remembered how hard it had been for her. Her mother had been alive, yes, but she had not been very interested. She'd come to Mathering to visit only once in fifteen years.

"I'm so sorry to hear about your mum," she told Jane. "That must have been very hard."

"Yeah, it was." Jane blinked rapidly. "She was amazing.

So much fun. She had this incredible laugh…" She trailed away with a sigh. "Anyway, Dad's done the job of both mother and father since then, and I don't want him to think for a second that he's let me down somehow, because he hasn't." She looked at Anna with a fierce expression in her blue eyes as Anna hoisted Henry to her other hip. He *was* a little monster, she thought affectionately. He was certainly heavy. "He absolutely hasn't," Jane insisted, and Anna nodded her acceptance.

"Still," she replied gently, "I think he could probably take the truth from you. And maybe he needs to hear it. He sounds like he wants to be a help, and he needs to know how."

"I didn't really think about it like that," Jane replied slowly. "Still, I don't know how I would tell him. He can be a bit sensitive—not in a bad way, though!" She looked alarmed at the possibility that Anna might think badly of this paragon of paternity for so much as a millisecond.

"He sounds like a wonderful father," she told her, meaning it. The man had moved to Mathering for his daughter, and clearly wanted to support her in every way that he could. He really *was* a paragon, or close enough. "And like I said," she finished, "I think he can probably take it."

"Maybe," Jane allowed as she finished her tea. "He said he was going to pop round this afternoon." She nibbled her lip. "I think he's worried about me. Probably because when he rang this morning, I sounded a *teeny* bit hysterical about how little Henry has been sleeping."

"That *might* have caused him concern," Anna agreed gravely, her lips twitching. She imagined Jane shrieking into the phone while some kindly seventy-year-old became alarmed—and probably felt utterly ill-equipped to deal with a mother's rage about sleep deprivation and teething.

Jane let out a little bubble of laughter. "It might have," she agreed, and then she laughed again, shaking her head. "Thank you, Anna. I can't tell you how—how *normal* it feels, to talk to someone like this. I think part of the problem, besides the immense sleep deprivation, of course, is that I just haven't been able to *talk* to anyone here."

Anna frowned. "What about the other mums from the toddler group and that sort of thing?"

"They're nice enough," Jane replied, "but they've all known each other since the year dot. They all grew up here, and to tell you the truth, I can't always understand their Yorkshire accents!"

Jane gave a wry laugh of acknowledgement. "It can be hard," she agreed. "It took me a while to find my feet here, especially when I was a young mum."

"But you did eventually?" Jane asked hopefully.

Anna hesitated for a split second before replying, "Yes…eventually." Maybe just in the last week, though. "It will get better," she assured her. "Especially once Henry starts sleeping through the night!"

"By then I might have had another one," Jane replied with a groan. "Eric grew up with a brother only a year younger than him and he wants the same closeness for ours."

"Well, he's not the one having the babies, so maybe he can keep his thoughts to himself," Anna replied with smiling asperity, and Jane grinned.

"I might tell him that."

"I hope he doesn't hate me for it." She had yet to see Eric, except briefly in passing, but he looked like a real bloke's bloke, friendly in a rugby player sort of way.

"No, Eric's lovely, really," Jane said on a sigh. "He's worried about me, too. I really need to get my act together."

"You can start by nipping upstairs and having a shower," Anna told her. "Especially if your dad might stop by. You want to be in fine fettle when he does." And maybe she'd get to meet this paragon at long last. He was technically her landlord, after all.

With a few assurances that she'd be absolutely fine with Henry, Anna saw Jane off upstairs, and breathed a sigh of relief when she heard the sound of the shower running. Five minutes under stingingly hot water could be wonderfully restorative, and she certainly hoped it was for Jane.

With Henry seeming happy enough, Anna put him back in his high chair, strapping him in and bribing him with a rusk, which he gummed cheerfully as she set about cleaning the kitchen, which was a dispiriting mess of dirty dishes, smelly laundry, and half-drunk cups of stone-cold tea. It felt good to be helping Jane, in a way, she thought, that was different from helping Harriet or Rachel.

There was no history with Jane, she realised, no strings attached to anything, no need to tiptoe or cringe or apologise endlessly. Admittedly, things had got better between her and her daughters—a *lot* better—but they were not yet entirely uncomplicated.

And her bombshell today, Anna acknowledged ruefully, would complicate matters between the three of them even more. She could already guess what was going to happen when Rachel told her that Anna had admitted their father had loved another woman. Harriet would start firing questions at her, demanding answers, and probably leaping to some unfortunate conclusions. It was her daughter's defence mechanism, a way to keep from getting hurt, and unfortunately it didn't seem to work.

But Anna knew she'd have to deal with it sooner rather than later; perhaps she'd head back to the farm after she'd sorted Jane out. Harriet had said she would be back for supper, and Anna had a feeling Rachel wouldn't keep the news from her, wouldn't even want to. Yet more drama to look forward to that evening.

She'd just put a load of wash in and put away all the dishes she'd had drying on the rack when the sound of a car pulling up in front of the house had Anna pausing for a moment, only to stop completely when a few seconds later, there was a light tap on the door and a male voice called, "Jane, sweetheart?"

Ah, the dad had come at last! More curious perhaps than she had any right to be, Jane hurried to the front door and opened it.

"Jane's just upstairs—" she began smilingly only to stop abruptly, struck dumb by the sight of the man standing on the doorstep, a Tesco bag of groceries in one hand, his blue eyes creased in concern as he took in the sight of Anna on his daughter's doorstep. It was the man from the quiz evening.

Chapter Eleven

"OH!" ANNA EXCLAIMED, her voice full of recognition, and then she blushed. The man might not even remember her!

"The member of the Motley Matherings who led her team to fifth-place victory with the clutch knowledge of knowing where the cruciate ligament is," he replied with a ready smile. "In the flesh!"

Anna let out a rather wavery laugh. At least he hadn't said *the clearly unhinged woman who stalked me in Tesco an hour ago.* Thank goodness.

"You're responsible for that, as you very well know," she replied. "It's nice to meet you."

He transferred the bag to his other hand as he stuck his right one out to shake hers. "James Adams."

"Anna Mowbray," she replied, taking his hand. His palm was warm and dry, and his fingers squeezed hers gently, causing a thrill to go through her. *Get a grip, girl.* "Come in," she said, stepping aside. "Jane's just in the shower."

"I'm finally putting two and two together and making a reasonable four," James remarked as he strolled back to the kitchen, putting the bag of groceries on the table. "You're the new tenant."

"Got it in one," Anna replied as she followed him into the kitchen. She wasn't quite sure what to do with herself; Jane was still in the shower, but it wasn't her place to act as hostess, and so she stood hovering in the doorway, uncertain.

"And how's this fella?" James asked as he chucked Henry under the chin. The baby gave a screech of joy at seeing his grandfather and held his arms out to be released from the prison of his high chair. James, oblivious, turned away to glance back at Anna. "You've been helping Jane out, I gather?"

"You could hold him," Anna replied, a seeming complete non sequitur, except James clearly didn't take it that way.

He looked startled for only a moment before he remarked mildly, "Why does that sound as if you're scolding me?"

"No," Anna protested quickly, blushing in mortification. What on earth had possessed her to say such a thing? But then she recalled Jane's blotchy, exhausted face, and she found herself saying, "But you could."

James gazed at her evenly for a moment, his expression bemused but not annoyed—at least Anna didn't think it was—and then he said, equably enough, "Yes, I suppose I could. And should." He turned back to Henry and started, with the confidently competent attitude of a middle-aged male, to unbuckle the straps of the high chair. Except, for whatever reason, he couldn't quite manage it.

After a few seconds, he turned back to Anna with good-natured exasperation. "I fear I'm revealing my lack of expertise in this area," he told her wryly, which made her smile.

"These things are torture contraptions," she reassured him. "Back in the day, I lived in mortal dread of having to fold and unfold my daughters' double pushchair."

He laughed at that, a genuine sound of amusement and even joy that made Anna's heart sing. She forced the feelings back, knowing they weren't warranted in this situation. *And yet…* No. She couldn't think that way. "May I help you?" she asked.

"Please." He gestured widely towards the high chair and Henry, who had been looking between them both, clearly bemused by the interchange. "By all means."

Anna started forward, and it wasn't until she had reached for Henry's straps that she became, quite suddenly, conscious of James Adams's nearness, and in particular, the smell of his cologne. It was citrusy and fresh, so different from Peter's smell of soap and cow, back when they'd been married. And truth be told, she hadn't been close enough to any man to smell him since.

At this thought, her fingers fumbled with the straps, and she found herself bumbling as much as James had been, which made him laugh softly.

"Is this too much for us, do you think?" he asked, his mouth close enough so his breath tickled her ear, creating an absurd sense of intimacy that made Anna only fumble all the more. Henry, growing impatient, let out an ear-splitting screech.

"Sorry…" she said, a bit breathlessly, unsure if she was speaking to Henry or James. Maybe both.

Finally, the buckle came free and with an audible sigh of relief, she lifted Henry from his high chair. Thank goodness.

"There we are," she said cheerfully, and then, with just a *hint* of a knowing gleam in her eye, she thrust Henry in all his chubby, sticky glory, his mouth rimmed with gloopy rusk, towards James, who took him with a startled oof, and then a wry smile.

"Here we are," he agreed, and then to Anna's surprise, he blew a raspberry on the baby's tummy. "Hello, my little chum," he said, and with another squeal, Henry grabbed both of James's ears and tugged hard. "Ouch," he said wryly, as he sought to extricate himself, and Anna laughed.

"Dad." Jane sounded shocked, thrilled, and slightly scandalised all at once as she came into the kitchen.

For a reason she couldn't quite fathom, Anna took a step back from James and the baby, as if to distance herself from them.

Jane came forward, dressed in pyjamas, her damp hair knotted on top of her head. She had her arms outstretched for Henry. "Let me take him off you."

"Not so fast," James replied, dancing nimbly away from his daughter. "I'm enjoying this." He gave Anna a humorous glance that she saw his daughter definitely noticed, frowning slightly.

"Do you know each other?" Jane asked.

Once more Anna and James exchanged looks and then he replied easily enough, "Not quite."

"Not quite?" Jane replied, glancing between them both, the frown deepening between her brows.

Uh-oh. Anna suddenly had the crystal-clear sense that Jane would most definitely *not* approve of any kind of friendship between her father and her neighbour. She'd likely been the sole object of her father's attention for what—? Fifteen years?

Then, as quickly as Anna had had these thoughts, she told herself they were ridiculous. She and James had done nothing but have a tiny bit of chat. They did not know each other at *all.* Why on earth was she thinking like this?

"We saw each other at a quiz evening," James replied, glancing at Anna as if in query. She gave a little nod. She was definitely *not* going to mention Tesco. Ever.

"Yes, I'm afraid your dad's team trounced mine," she replied lightly. "But he did give me some help."

"It sounds like there's a story there," Jane replied as she took Henry from her father and clutched him to her. She did not sound all that pleased about that observation.

"No, no story," James replied, but something in his tone made the words *not yet* appear in Anna's mind like invisible thought bubbles. She really needed to get a hold of herself.

"Okay, well…" Jane glanced at Anna, and she realised this was, most definitely, her cue to leave.

"I should get back," she said hurriedly. "I think I might have left my shopping on my doorstep."

"If that included a large bottle of Bombay Sapphire gin," James interjected, his eyes twinkling at her, "then, yes, I think you did."

Anna would have been embarrassed, save for his smile. He looked far too kind for her to take offence. "It certainly did include such a bottle," she replied with an attempt at pertness. "But were you snooping in my groceries?"

"Not at all," he assured her, his mouth quirking up in a smile as his eyes glinted at her. "The bottle was practically rolling out into the street."

"Oh!" Anna shook her head at him, and he grinned, and belatedly she realised their behaviour was, well, rather *odd*. They were acting as if they'd known each other for years, and they really hadn't.

"I should go," she said, glancing at Jane, who was starting, she feared, to look a little bit annoyed. Anna hoped she hadn't jeopardised their friendship with her amateurish attempt at flirting with a man she barely knew. "Lovely to meet you," she threw at James, not quite looking at him, and then she blew Henry a kiss before hurrying out of the house.

Back in her house, having lugged the groceries into the kitchen and unpacked them all, including the gin, Anna found herself in too much of a flutter to settle to anything. She thought about going back to Embthwaite Farm as she'd originally planned, but she didn't think she could face a big emotive conversation with Harriet and Rachel just now, not in the mood she was in.

Yet what mood *was* she in? Feeling so fluttery and jittery and out of sorts? It was silly, in a woman her age. It was *humiliating*. Somehow, this realisation settled her down, maybe a bit too much. She started to feel quite flat. Really, it was positively ridiculous that she'd got in such a tizz, and over absolutely nothing.

With the groceries put away, Anna decided to do some ironing. It was, somewhat perversely, something that relaxed her. Maybe it was the satisfying way wrinkles were smoothed out with just a little heat and pressure. There was a metaphor for life in there somewhere, Anna thought wryly as she set up the ironing board, but she wasn't sure what it was—or at least she didn't really want to think too hard about it. She put on the television, choosing a mindless game show, and thought about breaking open the Bombay Sapphire, but decided against it. It was only just past five, after all, and she still might motivate herself to head back to Embthwaite Farm...maybe.

As if her daughter had sensed her thoughts from four miles away, a text from Rachel pinged onto her phone.

I'm going out with Ben tonight. Let's talk with H. tomorrow.

Phew. Anna felt only relief. She could have that gin, after all, and she'd enjoy it, too. She'd just finished mixing her drink, trying not to feel either guilty or like a lush, when a light tap sounded on her front door. Anna tensed, bracing herself for some kind of awkward conversation with Jane, although really what could Jane possibly say? *Don't smile at my dad.* Really, Anna was reading far too much into the situation, never mind Jane. And yet...why else would Jane come over?

Sighing, Anna put her drink down by the TV and went to the door, opening it to find not Jane but James Adams standing on her stoop.

"Hello again," he said with an easy smile, his bright blue eyes crinkling at the corners. "Do you mind if I come in?"

"Er..." Anna was dumbfounded. Despite his friendliness, she had not expected him to seek her out. To come right to her door...and *inside.*

"No, of course not," she said a bit belatedly, because what else could she say? She stepped aside and James strolled into the house.

"How are you finding it here?" he enquired as he headed

back towards the kitchen. Anna hurried after him, pausing in the lounge to turn off the TV and iron.

"It's lovely," she told him as she joined him in the kitchen, where he was standing by the French windows, his hands in his pockets of his chinos as he gazed out at the twilit garden. "You've done a fabulous job renovating it."

"It was fun," he replied, his back to her. He sounded distracted. Anna wondered why on earth he'd come. She didn't feel she could ask.

Finally, resolutely, he turned around. "You've been very kind, taking an interest in Jane."

Ah, so they were talking about Jane. Anna felt a confusing welter of relief and disappointment. "I'm sorry that I didn't realise she was struggling a bit, until today," she told him. "She seems so cheerful and on top of things most of the time."

"Yes, she doesn't like to cause trouble. Well." He smiled wryly. "Cause *me* trouble. Or worry. She's very protective of me, but she got married just eighteen months ago and then moved and had Henry almost right away—something of a surprise—and I think it's all been a bit difficult."

"Honeymoon babies often are," Anna replied with a small smile, impressed by his emotional astuteness on several levels. "I had one myself, and then another fifteen months later. Those first few years were a complete blur."

"I can imagine." He paused and then admitted, "Jane told me a little bit about you…that your daughters live here, and you've come to help them out with their father. I'm sorry about your ex-husband…his diagnosis."

"Thank you," Anna replied, and then felt compelled to

add, "And she told me a little bit about you, as well. Your wife..."

He nodded, a bit quickly. "She died fourteen years ago. Cancer. It was quick."

They both nodded, smiling a little wryly. It was odd, Anna supposed, to know such broad strokes about a person without any other detail.

"It sounds like you have a lot going on," James told her, "So I really don't want to impose, especially as you've already done so much for her today. Jane told me how you had a chat and a cup of tea," he explained, "and watched Henry and cleaned the kitchen while she had a shower. That really is so kind."

"It was no trouble," Anna assured him. "Jane's been so lovely and welcoming to me."

"Well, then." He gave a grimacing sort of smile as he rubbed the back of his neck; Anna got the sense that he didn't enjoy asking people for favours and also that he was genuinely concerned about his daughter. It made her like him all the more...and she was conscious that she already *did* like him, or at least what she knew about him.

"I wanted to ask if you'd be able to check on Jane once in a while," he said. "I don't mean more than that—you really went above and beyond today. Just to make sure she's coping. I come by as often as I can, but she doesn't like me to fuss, and I think she prefers being protective of me, rather than the other way round." He sighed as he dropped his hand. "It's a little complicated."

"Families often are," Anna replied. "I think it was the poet Mary Karr who said, 'Dysfunctional families are ones with more than one person in them.'"

James gave a huff of laughter, a genuine sound. "True enough. There's only Jane and me, and I suppose there is a certain amount of dysfunction just between the two of us."

"You seem very close," Anna remarked. As she said the words, she realised they caused her a funny little pang of envy. She wanted that kind of closeness with her own daughters. They were getting there, which heartened her, but they weren't there yet. They weren't really even near. A small sigh escaped her at the thought before she came to herself and gave James a bracing smile. "Anyway, I'd be very happy to keep an eye on Jane, and I could take Henry sometimes too, if it would be helpful. He's so gorgeous."

"I don't want to presume," James protested quickly. "You certainly have a lot on your plate as it is."

"Yes, but when you're living so close to death, being reminding of the joys of life can be a good thing," Anna replied quietly. "I'd be happy to, honestly."

"Thank you," James said simply, and then they were left staring at each other in a manner that felt a little uncomfortable, although not in a bad way. In a sort of exciting way, actually, Anna thought, as James cocked his head, his cerulean gaze sweeping slowly over her, making her tingle with anticipation—and hope.

"There was something else I wanted to ask..." he began, and she raised her eyebrows, smiling faintly.

"Oh, yes?"

"I wondered if you'd care to go out for a drink, maybe this weekend?"

That faint tingle of anticipation became a positive buzz

of excitement, coursing through her veins. Then, quite abruptly, Anna imagined heading over to one of Mathering's three pubs for a drink with a handsome man and knew the gossip would be racing around the town within minutes, with all its inevitable fallout. Harriet and Rachel would probably know about it before she'd even driven back home. She wasn't sure she could deal with that, on top of everything else. And yet…

"Still thinking about it?" James asked, his mouth quirking wryly.

"Yes, sorry, but not because… It's just Mathering is a small town," Anna explained in a rush. "And I haven't been back here in quite some time, and what with my daughters and ex-husband here, my presence is already causing something of a stir."

"Ah." He nodded in understanding. "The inevitable gossip mill going into overdrive."

Anna nodded, relieved he got it. "Yes, exactly."

"Well." He paused, his forehead crinkling. "If this doesn't sound too forward, you're welcome to come to mine. Unless someone follows your car all the way out of town, no one would know." The smile he gave her was charming and just a little bit whimsical. "But if you'd rather meet in a public place, I understand, of course."

Of course, it would be more sensible, as well as safer, to meet in a public place. Anna would have lectured both Harriet and Rachel about meeting a strange man in a secluded place, most certainly! But…she trusted James Adams, and she felt she knew him, both through Jane and the brief interactions they'd already had.

"I don't mind," she told him. "That would be lovely."

His smile widened in a way that made Anna feel like laughing. He looked so pleased, and she felt the same. Something about the way they interacted felt amazingly easy, and *right*. Or was that just wishful thinking?

"Great," he told her. "Friday, around seven? I'll give you my postcode, as well as my number, in case something comes up."

"Wonderful," Anna replied, and that buzzy sense of something good happening rippled through her again, so she felt positively electrified.

Chapter Twelve

THE NEXT MORNING, Anna headed over to Jane's with a dozen blueberry muffins and a packet of freshly ground coffee. There was a lightness in her step, a positive swing to it, after James's invitation last night. It was only Tuesday, but she could hardly wait until Friday. Did it count as a date? she'd wondered endlessly already. She thought it might. Was she too old to be feeling this way? She thought she was, but she didn't care.

"Oh, Anna!" Jane came to the door still in her pyjamas although it was ten o'clock in the morning. She looked exhausted. "Thank you for yesterday. I'm sorry I wasn't more together. You must have been appalled by the state of me—"

"Not at all, Jane, and you really don't need to apologise," Anna returned quickly. "I understand completely how a little one can take over your life. And the brain fog…! Please. I get it, I really do." She smiled, shaking her head, before holding out the muffins and coffee. "These are for you. A little pick-me-up."

"Oh." Jane brightened as she took the offerings. "Thank you so much. Do you have time to have a cuppa and a muffin?"

Anna hesitated, knowing she really needed to see Harriet

and Rachel, but then decided that an extra half an hour could hardly hurt. "That would be lovely," she said, and stepped inside.

Jane led her back to the kitchen which, despite Anna having tidied it just the night before, looked as messy as ever, or almost.

"Sorry, all your good work gone to waste," Jane remarked on a sigh, and Anna smiled.

"Isn't that always the way with children?" She glanced around the kitchen. "Where's the gorgeous Henry?"

"He's sleeping, the wretch," Jane replied good-naturedly. "After being up for four hours last night."

"Oh, Jane." Anna gazed at her in dismay. "Maybe you should take a nap yourself."

She shook her head resolutely. "I can't, I'm afraid, once I'm up. Maybe later."

Anna frowned, because she knew how important the sleep-when-your-baby-sleeps maxim could be…but she was also conscious that it was hardly her place to insist.

"Well, hopefully a cup of coffee will help, then," she said instead.

"It was so funny," Jane remarked as she set about making coffee, "how it seemed as if you knew my dad! He explained everything, of course."

Did he? Anna thought. What, exactly, had he explained? "Yes, that was strange," she replied after a moment. "We don't know each other at all, actually. Just saw each other across a crowded room." And were having a drink together in three days. It wasn't, Anna felt, her place to mention that fact, and yet she felt uncomfortable intentionally omitting it, because she had a feeling James hadn't said anything.

"Across a crowded room!" Jane let out a hoot of laughter as she poured boiled water over the coffee granules. "That almost sounds romantic." She slid Anna a speculative glance, as if daring her to contradict it—or admit it? Anna felt as if she were flailing.

"Well, he obviously cares about you," she remarked, and Jane nodded, seemingly satisfied, as if Anna had given the right answer.

WERE *ALL* RELATIONSHIPS fraught on some level? Anna wondered when she left Jane's house for Embthwaite Farm forty-five minutes later. Henry had woken up right as she'd been putting her coat on, and she hadn't missed the way Jane's face had fallen.

"He barely slept at all," she'd muttered, and then tried to rally. "Well, it's better than nothing, I suppose."

Anna had promised to pop in when she returned from the farm, but she had a feeling Jane was in for a long, tiring day. And when was Anna going to tell her about her drink with her dad? By not saying anything, it seemed to take on a greater significance than perhaps it had…although to be fair, it was feeling pretty significant to Anna already.

Still, a problem for later, she decided. She had to focus on her own daughters now.

The drive through Mathering and over the moors to Embthwaite Farm was beautiful on this sunlit, January morning, the grass sparkling with frost, the Derwent a winding, grey-blue ribbon in the distance. A few heavily pregnant sheep, looking rather stoical, munched on the icy grass, and Anna smiled to see them.

As she pulled into the farm's drive, her breath came out in a long, slow sigh. She had no idea what this conversation with her daughters was going to look like. How much they would ask. How much she would tell.

For a second, she simply sat in the car, remembering the first time she'd come to Embthwaite Farm, how she'd fallen in love with it, how she'd *wanted* to fall in love with it. It was so easy to love things—and people—when your heart was crying out to. Back then, everything had felt like a fairy tale. Peter had been charming, in his admittedly rugged and taciturn way, and he'd been excited to show her the farm. He'd loved her at the start, Anna knew. He'd told her as much, even while confessing his love for another woman. *Ruth.* The name had always felt like a stone in her mouth, hard and gritty.

She remembered as they'd driven up in his old Land Rover, how the sun had been setting over the hill behind the farmhouse, bathing everything in gold. How when she'd stepped out, the air had felt as fresh as a drink of water, and she'd been able to hear the cattle lowing from the barn, an unfamiliar yet comforting sound.

Inside, admittedly, she'd faltered a bit. Squat, grey, and from the Victorian age, the farmhouse had seemed terribly dreary inside, full of dark, heavy furniture and thick, dusty curtains, faded, aged wallpaper and muddy-looking portraits. But the kitchen had been warm and welcoming, and she'd imagined how she could make it a home. She'd even romanticised its dreariness—she would transform this melancholy pile into something both beautiful and cosy. She'd fashioned herself as the heroine of a Gothic novel, Anna acknowledged wryly. That otherworldly excitement had lasted, for a little while.

The front door of the farmhouse opened, and Rachel poked her head out, frowning. "I could see you from the dining room," she called. "Are you coming in?"

"Yes," Anna answered, and shaking her head to banish all the memories, she got out of the car and headed inside the house, her boots crunching across the gravel.

Rachel was waiting for her in the hall, lowering her voice as she confided, "I haven't told Harriet anything. Just that we need to talk."

"All right," Anna replied mildly. She suspected that would be enough to put her younger daughter on high alert. "How's your dad?"

"The same, really." Rachel gave an unhappy little shrug. "Sleeping a lot, talking a bit, although I can't always understand what he says. He only eats about half of what I bring him up on a tray. The nurse upped his pain relief *again*." She paused and then admitted quietly, "It's all happening faster than I expected it to, except it *isn't*, really. At the beginning, the doctor said three to six months. It's already been over two." She frowned unhappily. "But at the beginning…Dad seemed at peace with it. He said he had enough time to get things in order, and that was a—a gift." Her voice wavered. "But lately, he's just seemed…angry. Or confused. Or both. Or worse." Rachel shook her head, blinking back tears.

"A brain tumour can change someone's personality,"

Anna told her gently. "And even if you're not scared of death itself, I can imagine it's still frightening to lose your capabilities. To not be able to talk, or to forget where you are…" She felt a rush of pity for her ex-husband, as well as her daughters, having to deal with him like this. He'd always been a proud, stubborn man, secure in how capable and competent he was. To lose all that…it had to be devastating, even if he'd been prepared for it, or at least had thought he was.

"I just…don't want this to go on forever," Rachel confessed quietly. "I know it won't, obviously, but even—even a few more weeks like this feels like too long. I think Dad would want to go—to die, at this point, if he could say so."

"He might," Anna agreed. "But remember what he said before? That this time was a gift. It was a gift to him, and it can be to you, as well." She glanced seriously at her daughter. "This is the time to make peace with your father, Rachel, both you and Harriet. And love him for who he was, not who we all wanted him to be, which I know is a big ask."

Rachel wiped her eyes. "*You* can say that, even experiencing what you did?"

And her daughter didn't even know the half of it. "Yes," Anna said firmly, surprised by how much she meant it. A few weeks ago, she might have been in a different place, but now? When her life felt as if it were finally expanding, if only a little? She could, and she was glad.

Rachel drew a shaky breath as she composed herself. "Harriet's in the kitchen," she said, and Anna nodded and followed her daughter back.

Harriet was sliding scones off a griddle pan on top of the

Rayburn; as Anna came into the kitchen, she gave her a swift glance before looking away again, back to the scones. Fred, from his usual position in front of the Rayburn, lifted his head and thumped his tail once or twice in greeting.

"You're an expert at stepping around dear old Fred," Anna remarked to Harriet as she stooped to pat the dog's head. "What are the scones for?"

"Afternoon at the hotel. Quinn wants three deliveries a week."

"Wow, you're really taking on a lot, aren't you?" Anna exclaimed, pleased for her. "Well done, Harriet. That's wonderful."

Another quick glance from her daughter; Anna couldn't tell how she was feeling. In a moment of confidence, she decided to grasp the nettle. For too long, she'd waited for her daughters to ask questions, make overtures. She hadn't wanted to press, or maybe she'd felt as if she didn't have the right to force anything, and so she'd always acted the supplicant, silently begging for the scraps of their attention.

Not today.

"I know Rachel told you we should talk," she stated carefully as she sat down at the table and folded her hands in front of her. "It might be that we should have talked about all this before. But I said something to her that I want to say to you, just so you understand where I was coming from, when I left all those years ago."

Harriet finished sliding the scones off the pan and then moved it off the Rayburn and closed its lid. "All right," she replied neutrally, and Anna was grateful she was being so even-tempered about it all. Rachel sat opposite Anna, and

Harriet took the seat at the end. They both waited expectantly.

Anna decided she might as well rip the plaster off. "I told Rachel that your father was in love with another woman," she stated baldly. Rachel gave a little nod while Harriet's jaw dropped.

"What…"

"I found out about her a year after we got married, when I'd just had Rachel."

"You mean…they were having an *affair*?" Rachel asked, and Anna almost laughed. What had her daughter thought she'd meant, when she'd said Peter was in love with another woman? That he'd gazed longingly at her photograph every night before bed?

"Yes," she confirmed. "They were."

"But Dad never went anywhere," Harriet protested. She didn't sound disbelieving, just confused. "How could he have had an affair?"

"He didn't go anywhere *much*," Anna agreed, "but he did go to the livestock market in Selby almost every month."

"What are you saying?" Rachel asked. "That's where he first met her?"

"He knew her before we were married," Anna explained. She was surprised to realise reciting these facts didn't hurt her anymore, although they still made her feel sad. "He proposed to her, actually, I found out later, before he met me, but she's a farmer herself and she didn't want to leave her farm for his. He didn't want to leave his for hers, so they ended it. He met me a few months later, and we had a whirlwind romance. I think I was the opposite from her in just about every way, from what I've gathered, and of course I didn't have a farm myself, so there was no problem there."

She fell silent, remembering how *enchanted* Peter had seemed with her, at the start. She'd realised later it was because she'd been so naïve, so thrilled with the idea of the farm, the moors, the *life*. So different from Ruth, who had been completely self-sufficient and hadn't wanted to fit herself into someone else's life at all. Anna, meanwhile, had been doing backbends to make it happen.

"I can't believe it," Harriet said, her voice hollow. "So, Dad was…what, visiting this woman every month in Selby?"

Anna nodded. "Something like that."

"How did you find out about it?" Rachel asked, and she sighed in memory.

"In the most unlikely way, really—from an old school friend who had come to our wedding. She saw your father with—with her out in York. She'd been there for a holiday, and she walked up to him. He went completely red, apparently, and blustered something about how he was visiting a friend. She felt she had to tell me."

"And did you confront him?" Harriet asked. She had the hushed tone of someone who was listening to a fascinating story and maybe that was what it seemed like—nothing more than a story, and certainly very little to do with the man upstairs in bed, barely tethered to this life.

"Yes, I did. I was heartbroken and furious, plus sleep-deprived and emotional from having a newborn, and so I burst into tears when I told him what I'd found out. He didn't deny it." She paused. "To be honest, he didn't even apologise. He just said he'd always loved her, and he had room in his life for both of us."

"What!" Rachel smacked the table with the palm of her hand, half-rising in indignation.

Anna smiled faintly. "Would you really expect your father to be any different, Rachel? The funny thing is, I could almost see his point. He'd chosen me…mostly. He only went to Selby once a month, sometimes not even that. He told me he would never leave me, especially not with you in the picture, Rachel. In his own way, your father was a family man. So, the end result was, I had to like it or lump it."

"But couldn't you have left?" Harriet asked quietly. "You'd only been married a few months…"

"I thought about it," Anna admitted. "And in some ways, it was as much pride as practicality that kept me where I was. My parents had warned me not to marry him, and I didn't want to prove them right. But there were also the facts to consider—I had a newborn baby, and I was more or less estranged from my parents at the time. I'd never held down a proper job. I had no money. And," she admitted fairly, "whether you can believe or not, I still loved him. I convinced myself that eventually, I'd be enough for him, but I never was."

"Are you saying he kept up this affair the whole time?" Harriet demanded. "All those years? And we never knew?"

Rachel leaned back in her chair. "So much makes so much sense now," she murmured, shaking her head, and Anna suspected she was thinking about how unhappy she'd seemed, so much of the time.

"It came and went, a bit, I think," she told Harriet. "Sometimes he was too busy to go to Selby. Sometimes I was too unhappy, and I think he felt guilty about that. But whenever he went to Selby…well, I knew. I could tell he'd been with her."

Rachel grimaced. "And afterwards? When you left him?"

Anna shook her head. "I don't know. I suppose I thought he might make more room in his life for her, but the impression I got was that she was as happy with the way things had been as he was. She had her own…" She paused and then shook her head. She couldn't tell Harriet and Rachel the rest. She feared it might devastate them, and in any case, it didn't feel like her part of the story to tell. It was Peter's, or maybe it was Ruth's. "She had her own life," she finished.

"Why did you leave when you did?" Harriet asked abruptly, clearly still processing all she'd heard. "If you'd been putting up with it for years, why then? Why was that the breaking point?"

Anna hesitated. *Should* she explain? But no. She didn't have the strength for that conversation, not then, anyway, and she still wasn't sure it was her place. "I don't know, exactly," she said quietly. "To be honest with you, that day is something of a blur. I remember standing in the middle of the kitchen, and then I remember walking out to my car. The next moment it felt as if I'd blinked and arrived in Reading. I know I drove there, obviously, but I can't remember a single minute of that journey." She gave them both an apologetic smile; she knew it wasn't a very satisfactory answer.

"Where did you go, Mum?" Rachel asked. "Your parents were gone by then…"

"To my aunt's. She was the only person I could think of, and she'd always tried to stay in touch with letters. She used to send you two hand-knit booties when you were babies, and then jumpers when you were older. They had sheep on the front. She knit them every year."

"I remember those," Harriet recalled, her eyes lighting up. "They were darling. Did we visit her? I can't remember..."

"When you were little. Then she became a bit frail, and couldn't travel, and going all the way down to Reading was harder. I think you must have been twelve or so the last time we went."

Harriet nodded slowly. "I think I remember that, actually. She used to give us toffee that just about broke your teeth."

"That's right." Anna smiled. Aunt Pauline had been, in her fusty, no-nonsense way, exactly what she'd needed at that time. "Anyway," she resumed, determined to say it all now, "I went to her. And after about twenty-four hours she realised I wasn't coping very well at all, and she called the GP, who referred me to the psychiatric intensive care ward at Prospect Park Hospital. I was there for two weeks, and then in an inpatient ward for another two months."

This statement had the effect of making Anna feel as if they'd all become frozen in pools of silence. Despite her having told them she'd been sectioned earlier, Harriet and Rachel were looking shell-shocked by the specifics.

"Psychiatric intensive care..." Rachel repeated faintly. "Mum, what do you mean, you weren't coping? How bad was it?"

Anna sighed, briefly closing her eyes as she remembered—or tried to—that awful time. It felt like a blankness in her life, a dark space where memory should be. "Honestly, I don't entirely remember how I was. I shut down in a lot of ways—wouldn't eat, couldn't sleep, could barely talk. It was as if…" She paused, reflecting. "It was as if my body was finally responding to twenty years of trauma. Not physical," she clarified quickly. "I told you before your father never hurt me that way, and he didn't, not ever. But emotionally…there was a lot to deal with, and for some reason, it hit me all at once. I'm sorry, though," she said quietly, as she glanced between them both. "I wish I'd been able to handle it. I wish I'd been a better, more present mother for you. I know sometimes when you were younger, I let the sadness get the better of me. And of course, leaving the way I did…well, that was very hurtful. I've always understood that."

Slowly Harriet shook her head. "Mum…" she began, and with a jolt, Anna realised it was the first time Harriet had called her mum in…*years.* "I wish you'd told us this before, but I understand why you didn't. Why you couldn't, I mean, and maybe I wouldn't have been able to listen. Maybe we both needed…to go through some things." She drew a shuddery breath and reached for her mother's hand. "I'm just sorry you had to go through it all, and alone, too."

"So am I, Mum," Rachel said softly, and she put her hand on top of Harriet and Anna's. "Really sorry."

They all sat there for a moment, their hands on top of one another, absorbing the significance of the moment. Was there anything more than this? Anna wondered, a sob caught in her throat. Her daughters' understanding. Their forgiveness. It had taken a long time to get here, but oh my goodness, it was so worth it. She was so grateful.

"Thank you both," she said quietly, "for understanding. It means…it means the world to me." They were all silent for a moment, giving each other watery smiles and struggling not to cry.

It felt, Anna thought, like the best thing in the world.

Chapter Thirteen

THE MOORS WERE cloaked in darkness when, three days later, Anna followed James's texted directions to his house on the other side of Mathering. The last few days had been good—wonderful, really—but also hard in their own way. Harriet and Rachel were clearly absorbing everything Anna had told then, and that was an emotional process.

In the meantime, Peter was continuing to decline, and Anna feared he didn't have very long left at all. Time was measured in days and maybe weeks, certainly not months and years. Soon, she suspected, it would be in just hours and days, and the thought filled her with sorrow. She wanted her daughters to reconcile with their father, to make peace with him, and she feared what she'd told them would make it impossible.

Had she been wrong to admit the truth, and tell them about Peter's affair? It was something she continued to wrestle with, all the while glad that she had, because it meant she was closer to her daughters than ever. Things weren't perfect, and everyone could still feel and act a little spiky, but there had been progress. A lot of progress. And Anna found she could not regret that.

But now she had something exciting and more than a

little nerve-racking to think about—her drink with James. He'd texted her twice since inviting her, once with directions and once, just an hour ago, to say he was looking forward to it and asking her to bring her bottle of Bombay Sapphire, accompanied by a wink emoji so she wasn't sure if he was serious or not. She'd brought it just in case, but the whole thing was making her rather nervous.

She hadn't done the dating thing pretty much ever; her relationship with Peter, whirlwind that it had been, couldn't really count and in the last twelve years she'd gone on exactly two dates, neither of which she cared to remember. But maybe, she reminded herself, this wasn't a date.

It had taken her an hour to choose what to wear for this was-it-or-wasn't-it-a-date, and she'd finally settled on a pair of wide-legged black wool trousers and a cowl-necked top in deep blue cashmere—elegant and understated, she hoped. She hardly ever wore make-up except the prerequisite lotions and potions to smooth away fine lines, but she'd dared to add a bit of mascara and subtle lipstick just in case it really was a date. Her hair was in its usual sleek, silver bob, nothing much to change there. She'd gone completely grey in her early forties, when she'd first left Peter, and she'd never bothered to dye it since.

The sat nav directed her to a lonely looking farm track that cut through the moors, the twinkling lights of a house barely visible in the distance. The man clearly enjoyed his space, Anna thought, bemused, as she started down the track, passing over two cattle grids before she finally pulled up into the courtyard of a very impressive barn conversion.

When Jane had told her that her father lived in a barn

conversion, Anna had pictured something simpler and more, well, barn-like. The house in front of her was something else entirely—sprawling, with huge glass skylights and a wrapa-round deck that took in the spectacular view of the moors, now cloaked in darkness, stretching endlessly in every direction. *Wow.* Anna felt impressed and intimidated and more than a little out of her depth all at once.

James came to the door before she was halfway across the slate-tiled courtyard, throwing it open wide.

"Welcome!" he called, and his enthusiasm made her smile.

Deciding to own it, she brandished the bottle of Bombay Sapphire. "As requested."

With a laugh, James shaded his eyes with one hand. "That was meant to be a joke. I hate you to think I'm so stingy that you have to bring your own booze."

"Well, better to drink it with someone than alone in my house while watching *The Traitors*," she replied, smiling as she handed him the bottle.

"I love *The Traitors*," he told her, and she laughed. As she stepped across the threshold, he put his hand on her lower back to usher her in, so lightly Anna barely felt the pressure but her whole body tingled all the same.

"And I thought the rental you renovated was impressive," she murmured as she walked into the soaring, open-plan space. The skylight was even bigger from the inside than the outside, a huge, vaulted dome of glass that now showcased a patch of velvety black sky twinkling with the first stars. A massive stone fireplace dominated one end of the space, flames crackling cheerfully within and surrounded by squashy leather sofas and armchairs, bright, cosy-looking rugs scattered across the slate-tiled floor. By the bi-fold doors leading out to the deck there was a table that seated eight, its top looking as if it had been from one of the original barn doors, now varnished to a high gloss. And then the kitchen, on the other end…

It was a dream kitchen, with a huge marble-topped island complete with sink, a massive Aga in cherry red, and Shaker cupboards, some fronted with glass to showcase pieces of pottery in a pretty slate blue.

"This is just about the nicest house I've ever seen," Anna exclaimed, too impressed by it all to be embarrassed by her own enthusiasm. "It looks like it could be in *Architectural Digest* or *Beautiful Homes* or something."

"Well, I like a project," James told her with a smile. "And, as it happens, I was an architect before I retired last year."

"Wow." Anna shook her head slowly. "I love it."

"I'm glad." He held up the bottle of gin. "G&T or something else? I have wine, beer, a few spirits, something soft if you'd rather." He headed over to the kitchen and Anna followed, noticing several bowls of crisps and nuts already laid out. This little thoughtfulness touched her in a way she couldn't explain.

"Wine, actually, and just the one glass," she told him. "Since I'm driving."

"Fair enough," he replied equably. "Red or white? I have both."

She hesitated, amazed at how easy it was to talk to him, and yet how unfamiliar navigating these social niceties had become. When had she done them, really, if ever? A few town or school events when she'd lived in Mathering, a few quiet evenings with friends back in Stroud. Not much more. "What are you having?" she asked.

"Whatever you are," he replied, smiling, his blue eyes sparkling amidst the weathered creases of his face, and she laughed and shook her head.

"Red, then, please."

A few minutes later James was handing her a glass and then ushering her over to the sofas before going back to bring the bowls of crisps and nuts.

"This is so lovely," Anna remarked with a sigh as she settled into one squashy armchair, tucking her feet up under her. The fire was blazing, sending a lovely warmth over her, and she'd taken off her ankle boots and slipped them under the chair. Outside the shadows were deepening and between the skylight and French doors, there was a lot of darkness to see, somehow making the room they were in, despite the soaring space, feel cosy and warm. "Do you mind living out here on your own?"

"No, I've learned to like my own space," James replied. He'd settled on one corner of the sofa, his arm stretched out along the back, almost making Anna wish she'd chosen the other end of the sofa, just for the thrill of wondering if his fingers might accidentally—or not-so-accidentally—brush her shoulder. She was really acting like a lovesick teenager, she thought ruefully. Yet she didn't actually mind the feeling; it felt too exciting, too *fun*, to be this buzzy inside. It had been a long, long time since she'd felt this way, and she realised she wanted to enjoy it…for what it was, and no more.

Just a feeling. An evening.

"How have you found Mathering?" Anna asked. "How long have you been here?"

"I was up and down for a bit, checking on the house," James told her. "But I moved here permanently just before Christmas."

"Oh!" For some reason, she was surprised; it was around the same time she'd come back. "Not long, then."

"No, not long." He smiled faintly, his eyes creasing. He was a handsome man, Anna thought with a pang; somehow the lines on his face and the silver hair just added to his appeal. He was a man who had lived, and suffered, and survived. Just like she had.

And yet… Anna couldn't shake that he was somehow far more deserving of the approbation of a hard life well lived than she was. It occurred to her, as she took a sip of wine, how *complicated* it was going to be, to have to explain things when he started asking the inevitable questions about her marriage, her children, her *life*. And what would her answers be? Did she really want to burden both of them—and the start of whatever this was between them, if *this* was anything—with the truth?

"What happened?" James asked, breaking into her thoughts, and startled, Anna blinked him back into focus.

"Sorry, I was miles away there for a moment," she apologised with a shaky laugh.

"Yes, I realised." He cocked his head, his expression nothing but sympathetic. "How come?"

He didn't pull any punches, did James, Anna thought

wryly. And maybe she shouldn't, either. After all, it wasn't as if they were in their twenties, naïve and a bit silly, trying to be the perfect whatever, because they still believed they could, that life worked that way.

"I was just thinking how complicated life is," she admitted baldly, taking a glug of wine for a bit of Dutch courage. It was very good—rich and velvety, sliding down her throat, trickling through her limbs. "Especially when you get to our age."

He cocked an eyebrow. "*Our* age? I think I might be a bit older than you."

She laughed, amused but also gratified by the remark. It made her feel not just like a lovesick teenager, but a giggly girl. "So, you're a cradle robber?" she teased, only to blush at the obvious innuendo. This wasn't a date. At least, it hadn't been explicitly *said*.

"Tell me how old you are and then I'll tell you if you're right," James replied, utterly unfazed by her remark, its implication.

Anna took a breath, met his bright blue eyes directly. She felt as if everything in her was tingling. "Fifty-three."

"Fifty-seven," he answered. "I don't think that *quite* makes me cradle-robber territory, does it?" He held her gaze, and it felt like a challenge.

What was happening…and already?

"No," Anna answered after a pause. She found she had to look away, his gaze was that piercing. "Not *quite*."

"What a relief," James remarked dryly, and she laughed.

Oh, this was *fun*, being here like this. She could become drunk on the sheer possibility of it, never mind the wine she was trying to cautiously sip, considering she had to drive home tonight. She *liked* this. She liked feeling so…*alive.*

"I'm glad to put your mind at ease," she quipped before adding, "but you haven't actually told me how you've found Mathering."

James paused, his eyes cast to the ceiling, his gaze distant and thoughtful. He was wearing chinos and a button-down shirt in light blue with a grey cashmere V-necked jumper, and she suspected this was his uniform for 'smart casual'. It was so *odd,* how she felt she knew him already, could surmise or at least guess what made him tick. Or was she just being fanciful?

Did she even care if she was?

"Small," he said at last. "I spent most of my working life outside London. I didn't think of myself as a city man, per se, but I grew up in Solihull, outside Birmingham, and so North Yorkshire is…different." He smiled, his eyes crinkling at the corners. "What about you? You must have spent a good amount of time in Mathering…?"

"I grew up in Reading," Anna told him, "but yes, twenty years in Mathering." Twenty long years.

James must have understood something from her tone, or maybe just the fact that he knew she was divorced, for he asked cautiously, "I know we're just getting to know one another, but…has it been hard? Coming back here?"

Anna rested her head against the back of her chair as she closed her eyes. "You have no idea," she stated quietly.

James was silent, and she wondered, with her eyes still closed, if she'd shocked him. Scared him off, maybe. So much for that fizzy feeling. She forced herself to open her eyes and look at him, and saw that he looked neither scared nor shocked, but rather understanding, his head cocked to one side, his eyes crinkled and full of warmth. She also realised she was not surprised by this. She'd *expected* him to be understanding, even in the middle of fearing that he wouldn't. Still, she felt she had to say something. "Sorry," she offered with a faint smile. "That's probably a bit grim for a getting-to-know-you chat."

"Not at all," he replied. "If we can't be honest in a getting-to-know-you chat, when can we be?"

Anna wrinkled her nose. "I always assumed people doled out the more gruesome parts of themselves in medicinal sips," she said, and James let out a bark of genuine laughter.

"They probably should," he agreed, "but there's something to be said for a warts-and-all confession, don't you think? I like to take my medicine in one big gulp."

Suddenly feeling very sober, Anna shook her head. "I don't know. It's a lot to take in, when you're getting to know someone."

Again, James was quiet for a long moment and then he finally stated, his tone sombre, "We're both in our fifties, Anna, and truth be told, I'm staring at sixty. We both have battle scars. No one goes through life unscathed."

She swallowed past the tightness in her throat. "Some people might appear a bit more battle-worn than others."

"They might," he agreed, "but scars mean you've survived. They're badges of honour, in my mind."

"That's a good way of looking at it," she replied with a smile. She realised she didn't want to go through their messy pasts just then, dragging them into this cosy, welcoming room like a cat bringing in a dead mouse, stinking up the air. The evening felt far too pleasant, far too full of possibility, for that.

"So, if you don't live in Mathering," James resumed after a moment when the only sound was the comforting crackle of the fire, "where do you live?"

"Stroud, in Gloucestershire, but…" Anna trailed off, and James raised his eyebrows, his mouth quirking upwards.

"But?"

"But there's nothing really holding me there," Anna explained slowly, feeling the words out for herself. Since coming back to Mathering, she hadn't really thought about returning to Stroud, save for getting some of her things and bringing them back here. But to return to Stroud for *good*, when both Harriet and Rachel were finally talking to her, and living up here? It made no sense.

But as for an alternative…

"I have a few friends there," she continued, "but no family. And my job is just at a garden centre, nothing very career-based, although I do enjoy it." She paused to take a sip of wine as James continued to gaze at her thoughtfully. "I don't really know what I'm trying to say," she admitted.

"It sounds," he replied after a moment, "as if you're thinking about moving to Mathering. Or," he corrected, while Anna tried to figure out how she felt about that, "at least move from Stroud, maybe closer to your daughters." He raised his eyebrows. "As someone who has done it, I must say, I think it makes sense."

"Yes, I can see how it would for you," Anna replied slowly. She took a sip of wine, gazing into the glowing depths of the fire as she tried to envision living the rest of her life in Mathering. It was oddly difficult to imagine, because this place was so tangled up with the past and all its painful memories.

"But not for you?" James filled in gently, breaking into her thoughts.

Anna turned back to him. He looked relaxed, one arm still stretched along the back of the sofa, his head cocked thoughtfully, but there was also an alertness to his expression that made her think he really did want to know the answer.

"I don't know," she admitted. "I lived here for twenty years…and they weren't all that happy." Although since returning, she acknowledged fairly, she had remembered some happy times. It was just that so much of her marriage had the sepia tint of sorrow to it.

"That may be so," James answered after a moment, "but what about reshaping the future?" He paused, his gaze steady on hers over the rim of the wine glass. "Or are the memories too painful?"

Were they? Anna considered the question. Since returning to Mathering, she'd made so many strides towards healing her relationship with her daughters. She'd reconnected with people, too, like her old neighbour Diana. And she liked both Quinn and Ben and wanted to get to know them better.

"I don't know," she told James again. "I'd like to think that they weren't, or at least they don't have to be, because I don't want to be shaped or controlled by my past. And a lot of good things have happened while I've been here, even though it's been hard. Maybe I need to return to Stroud to figure it out," she finished. "I'm actually planning to go there tomorrow."

"Tomorrow?" James did a double take.

Anna hastened to add, "Yes, just for the day. I don't want to leave my family for longer than that, but I'd like to get a few of my things."

"That's got to be an eight-hour round trip," he remarked, frowning, and Anna grimaced.

"Probably more like nine. It's going to be a very long day of driving, I'm afraid."

"I could go with you," James said suddenly, seeming to surprise them both with the entirely unexpected offer.

Anna simply stared at him, having no idea how to respond. *Go with her…?*

"Sorry," James said with an abashed laugh. "That clearly shocked you. I just meant that it seems a pity to have to do all that driving by yourself. If I went with you, I could share the driving, and you'd have some company, if you wanted it, that is. But feel free to tell me absolutely not. I wouldn't blame you."

"I…I don't know what to say," Anna replied, still startled. "You have shocked me, mainly because that's such a generous offer when you barely know me—"

"I don't feel as if I barely know you," James interjected quietly. "I haven't felt that way since I first saw you in the village hall, trying to figure out that quiz." He paused, ducking his head before returning his resolute gaze to her. "Maybe that's mad, but it's how I feel. Or how I don't feel, I suppose." He fell silent, taking a sip of wine, his gaze remaining steady on her.

Anna's mind was spinning. She knew exactly what James meant, because she felt it, too. Like she *knew* this man…even when she didn't. It wasn't anything as fanciful or foolish as love at first sight, but something weirdly almost deeper.

But did she want to spend nine hours in the car with him?

A sudden, heady reckless, perhaps fuelled by half a glass of wine, fizzed through Anna. She lifted her chin, smiling as she met his gaze.

"All right," she told him. "I'll take you up on that. Let's do it."

Chapter Fourteen

IN THE GREY light of a cold, drizzly morning, the heady recklessness Anna had felt last night was replaced by a wary uncertainty that, when she let herself think about it too much, bordered on something close to terror. After she'd agreed to James's offer to accompany her to Stroud, they'd ended chatting about desultory things for the rest of the evening—movies and hobbies and even the weather. It was as if they'd skated too close to the edge of a yawning precipice, and then, by mutual, silent agreement, decided to inch back, just a little, whether for form's or sanity's sake, Anna wasn't sure, but she'd been relieved.

She'd left fairly early, just after nine, claiming she needed her sleep for the big drive tomorrow, and in any case, they'd have plenty of time to talk in the car.

"Are you sure about this?" she'd asked him frankly as he'd helped her on with her coat. "Coming to Stroud, I mean. It is a long way, and I would absolutely not blame you one bit for backing out."

"I'm not going to back out." James's voice was as warm as his hands as he slipped her coat onto her shoulders, resting them there for just a split second before he stepped away. "I had a lovely time tonight, Anna, and I'll see you tomorrow, bright and early."

Bright and early was eight o'clock, as Anna headed across the moors that looked soggy under a damp grey sky. She'd packed snacks and a flask of coffee and in something of a panic, had hoovered out her car. James had offered to take his SUV, but Anna couldn't justify adding hundreds of miles onto his car when he was already being so kind.

Her stomach was a swirl of butterflies as she pulled up into the courtyard of James's house. The barn conversion looked even more magnificent in the daylight, with the moors stretching out all around it; she saw several rattan sofas and chairs on the deck, along with a hot tub, and for a second, she imagined lounging in its bubbly depths with James…but no. She could not think that way, not when she was about to spend the entire day with this man.

She'd barely turned off the car when James stepped outside, ready to go. He was wearing corduroy trousers and a checked shirt with a fleece gilet underneath a waxed jacket and wool scarf, every inch the dashing country gentleman.

"No second thoughts, then?" Anna called out as she got out of the car. She'd taken care with her appearance, trying for a similar country casual look, with an oversized cable-knit sweater and skinny jeans with knee-high leather boots.

"Not a single one," James replied easily. He locked up the house as he strolled towards the car. "I would have brought coffee, but you beat me to it." She'd texted him that morning, saying she would bring a flask and travel mugs. "So, I brought these instead," he told her, and she saw he was holding a paper bag. "Pain aux raisins from the bakery in town."

"You went into town already this morning?" Anna asked in surprise.

He shrugged. "I'm an early riser. I hope you like raisins."

"I do," she assured him, touched by his thoughtfulness. He was a man who seemed to think of just about everything.

"Shall I pour the coffee while you drive?" he suggested as they both got in the car. A few moments later, they were heading down the track, their travel mugs of hot coffee tucked in the drink holders between their seats, a pain aux raisin each on their lap, along with a much-needed napkin. The sky was still grey, and it was starting to drizzle, but Anna felt as if she was all sunshine inside. *I'm happy*, she thought with something close to incredulity. *I can't remember the last time I've felt this happy.*

James glanced at her and smiled.

ANNA HAD BEEN worried about how to fill four hours of silence as they drove southward, but she realised she needn't have worried—first, because they'd both soon discovered that not all silence needed to be filled, and second, they had enough to talk about, anyway. James asked her plenty of questions about her life—easy ones, softballs he was gently lobbing and which she gratefully batted back. He asked her about her job, and what she loved about gardening, and why she'd chosen Stroud as a place to land. In return, she asked him the same sort of get-to-know-you questions back—why he'd gone into architecture, the most interesting projects he'd worked on, and whether he thought he'd ever feel like a true Yorkshireman.

By the time they'd stopped on the far side of Doncaster for a break, Anna felt as if they'd got to know a bit more about each other. Just the basics, it was true, but she felt comfortable in his presence in a way that was both gratifying and reassuring.

"Shall I drive now?" James asked once they were heading back to the car. "But only if you want me to."

"That would be lovely," Anna replied. After nearly two hours at the wheel, she was ready to relax a bit. James slid into the driver's seat and began to reverse out of the parking space with the same air of calm competency he seemed to do everything; it wasn't arrogance, Anna reflected, but assurance. Already, amazingly, he felt like a steady presence in her life. Was she being ridiculous, thinking that way? Probably, but she still enjoyed the feeling.

"So now we've done all the easy chitchat," James remarked once they were back on the motorway. "Shall we level it up?"

"What?" Anna couldn't hide her immediate discomfort at that alarming suggestion. "Level it up…how?"

He shrugged, smiling. "Tell me something a little more personal. Or I'll tell you something since I'm the one who suggested it. Only fair."

"How personal?" Anna asked, trying to sound light and not somewhat terrified. She'd been enjoying the chitchat so much, but she knew she wasn't remotely ready to delve into the deeply personal, not yet, not when they'd been having such a lovely time.

"Let's see…" James screwed up his face in concentration

while Anna braced herself for some semi-hideous revelation. How should she respond? And more frighteningly, how should she reciprocate? "I'm scared of the ocean," James stated, "and when I was a kid, I bit my toenails." He slid her a laughing glance. "So now you know."

"*Oh.*" Anna couldn't hide her relief. *That* kind of personal she could handle. "Scared of the ocean? Really?"

"Deep ocean, without land in sight. I went snorkelling off the side of a boat once when I was about eight, nothing around but blue, and I inhaled about half the Pacific in one mouthful. It was terrifying."

"And biting your toenails?" Anna grinned and grimaced at the same time. "Ew."

"I know." James nodded soberly. "I stopped when I was about ten. But still...deal breaker?" He glanced at her expectantly, while Anna stared back at him, flustered and flummoxed. *Deal breaker?* Did that mean...?

"That was a long time ago," she managed lightly, after a moment. "But still, a bit disgusting."

"So, my mother told me, many times. What about you?" His smiling glance turned appraising. "What disgusting habit did you have as a child?"

Anna smothered a laugh. "You really want to know?"

"Absolutely."

She shook her head, trying to think of something suitably gross without being entirely off-putting. It was, she realised, a rather delicate balance. James had got it just about right with his toenails remark. "Well, this isn't gross," she finally said, "but it's a bit weird, I suppose. I used to have to line all my shoes up exactly, their tips completely in line, before I went to bed."

James was silent for a second, and Anna wondered if that was not the kind of thing he'd meant. Instead of being goofy or even gross, she realised, it just sounded…sad.

"Funnily enough," she finished lightly, "by the time I went to university, I had completely lost the habit. My room was an utter tip all three years."

"That sounds about right," James replied with a smile. "But you know, I realise in all our getting-to-know-you chat, I don't actually know much about your childhood. You said your parents were university lecturers?"

"Yes, very academic. I went to uni in Sheffield for art history, which was something of a disappointment to them, I think, although they never said." Again, that felt more revealing than she'd meant it to. She had to stop doing that.

"And then you must have married quite young," James remarked. She'd already told him Harriet and Rachel's ages as well as her own, so he'd clearly done the arithmetic.

"Yes, I was twenty-one." She paused. "Peter was—is—twenty years older than me."

James raised his eyebrows as he glanced at her. "How did your parents feel about that?"

She smiled wryly. "Not amazing."

He nodded in understanding. "I can imagine. I don't know how well it would have gone over, if Jane had wanted to marry someone so much older."

"And after only knowing him for two months," Anna added. "Really, it was mad."

"So why did you marry him, if you don't mind me asking?" He gave a little grimace. "I know it's a bit of a nosy question."

Anna glanced out the window at the wintry landscape blurring by. "Why did I marry him..." she murmured thoughtfully. "Well, I loved him, or I thought I did. I loved what he represented—the whole *Country Living* lifestyle, the rugged farm, the home he'd had for generations, although by the time I came along both his parents had already died. It was all so different than what I'd experienced growing up—dry, stuffy academia in a semi-detached in a grey Reading suburb."

James let out a dry chuckle. "Yes, when you put it that way, I suppose I can see the appeal."

"I was young and far too romantic," Anna told him. "I'd barely had a boyfriend all through university because I was so shy. Peter swept me off my feet, in a manner of speaking, but to tell you the truth, I don't know that it took all that much. I was ready to fall in love with the whole fairy tale."

"You wouldn't be the first," James replied after a moment. "So, what went wrong? Or are we ratcheting up the levels too fast?"

Anna sighed, knowing she had to give at least some sort of answer. "We weren't suited, for a start, and I had no idea what I'd let myself in for, in terms of the endless drudgery of farming life, as well as...other things." She considered telling James about Peter's affair, but for some reason it didn't feel entirely fair, when the man was on his deathbed. She also, she realised suddenly, didn't want to be an object of James's pity. He seemed to have it all together—a successful career, a productive retirement, a beautiful house and a loving daughter. What did she have?

"There were some other issues that caused problems," she finished, her tone both vague and final. "After twenty years, I suppose we'd simply run our course." Which, Anna realised belatedly, made it sound like they'd just got tired of each other, and it had been so much worse—so much more scarring—than that.

"I'm sorry," James murmured after a moment. "It sounds like it was hard."

It felt like an ending to the conversation, and Anna was glad. Surely there were other, better, nicer, funnier things to talk about? As if sensing her thoughts, James asked suddenly, "What's your favourite ice cream flavour?"

Anna laughed. "Rum raisin," she said impulsively, while James's jaw dropped. She laughed again, the sound ringing out in a joyful peal. "No, I'm teasing. Does *anyone* like rum raisin? Salted caramel probably, or anything with peanut butter and chocolate."

"Phew," James replied, pretending to wipe his brow. "Because liking rum raisin *might* be a deal breaker."

BY THE TIME they arrived at her little house in Stroud, Anna was feeling happy and relaxed but also tired; it had been a long drive through the rain, and she wasn't quite sure what to expect when she arrived back home, how she would feel.

As it turned out, as she stepped out of the car, she didn't feel all that much beyond a sense of unreality that she was there at all.

"Nothing on your barn conversion," she felt compelled

to say as she fished out her key.

"It looks lovely," James replied. "And you clearly love your gardening." He nodded towards the neatly tended flower bed in front of the sitting room window, now, in late January, filled with winter jasmine and hellebore and scattered with snowdrops. Anna always planted her flower beds in a way that ensured they were never bare.

"I do," she agreed, and then unlocked the front door.

After nearly a month away, the house smelled musty and unlived-in. A thin layer of dust covered the hall table. As Anna stepped in and looked around, she felt as if she were inspecting something unfamiliar, or at least half-forgotten. There was the gilt-edged mirror she'd bought at an antiques fair; there was the aspidistra her neighbour had offered to water, looking healthy but a bit dusty. Here was the armchair she curled up most nights with a glass of wine and a book. Here was the little kitchen table with its two chairs. Everything about this place, she realised, spoke to a solitary life.

A lonely one.

"It's a lovely place," James said, and Anna let out a huff of laughter, although she wasn't sure what she found funny—or sad. She felt as if she were looking at her life from a distance, a spectator to her own self, at least for these few moments. It was the oddest feeling.

"I'm not even sure what I want to bring back," she admitted as she looked around. "I should have made a list." That clearly would have been the obvious and sensible thing to do. Right now, she felt overwhelmed, gazing around at all the vestiges of her old life, a life that just a month later she didn't quite recognise anymore.

"Why don't we go room to room?" James suggested. Anna heard a gentleness in his voice that almost made her eyes sting. "Or you can do it by yourself, if you'd rather, and I'll find my way to the kettle and make us both a cup of tea."

Again, Anna was struck by how understanding he was, how emotionally astute, sensing she might want to be alone, but willing to be there with her if she wanted him to be. They really did barely know each other, and yet…

Just as James had said, it didn't actually feel that way at all.

"A cup of tea would be nice," she finally said, "and I'll start upstairs." She didn't particularly think she was ready to usher James into her bedroom just yet, even if it was just to fill a suitcase.

"All right," he said easily enough, and he made his way back to the kitchen while Anna headed upstairs. She stood in the doorway of her bedroom for a few moments, just breathing in and out. She didn't know why coming back to her little house was making her feel so emotional; surely it was going back to Mathering that should have stirred all the old feelings up, and it *had*, but this was something different.

This, Anna realised as she opened the wardrobe doors and surveyed its contents, was her looking around and realising this—these few rooms and their objects—was the sum of her life. This was what she'd made of it, on her own. It wasn't bad; on the contrary, many parts of it were quietly good. She could honestly say, even with the sorrow of her estrangement from her daughters, she'd felt content here in Stroud, with her little house, her little job, her quiet evenings and her small circle of friends. She'd *learned* to feel content, because after the tribulations and tumult of her marriage, all she'd wanted was solitude and peace, and she'd found both.

But somehow, right now, it made her feel sad. Thirteen years of her life felt—not wasted, no, but *small*. Very small.

Anna heard the kettle switch off downstairs and decided she needed to get a move on. Hurriedly she grabbed some of her clothes out of the wardrobe and flung them on the bed before she grabbed a suitcase from the cupboard in the hall. She started throwing things into it willy-nilly—the clothes, a soft throw in rose pink she'd always loved, a few pillows, her favourite books. Things that felt like they were truly hers.

There wasn't much to take from the bathroom and the other, smaller bedroom she'd used mostly for storage. She headed downstairs with the single suitcase and left it by the front door.

"Done already?" James asked as he came from the kitchen with two cups of tea. He nodded at the suitcase as he handed her one. "There's not much there."

"In the end, I'm not sure how much there is to take. If I do move to Mathering, I suppose I'll have to do the big clear-out, but I'm not quite at that point yet."

"This place seems very cosy," James remarked. "You must have been happy here."

"I was content," Anna replied, not so much an agreement as a correction.

"Sometimes that's even better," he replied. "A sort of settledness in yourself. Happiness, I've found, can be fleeting."

This conversation was getting very deep, but for once Anna didn't want to shy away from it. "Yes, I think you're right. It took me a long time to get to that point."

"It did for me, as well," James replied quietly.

Anna had not asked him very much about his wife. It had felt, for a reason she couldn't quite discern, like a no-go area, but maybe that was down to her apprehension rather than a lack of willingness on James's part. She decided to broach the subject now.

"It must have taken awhile," she offered hesitantly, "after your wife died."

"Yes." He nodded slowly. "Helen's diagnosis was so sudden, and she deteriorated so quickly. They didn't catch it until it was well advanced—apparently that happens more often than anyone would like. She died just three months after we'd first learned she had it, just a few weeks after she'd started treatment. My head was still spinning, and poor Jane was only seventeen, doing her A levels. To lose her mother right then…just about the worst time, really."

Anna took a sip of tea to hide the expression on her face. Harriet had more or less lost her mother at the same age, although hardly in the same way. How would James feel, she wondered, to know she'd walked away from her children in the way that she had? Considering how close he was to his own daughter, how he would react, realising she'd been estranged from hers for over a decade?

Her stomach churned at the thought. They'd been having such a pleasant time getting to know one another, but right then it felt as if it was all based on lies…and Anna didn't think she was brave enough to trust James with the truth.

Chapter Fifteen

IT WAS DARK by the time they made it back to Mathering, and Anna was feeling exhausted. James was, as well, she suspected; they'd both been quiet in the car for the last two hours of the trip, although not in an uncomfortable way…she hoped. The truth was, ever since she'd realised how much she hadn't told him about herself, she'd been feeling a little awkward. A little guilty, like she'd lied without meaning to, and was now continuing to lie, by omission.

And maybe James, in his usually astute way, sensed something of that, because they'd both backed off any emotional or intense subjects, and concentrated simply on choosing what belongings to bring back as well as loading them into the car. Three boxes of books, two of kitchen stuff, and one of photos and knick-knacks later, they were heading back towards North Yorkshire.

They'd stopped for dinner at a pub outside Sheffield, and then Anna had dropped James off at his house before coming to hers. He'd offered to help her unload, but Anna had told him there was no need; he looked tired, and, in any case, he'd been helpful enough already. Besides, they were two people used to their own company and they'd spent nearly twelve hours with each other. Anna had found it a bit intense, and she suspected James had, as well. And while he'd promised to call her soon, she thought they could both use a bit of a breather.

And somehow, she reflected as she pulled in front of her house, in that time she had to figure out a way to tell James about those battle scars she'd mentioned. Scars he'd said were signs she'd survived, badges of honour, *but*...they were still scars, and there were reasons for them. Reasons he might not entirely understand or accept.

She was still sitting there, staring into space, when a rather determined tap on her window had her jumping as she let out a little shriek of surprise. She turned to see Jane peering in her window.

"Jane..." Anna rolled down the window. "Sorry, you startled me."

"Sorry, I was just wondering where you were all day," Jane replied. "I made brownies as a thank-you for being so kind the other day." She brandished a tray of brownies while Anna blinked at her. There was something *slightly* off about Jane coming to find her in her car at this time of night, with the brownies in hand.

"That's very kind of you," Anna replied as she opened the door and stepped out of the car. Jane's gaze narrowed.

"Is that my dad's *scarf*?" she asked, sounding incredulous, and Anna glanced back to see, with a sinking sensation, that James had left his scarf, a lovely cashmere one in blue and grey stripes, on the passenger seat.

"Er...yes, it is," Anna replied, knowing she couldn't deny it, and why should she? Jane was a grown woman, and she and James were just friends. And yet she felt the need to brace herself, for whatever came next.

"Why…" Jane shook her head as if to clear it. "Sorry, I'm just really confused. I thought you were in Stroud today." She spoke accusingly, like she thought Anna had been lying to her.

"I was," Anna admitted. This was, she realised, sounding worse and worse. "Your dad came with me."

"To *Stroud*?" Jane goggled at her, looking, Anna hoped, more incredulous than angry.

"Yes," she confirmed, wishing she and James had talked about how to handle telling Jane—although, what really, was there to tell? Basically nothing. Besides, why should Jane, at thirty-odd years, need *handling*? Maybe she was just bruised from the way her own daughters did, or at least had used to. "He offered to help with the driving and things," Anna explained.

"But didn't you just meet, like, four days ago?" Jane demanded. She was clutching the brownies to her chest, heedless of the chocolatey crumbs now caught on her fleece top.

It *did* sound strange, Anna knew. It *was* strange, and yet it had also been wonderful. "Yes," she admitted, "that's right. But I suppose we've become friends."

"*Friends…*" Jane huffed. "He didn't tell me he was going. I was texting him today, wondering if he wanted to come round and see Henry, and he just said he'd come tomorrow."

That, Anna knew, had nothing to do with her, and she wasn't about to wade into it.

"He was just helping me out, Jane," Anna told her. She

suddenly felt very tired, practically swaying where she stood. "I'm sorry, it's been such a long day. Shall we talk tomorrow?"

Jane gave her a look that was not quite a glare, but almost. There was clearly some hostility in the air, and Anna knew she would have to figure out a way to deal with it. "Yes, all right," she said frostily, and then she turned to go back inside without giving Anna the brownies she'd baked.

Anna stifled a groan. Clearly Jane was not happy with the thought of her being friends with her father, something Anna found unsurprising but dispiriting all the same. Yet another fraught relationship in her life...but, she decided, she'd think about Jane tomorrow. And for that matter, she'd unload the car tomorrow, as well. Right then all she wanted was a hot bath and bed, and not to have to think at all.

ANNA WOKE SLOWLY to weak sunlight filtering through her curtain and her mobile, charging next to her bed, pinging with texts. She scrabbled for it, pushing her hair out of her eyes, wondering who on earth was texting her with such urgency at just past seven in the morning.

She saw, with much trepidation, that it was Rachel.

Can you come? Dad's asking for you.

Peter was asking for her? Anna thought with a ripple of uneasy incredulity. Why—and what did that even mean? She feared she knew...that the end was close.

It had been coming—they'd all known that. Rachel had said as much the other day, and there could be no denying that Peter was becoming frailer and more disorientated by the day. And yet…somehow death always felt like a surprise. Unexpected no matter how much you were bracing for it. Anna recalled the numb shock she'd felt when the carer had called to say her mother had passed away. She'd been told it would be a matter of days, and yet somehow, she hadn't quite believed it could happen. And here she was again.

She dressed quickly, running a comb through her hair, and bolting a cup of coffee although her stomach was churning. *Peter was asking for her.* Why? What did he want to say? What would she say to him?

As she left the house, she glanced uneasily at Jane's closed door. She didn't have time to explain what was going on, but she had a feeling Jane would have put a lot of stock in her promising to come over that morning to explain things. Well, it couldn't be helped. She'd stop by later, if she could.

It was just half past seven when Anna pulled up to Embthwaite Farm. A single, lonely curl of smoke rose from the chimney; otherwise, the house looked dark and empty. Rachel met her at the door, a long cardigan thrown over her pyjamas.

"He woke up early," she explained in a low voice. Her eyes were red-rimmed, her hair in a wild tangle she pushed behind her ears. "Maybe five? He was agitated and wouldn't settle. It took me a bit to understand what he wanted…*you*." She shook her head slowly. "Then he got very clear, clearer than he's been in weeks. He said, 'I need to talk with Anna.'" Her eyes filled with tears. "This is the end, isn't it? Nearly."

"I don't know, darling," Anna answered, pulling her daughter into a quick hug. "It might be."

"I've read about it," Rachel said with a sniff as she pulled back to swipe at her cheeks. "Often people seem better right before they die. They get a burst of energy or a moment of clarity or something. Do you think that's what this is?"

Anna stared at her helplessly. "I don't know, Rachel. We'll just have to take each moment as it comes."

Her daughter nodded slowly. "Harriet's making breakfast. You'd better go up."

"All right." Anna would have rather checked in on her younger daughter first, but she decided to do as Rachel said, in case time was of the essence. Could the end really be that near? It gave her a sense of loss and regret that she hadn't expected. She'd come to terms with Peter's infidelity a long time ago, and she'd made peace with it as best as she could. But what did Peter have to say to her now?

She tapped once on the door and he grunted a greeting before saying in a voice that was clearer than she'd heard before, "Come in."

Slowly, with trepidation, Anna opened the bedroom door. Peter was sitting up in bed, propped against the pillows. Anna hadn't actually seen him in weeks, and she was shocked at how *diminished* he seemed. Once a brawny, broad-shouldered man, he now looked small and frail, engulfed by his pyjama shirt, his pink scalp visible through his sparse white hair.

"Hello, Peter," she said quietly as she stepped into the room, closing the door behind her. "Rachel said you wanted to see me."

He nodded once, his chin tucked towards his chest, the look on his face one Anna recognised—stubbornness. She hoped he wasn't going to berate her for something. That was the kind of deathbed confession she'd rather not have, but maybe Peter needed to get something off his chest.

"Sit down," he said, his voice raspy, and he pointed to the end of the bed.

Gingerly, Anna perched there. "How are you?" she asked, and he gave a croak of rusty laughter.

"How do thee think I am, lass? About to die. Ready to."

"I'm sorry," Anna said quietly. She had no other words.

"So am I," Peter replied frankly. The words were clear, although it was obvious he had to take his time saying them, fishing each one out of the deep pool of his consciousness. "So am I, Anna."

She gazed at him uncertainly, sensing the import of his words but not sure how to respond to them.

"I wasn't fair to you," he stated flatly. "I know it."

That jolted her, because she'd never expected him to say it, and yet looking at his resolute expression, the sorrow and resignation so evident in his eyes, she didn't feel gratified or vindicated, the way she'd expected to feel…just sorrowful and full of pity for a man who clearly felt so much regret as he looked back on his life.

"No, you weren't," she said at last. "But maybe I wasn't fair to you, either. I resented you the whole of our marriage, in one way or another." Once she'd found out about Ruth it had been like a stone in her shoe, a thorn in her side. As well it should have been—Anna wasn't about to sanction any sort of infidelity whatsoever. *And yet…*if she'd been prepared to accept it and live with the man, then maybe she should have actually accepted it. She never had.

"You had cause to, though, didn't you?" Peter replied. He closed his eyes briefly, the act of speaking having clearly exhausted him. "You were such a pretty little thing when we first married," he remarked, a smile in his voice, his eyes still closed. "All eyes and hair. I could have picked you up in one arm." He opened his eyes. "I loved you, you know."

"I know," Anna replied quietly, a soreness starting in her throat, an ache in her chest.

"Not enough, though," Peter said slowly, each word laboured. "I…I shouldn't have been so…stubborn…about Ruth." He paused, his face screwed up from the effort of finding the words, forcing them out. "About a lot of things."

She'd never expected him to admit to any of this, and Anna knew she couldn't let the opportunity pass. "Peter, you do know Harriet is your biological daughter, don't you?" she said, her voice low and insistent. She knew, from Harriet, that Peter had acted as if she wasn't, whether from times past or as a result of his brain tumour, she didn't know. "I know," she continued, "when we were having a fight, all those years ago, I said something to make you think she wasn't, but she was. Is. She always has been."

She remembered the moment well and had kicked herself a thousand times for it. She'd been heavily pregnant with Harriet, and Peter had gone to see Ruth. Again. He'd come back unrepentant, indifferent, and that had hurt most of all. In a temper, which had felt better than tears, she'd flung at him, *"And what if this baby isn't yours? When the cat's away the mice will play, after all, and you're away a bloody lot of the time, Peter."*

His face had frozen, his expression turning stony, and

then he'd turned away without a word while Anna had tried to hold back her sobs. They'd never spoken of it again. And in all that time, she'd never actually believed that Peter thought Harriet wasn't his. It had been heart-wrenching to learn that he might have acted that way because of her, but who was to say? Maybe it had just been a belief born in the muddle of the brain tumour.

Harriet claimed he'd always favoured Rachel rather than her, but he hadn't been the cuddliest of fathers, and Anna had gravitated towards Harriet anyway. She'd been feeling so needy, and as a baby and toddler Harriet had been all smiles and cuddles, a balm to her soul. But until Harriet had confessed what Peter had thought a few weeks ago, she hadn't believed he'd really taken that pain-filled remark to heart.

"I know that," he said now, closing his eyes again. "I've always known."

Then why did you cause her so much pain? Anna wanted to cry. Was there any point now? Peter was dying. "You should tell her, Peter," she said quietly. "Because she believes you don't think she is, and it has caused her a lot of heartache."

He grimaced, and she decided to press the point. "You still have a chance to make things right. To be at peace with those who love you, before..." She couldn't finish the thought.

With his face still in a grimace, he nodded slowly. "I know."

Anna let out a long, low breath. What more could she say, or *should* she say?

Peter angled his head to gaze at her directly. His eyes

looked faded, as if the life was draining out of him as they spoke, his grizzled cheeks hanging slackly, his face full of pain that she suspected was both physical and emotional. "Anna," he said. "I'm sorry."

His words caused her to feel a settling inside herself, a surprising sense of peace along with a sorrow too deep for regret. Somehow, they existed together, entwined, one feeling giving life to the other. Slowly she nodded. "So am I," she told him. "For a lot of things. But we have two beautiful daughters, and that's something, Peter."

A smile flitted across his lips and then faded. His face was now grey with fatigue and pain, and she felt as if she could see his energy, his very life, ebbing away. "I should go," she said, starting up from the bed. "Let you rest."

"Wait." The word came out in a croaky command, and he flung one hand out to her before letting it fall to the bed.

"Peter…?" Anna prompted uneasily when he didn't seem capable of saying anything more.

"Anna…I need to ask you something. Something…"

"What do you need to ask me?"

His gaze turned bleak but determined as he looked at her. "I need you to contact Ruth. She doesn't know… We haven't… She ought to know."

Anna stiffened. *Contact Ruth…!* As much as she instinctively recoiled against such an idea, she realised it didn't cause her the pain it once might have. She didn't love Peter anymore. And he was right, she supposed; Ruth *should* know, even if some part of her still rebelled against the notion.

"You haven't been in contact?" she asked, and he shook

his head.

"She ended things years ago," he admitted, the words coming now with slow, laboured breaths. He really needed to rest. "I haven't seen her…or Daisy…in years."

Daisy. Anna pushed the thought of her away, knowing she couldn't think about her now. She *never* thought about her. She simply didn't have the strength. "I'll tell Ruth," she agreed heavily. She—and Daisy, Anna supposed—both needed to know. "But I don't know how to contact her…"

"My address book…" He nodded towards the bureau in the corner of the room, piled with old bills and receipts. "It will be there. Ruth Hatch."

Anna swallowed the taste of bile in her throat. Ruth Hatch. A woman who had given her so much heartache in her life. "All right," she said. "I'll do it."

He tried to reach for her hand, but his fingers barely twitched on the sheet. "Thank you…Anna."

She nodded, a lump forming in her throat, and then she stooped to pull the cover over his thin shoulders. "You should rest," she said quietly. She feared their conversation had utterly exhausted him.

Peter nodded, his eyelids already fluttering closed. Anna stood and watched him for a moment, her heart feeling as heavy as a stone in her chest. Peter had been so aggravating, and stubborn, and hurtful, for so many years. Yet somewhat to her surprise, she'd let go of all that emotion, cast it off like the useless flotsam and jetsam it was. What was left, though, was only sadness for the wreck of this man's life, the mistakes he'd made that he could only now, on his deathbed, acknowledge.

It was, she thought, a salient reminder to live your life well…and make amends as soon as you could, when you needed to. She wished she'd been able to do that sooner with Harriet and Rachel, but she had now, and now, more than ever, Anna wanted to look towards the future…whatever the future looked like.

Chapter Sixteen

ANNA DIDN'T LEAVE Embthwaite Farm till after supper-time, which had been a subdued affair. The whole day had been subdued, a shroud of grief already seeming to be draped over the house, even though Peter hadn't died yet. It was coming closer, a looming reality, and Anna knew they all felt that. It was only a matter of time, and a short amount of time at that.

In the afternoon, Rachel had broached the subject of funeral arrangements, and Harriet had snapped at her, then apologised, then became tearful. Anna had hugged them both and made soup and fresh bread for supper. It felt like the only thing she could do—tangible ways to show her love for these girls of hers who were grieving a man they'd been desperate to love and be loved by, but it hadn't quite worked out that way, or at least not as much as they'd hoped.

She still longed for Harriet and Peter were able to reconcile, in some way, no matter how small, and she'd encouraged Harriet to try to talk to him.

"He doesn't want to talk to me, Mum," Harriet had replied. "I don't think he ever did, but even less so now."

"He wanted to talk to me," Anna had pointed out gently. "I think he's trying to make amends, Harriet, as best as he can. I know it's late, almost too late, but I think you will feel better for it, if you listen to him." She wanted Harriet and Peter to reconcile for Harriet's sake more than Peter's, as sad as she felt for her ex-husband. She hoped Harriet might feel released from the burden of feeling like a disappointment to her father, if she and Peter could finally talk.

Harriet had looked doubtful, and she hadn't ventured upstairs all afternoon.

Could any parent keep from disappointing their child, Anna wondered as she started the drive through the dark back to her house in Mathering, after promising to return in the morning. Of course, both she and Peter had disappointed Harriet and Rachel in specific, tangible ways, but it was so easy to let that tangle you up and keep you back, rather than moving forward in a way that helped both parent and child.

Maybe the very nature of the relationship—the importance and expectations parents and children invariably put on each other—made disappointment inevitable, something to work through and deal with along with everything else. Maybe, she reflected, feeling a bit too emotionally weary for such deep thoughts, and yet having them anyway, disappointment wasn't so much about failure as simply another emotion to process and accept. A normal part of life.

Her phone pinged with a text from James and, with her heart skipping a slightly apprehensive beat, she pressed the car's touch screen to listen to it over the speaker.

"Hello, just wondering how you're recovering from our long drive! Hope to see you soon—maybe even venture out to a pub for a meal?"

Even in her phone's automated computer voice, Anna fancied she could hear James's whimsical tone, the hint of a smile. She was glad he'd texted; she'd been semi-worried—okay, a *lot* worried—that yesterday had somehow scared him off. Nine hours in the car could be too much, too soon for anyone, and towards the end of their journey it had started to feel both intense and morose.

And yet, when she thought about all the stuff she still had to tell him, *too much too soon* didn't even begin to cover it. There was so much more to come. When was she going to tell him about leaving Peter, the girls, spending three months in a psychiatric facility? Her stomach clenched at the thought of it all.

Her phone rang, startling her, and with another ripple of apprehension as well as excitement, she saw it was James. He'd just texted, and now he was calling? Anna couldn't decide if that was a good or bad sign. She pressed the screen to answer the call.

"Hello?" She sounded cautious.

"Anna." His voice was warm and rich, with that hint of a smile she remembered, and it made her smile in return.

"In the flesh," she replied breezily, only to amend, "well, not actually."

"No, indeed not," James agreed. "I was wondering how you were. Unpack everything yet?"

Anna glanced back at the still-full back seat and boot of her car. "No, actually, I haven't even taken anything out of the car yet," she admitted. "I was exhausted last night." Now, she decided, was not the time to mention her little run-in with Jane. "And this morning Rachel rang me to say Peter was asking for me. I came right away, and I've spent the whole day at the farm. He's…he's starting to slip away." Her voice caught as the reality of it hit her all over again.

"I'm so sorry," James said, his voice full of quiet warmth. "That sounds incredibly difficult."

"It was…sombre, I suppose," Anna replied. "Honestly, I don't know how I'm supposed to feel in this situation. I'm sad, yes, but more for what never was rather than what once was, or even what could be, but maybe that's the nature of any relationship…" She was blathering, she realised, because she'd been so wrapped up in deep thoughts. "Sorry, I don't know if I'm making any sense. I'm probably not."

"You are making sense, but I'd love to hear about it in more detail," James told her. "Have you eaten?"

Anna thought of the bowl of soup she'd barely touched at supper. "A bit."

"I was asking in case you felt like coming by here for a quick kitchen supper. Nothing fancy, mind. I didn't learn to cook until after Helen died, I'm sorry to say. But maybe you'd rather head straight home to bed, by the sounds of it?"

Anna thought of James's lovely house, with the fire burning cheerfully and a warm meal prepared for her, and most of all *him*, being so lovely and understanding, and she knew what she wanted.

"I'd love to come over," she told him, "if you're sure?"

"I'm sure," James replied, and that seemed all there was to say.

Ten minutes later, Anna was pulling up into the courtyard of James's house as if she belonged there. Considering it was the fourth time in just over two days that she'd driven over, she was starting to feel like she did. And just as before, James threw open the door in welcome before she'd crossed the courtyard.

"I've made a coconut curry," he called in greeting. "But don't worry, it's not too spicy." At some point in their journey yesterday, Anna had mentioned her intolerance for spicy foods. The fact that he'd remembered made her soften inside, and she smiled in return.

"Phew," she replied. "It sounds delicious." She paused at the door, feeling an urge to hug him or, shockingly, even kiss his cheek, except that would be inappropriate, wouldn't it? Or would it? She gave him a smile and an awkward hand wave instead before slipping inside.

"I thought you'd be tired of me," she confessed as he took her coat, "after yesterday. Nine hours in the car is probably too much for anyone."

"Not at all," James replied. "But truthfully, I wondered if you were tired of me." Something about the seriousness of his tone made Anna hesitate. "Only because you went rather quiet, towards the end of our journey," he explained. "But you were probably tired. It was a big day."

"I was tired," Anna answered slowly. "But I suppose I was thinking through a lot of things, as well."

James nodded. "I was too, which was why I went quiet, as well," he admitted as he walked back to the kitchen. "I wondered if you were feeling the same as I was."

Anna followed him back, taking a moment to savour the cheerful blaze in the fireplace, the delicious smells of coconut and coriander coming from the kitchen, the whole, homely warmth of the scene that felt like a cosy blanket enveloping her. "I suppose it depends on what you were feeling," she replied, wondering how long they were going to tiptoe around each other, talking about what they were feeling without actually saying anything remotely specific or important.

In truth, right then she wasn't sure she felt brave or energetic enough for anything else, but James obviously did, because he stopped with his stirring and placed his hands flat on the marble counter as he gave her a direct look, his blue eyes seeming very bright.

"Well, this is how I was feeling," he stated. "I was feeling like I really like you, and we get along really well, and we're both in our fifties so there might not be time to waste when it comes to a potential relationship."

"*Oh…*" The syllable slipped out like a sigh between Anna's parted lips. She hadn't expected all of that. Not remotely, although maybe she should have. James had been pretty direct since she'd first met him.

"But I was also feeling," James continued steadily, his gaze never wavering, "that life is complicated, maybe more for you than for me right now, although it's certainly been complicated for me in the past…more than you know. And I'm also feeling that there's a reason people take things slowly, no matter what age they are, and I don't want to scare you off by coming on too strong, which I probably am, simply by having this conversation and saying all the things that maybe are better said slowly, like the medicinal sips you talked about the other day." The smile he gave her was crooked and utterly endearing. "But then I decided, when I started, that it was better to say it all and simply have done with it so there are no secrets, no misunderstandings...although now that you're looking at me like I've grown two heads, I'm seriously starting to question the wisdom of my thought process."

"No," Anna said quickly, taking an involuntary step towards him as she let out a startled laugh. "No, not at all. That is...you're right. It's good to get it all out in the open, I think. I'm just surprised you said it all, and as plainly as that."

"Well, I've never been great when it comes to tact," James replied wryly, "as both Helen and Jane have told me in the past." He reached for two plates and began doling out the curry and rice. "But I guess the real question," he continued slowly, his eyes on the plates, "is, are those the sorts of things you've been thinking about...or not?"

Anna hesitated. Her mind felt as if it were crammed full of thoughts and feelings, a hopeless jumble she couldn't even begin to process. Her conversation with Peter, with her daughters, even with Jane last night. After living a life of quiet reserve for the last thirteen years, it all felt like a bit too much. All these *people*, people she cared about, needing or wanting things, and then her needing and wanting things in return.

On top of all that, she hadn't come here tonight expecting a full-on discussion of her and James's relationship, such as it was, which was basically nothing, and yet...

For a second, she pictured Peter's face, weathered with age and shadowed with regret. She wanted to make different decisions than he had, and yet right now she felt overwhelmed by it all, and she wasn't sure she could even decide what she wanted to drink. Still, the silence stretched on.

"I'm an idiot," James exclaimed suddenly as he shook his head. "Anna, forgive me. I shouldn't have said anything about all of this, if either of us even knows what *this* is. Dear Lord! You've just come from the deathbed of your ex-husband and I'm spouting off about feelings and whether you're ready to talk about them." He did a rather adorable face palm. "Please. You don't have to say another word. Just have some curry, and maybe a glass of wine, and enjoy the fire. And I will shut up, I promise."

She let out a wobbly laugh. "Actually, that all sounds marvellous," she admitted, "although not the shutting up part."

"No, definitely the shutting up part," James replied with a quick smile. "Forget I said anything. Truly. I mean it." He took their plates over to the table, and then went back for the bottle of red they'd opened the night before last. "A glass?"

"Just one, maybe," Anna replied, and he took two wine glasses from one of the glass-fronted cupboards and filled them both up nearly to the brim.

"What do you want to talk about?" he asked as he handed her a glass. "The weather? *The Traitors*? Very good TV, I have to say. Or maybe you just want to sit in silence, which is absolutely fine." He took his seat opposite her, and Anna let out another tired laugh.

"Maybe just sit in silence," she admitted, feeling badly about it, but also grateful for James's understanding. Her brain really did feel too full, and she didn't think she could cope with even desultory chitchat right then.

"All right, then," he agreed with alacrity, and they both

started eating, so, after a few seconds, the only sound in the room was that of their chewing, and the silence started to feel heavy, like something else that needed to be managed. After several minutes of this, Anna realised this wasn't what she wanted, after all.

"I didn't mean we had to take a vow of silence," she teased, trying for a smile, although she suddenly realised she was feeling more fragile than she'd thought. Her lips wobbled at the edges, and she had to press them together to keep them firm. She was, she knew, far too close to tears, and she wasn't even sure what about. Everything, maybe. Right then, life itself felt fragile, beautiful, and exquisitely painful.

To her surprise, James reached his hand across the table to brush her fingers with his own. "Do you want to talk about it?" he asked, and Anna gazed at him uncertainly.

"Talk about what?"

"Whatever it is that's upsetting you," he replied, "because you look as if you might cry."

Well, if that wasn't enough to set her over the edge! "Oh…" Anna began, and then, to her horror, an unruly sob escaped her. She pressed her hand to her mouth, but it was too late. Another one, and then another one, escaped until she realised, somewhat distantly, that she was full-on ugly crying and there wasn't a thing she could do about it except let it happen. In the midst of her deep embarrassment, it felt like such a relief—a pressure released, a burden laid down.

Somehow, she wasn't quite sure how, she found herself seated on the sofa facing the fireplace with James next to her, his arm around her as she pressed her cheek against his shoulder and soaked his jumper with her tears. How had *that* happened? He must have got her up from her chair and walked her over, but Anna couldn't actually remember it; she'd been crying too hard.

And now all she could think was how absolutely *wonderful* it felt to be held, and how long it had been since she'd felt this way. Years. Decades, even. How had she gone so long without someone's arms around her, someone's strong and solid shoulder to cry on, quite literally? Someone holding her and murmuring that it was going to be all right, so she hazily started to believe that it actually might be?

Except she really had soaked his jumper now, and she probably needed to stop. With what felt like superhuman effort, Anna pulled away from James just a little and wiped her face.

"Thank you," she managed shakily. "You're very kind. I didn't realise I was going to fall to pieces like that. I hope I haven't ruined your shirt."

"I'd be surprised if you hadn't fallen to pieces," James told her as he eased back, seeming wonderfully and remarkably unfazed. "You're dealing with so much." He paused. "And I know from experience how shocking the death of a spouse can be. I know you and Peter divorced a long time ago, but you were together for twenty years. That's no small amount of time, and you're bound to feel grief."

"Yes…" Anna murmured, conscious of all she still hadn't told him. Perhaps now was the time to admit at least a little bit of the truth. "But our marriage wasn't…your average marriage." She glanced uncertainly at James, who was gazing back with a small, sympathetic smile, everything about him alert and listening, ready to comfort, and the truth was,

Anna realised, she *wanted* to be comforted. Needed to, even. Needed to be honest…and, hopefully, understood. Right now, she was willing to take the risk.

"Peter was having an affair for pretty much the entire length of our marriage," she confessed in a rush. "I knew about it, almost from the beginning, and I accepted it because I didn't know what else to do." She bowed her head, feeling a dart of shame. What kind of wife—what kind of woman—went along with something as messed up as that? Why had she stood for it, for so long, even when it caused her so much heartache?

"Oh, Anna." James's voice was low and laced with sadness. "I'm so, so sorry."

"I am, too," she agreed, drawing a breath. "I'm sorry he had the affair, and sorry I stayed for so long when I was so very unhappy, and it should have been clear he was never going to change. Maybe I should have left earlier—far, far earlier, really—but Harriet and Rachel were so little, and the truth is, I really thought he might give her up." She glanced up at him with damp eyes. "Does that make me pathetic?"

"No," he replied firmly, his smile softening. "Just hopeful."

She sighed, a long, watery sound. "Hopeful with no good reason."

"If hope needs a reason," James countered philosophically, "is it really hope?"

She leaned her head against the sofa and closed her eyes, feeling spent. "That's too philosophical a question for me."

"Did your daughters know about it?" James asked after a moment.

"No, I kept it from them," she replied. "Looking back, I'm not sure why. I thought I was protecting them, but maybe it was just pride. I told them about it a few days ago, and they wondered why I hadn't said anything before."

"It can be so hard to know what the right thing to do is," James mused, "in regard to your children. I'm not sure there is even a right thing—what works with one child might go down like a lead balloon with another. Sometimes it can feel like you're just groping through the dark."

"Too true," Anna replied, thinking of Harriet and Rachel, and how different they were. Parenting had definitely felt like a grope through the dark for her. She hadn't had the kind of relationship with her mother to ask the important and necessary questions, and she'd been so very young and alone.

She glanced at James, giving him a small smile. "Thank you," she told him, "for listening, and for…for comforting. I think it was just what I needed."

"It was my pleasure, Anna," James replied. "Honestly." He held her gaze for a moment, and Anna felt it spin out into something else—something charged with promise, with deeper emotion. It thrilled her and alarmed her in equal measure, because she wasn't sure she was ready for it, not with everything else going on, and yet she wanted it. Wanted the possibility of something happening between them…eventually. Not quite yet, especially when there was still so much she hadn't told him. Still so much he might not understand. She broke their locked gazes first, deliberately, and she could tell James felt it.

"The real question is," she remarked, deciding to go for a

light tone, "how did you become so wise?"

"Old age," James replied, matching her tone with easy alacrity. "Do you see how white my hair is?"

She laughed, shaking her head. His hair was white, and thick and wavy, and just added to his appeal. Smiling back, he rose from the sofa to fetch their dinner plates and glasses of wine. "We might as well eat here," he remarked, handing her her plate and placing her glass on the coffee table. "By the fire."

By mutual, silent agreement, they shied away from the serious stuff and chatted easily instead, about all sorts of things. James regaled her with stories about the house renovations, and how difficult it had all been, and Anna talked about what she loved about gardening.

Her glass of wine slipped down nicely, followed by another that she hadn't realised James had poured until she'd drunk it, and it wasn't until it was after ten o'clock that she realised, with a jolt, how late it was—and that she'd probably drunk too much to drive safely. Two, maybe three glasses, at least.

"I've had such a nice time," she confessed, horrified by how thoughtless she'd been by knocking back so much wine without a thought. It had just felt so nice, to be curled up on the sofa, chatting inconsequentially, laughing at little things…and yes, drinking wine. "But I…I think I've drunk too much to drive home." She let out an embarrassed laugh. "I'll call a taxi, of course," she added hurriedly. "I'm so sorry. I know Mathering has a taxi service…" Although she didn't remember it being at all reliable—a one-man outfit that operated only when he felt like it, but maybe things had changed in twelve years. She could hope. Did Uber operate out here? Probably not.

"Anna, you don't need to take a taxi," James assured her. "I have three spare bedrooms. You're welcome to use any of them for the night, if you want to."

"Oh…" She hadn't even considered that as an option.

"Of course," James added hurriedly, "if you'd rather take a taxi, just say the word. I'd understand. Completely. I'll call it myself, if you'd rather."

She laughed, shaking her head, genuinely amused at how quickly he was tripping over himself to make her feel comfortable and safe—and she *did.* And once again, she knew what she wanted.

"Thank you, James," she told him. "That's a very kind offer, and I'll take you up on it."

Chapter Seventeen

SUNLIGHT FILTERED THROUGH the curtain as Anna languorously stretched, blinking the world into focus. She couldn't remember when she'd last slept so well. Maybe it had been all the wine—or the lovely double bed James had shown her to, with a thick duvet and soft-as-silk sheets. The only sound outside had been the calming hoot of an owl and the sweep of the wind over the moors.

James, of course, had been all hospitality, fetching her fluffy towels and assuring her he was right down the hall if she needed anything. He'd even brought a carafe of water and a glass for her bedside table, as well as a spare toothbrush and a tube of toothpaste.

"I feel like I'm staying at a posh hotel," Anna had told him. "With excellent service."

"I aim to please," he'd replied, and with a jaunty little mock salute, he'd closed the door and left her alone.

Anna had been too tired to reflect on the weirdness of the fact that she was staying over, which had probably been a good thing. She'd brushed her teeth and peeled off her clothes, slipping beneath the soft sheets with a sigh of pure pleasure. Then she'd fallen promptly asleep, only to awake now, eight hours later, feeling both relaxed and refreshed.

Pushing her hair out of her face, Anna reached for her phone. It was just past seven, which filled her with relief because she'd been a bit worried she might have slept in and missed an important message from Rachel or Harriet. Thankfully, there were no texts telling her to come quickly because the end was near.

The end *was* near, Anna knew, but at least she didn't have to rush over without having showered or eaten. She slid out of bed, her bare feet hitting the tiles that were nice and toasty from the under-floor heating. She grabbed one of the fluffy white towels James had given her last night and headed for the en-suite bathroom, which had a full tub in grey marble and a separate, glassed-in shower. Everything about his house, she reflected, was simple, streamlined, and elegant.

She put her clothes from the day before back on, finger-combed her damp hair, frowned at her make-up-free reflection, and the fine lines fanning out from her eyes that were very visible in the morning light, and then with a shrug for it all, went downstairs. The smell of fresh coffee wafted up as she rounded the stairs, and she saw James was already in the kitchen, cracking eggs into a bowl. He looked up as she came down and smiled.

"I was just making myself an omelette. Would you like one?"

"That sounds wonderful." Anna felt shy suddenly; it almost felt as if they'd spent the night together, but of course they hadn't. Not in that way. They hadn't so much as kissed, although right then she thought she would like to kiss James, quite a lot, actually.

He looked as handsome as ever, in yet another button-down shirt—did the man wear anything else?—and chinos. Like her, his hair was damp, and his eyes were creased in concentration as he cracked an egg one-handed into the bowl.

"How do you do that?" Anna exclaimed. "I think I'd get the egg yolk all over me."

"It took a lot of practice," James told her. "And a lot of broken eggs and messy hands. It was a trick I mastered for Jane when she was little. I think she'd seen some celebrity chef do it on TV and wanted me to try."

"And I thought you said you didn't cook," Anna teased.

"I don't, or didn't rather," he replied, smiling, "but pancakes and fry-ups were my two specialties. I was in charge of Saturday mornings. Helen made everything else."

Anna slid onto a bar stool and rested her elbows on the marble island. "You haven't told me much about her," she remarked. "What she was like?"

James gave a small, sad smile as he cracked another egg into the bowl. "She was lovely," he told her. "And fun. Full of energy, constantly moving, thinking, dreaming. I couldn't keep up with her. We used to joke that she'd tire of me once we retired, because she'd be running around and I'd be conked out on the sofa, watching TV."

"I struggle to believe that," Anna replied with a smile. "You seem like someone who is full of energy."

"Well…I wasn't always the way I am now," James answered, a remark that intrigued her. "Coffee?" he asked, and she nodded.

"Yes, please."

He poured them both coffees, handing Anna a thick,

ceramic mug that felt comforting to wrap her hands around. "So, what do you mean," she asked, "that you weren't always the way you are now?" Now she was the one levelling it up, but she was genuinely curious. It was hard to imagine James anything other than what he was.

He paused, his gaze on the eggs he was now whisking, as he considered his answer. "Well, when Jane was young, I was a bit of a workaholic," he finally said. "I wanted to become a partner in my firm, and then I wanted to start my own firm, and there was always some new goal I just had to achieve, by putting in the long hours, working weekends, whatever."

Anna took a sip of coffee before propping her chin in her hand. "That doesn't sound like someone who sits on the sofa and watches TV," she remarked, trying to figure out how to fit the pieces together.

"No, not at work," James agreed. There was a sorrow in his voice, a tension about his mouth, that Anna had never heard or seen before. "But that's the thing. When I was at work, I was a dynamo. When I was home…I was so exhausted I didn't want to do anything. I didn't want to read bedtime stories to Jane, or chat over a glass of wine with Helen, or…anything." His mouth tightened. "I threw away a lot of good years."

Just as she had, albeit in an entirely different way. "I'm sorry," Anna said after a moment. "I know how hard it can be, to live with regret."

He nodded slowly before reaching for a copper-bottomed omelette pan and setting it on the stove top to heat. "Helen's death was so quick," he continued, his back to Anna as he poured the eggs into the pan. "Her diagnosis so sudden. I didn't have time to think about how I could recalibrate, rearrange my priorities. One minute I was a workaholic, the next I was trying to manage a huge building project while my wife was having chemotherapy, and the next she was gone, and I had a daughter taking A levels and trying to figure out how to grieve." He shook his head slowly. "That was how it all felt, anyway, at the time. It wasn't until after, when I was watching her casket lowered into the ground, that I realised I wanted to live my life differently. It was too late for it to make a difference to Helen, but it could make a difference to Jane. To me."

"Oh, James." Anna gazed at him, his head bowed, with an ache in her heart that felt like a physical pain. Maybe she had been right yesterday, she reflected. You couldn't keep from disappointing your children, it was just a question of how…and how much.

"Anyway." He turned around, forcing a smile although his eyes still looked sad, drooping at the corners. "It was an important lesson to learn. I cut back on my work hours, I stopped trying to strive, all the time, for everything. It didn't happen overnight, and in some ways, it made things even harder, because I could have lost myself in work. Instead, I had to face up to my grief."

"That's not easy," Anna acknowledged, and he gave her a surprisingly shrewd look.

"You sound like you're speaking from experience."

"I don't think you can get to our age without having some experience of grief," she replied. "I lost both my parents—my father when I was in my twenties, my mother when I was in my late thirties. But I also had a kind of grieving to do, with my marriage. I know it's not the same as a death," she added quickly, "but it felt like it, in a certain way. It was its own loss."

He nodded. "I can understand that."

Could he? Could he understand even more—how she'd fallen apart, had to be in a psychiatric hospital, and had lost contact with her daughters for years? Would he be able to accept all that—or would that be a bridge too far? Several bridges, even, way past where either of them wanted to be.

And yet if she didn't tell him now, when? And how?

"So," James asked, and the moment for honesty, for better or worse, passed. "Will you head back to the farm this morning?"

"Yes, soon, I think," Anna replied. She thought of her car, still full of her things from Stroud, and her head, still full of all the conversations she'd had. "I might head back home first, unpack my car and change my clothes." She glanced down at her wrinkled jumper and jeans. "I feel as if I haven't been in my house properly for a few days." And, she realised, she needed to contact Ruth Hatch. She'd taken Peter's address book from his bureau, but she hadn't got any further than that.

"Sounds wise." He hesitated, and then said, "Look, Anna, about what I said last night…"

Anna tensed even as she smiled. "Which part?"

A sudden acrid smell of smoke reached them both and swearing softly under his breath, James turned around to rescue the burned omelette from on top of the Aga. He gave Anna a wry grimace before he scraped it into the bin.

"So much for that," he remarked. "And unfortunately,

I'm now all out of eggs."

"I've always been partial to toast," Anna told him. "Or cereal. Or yoghurt. Or just coffee." She held up her half-drunk mug. "Honestly, this is fine."

He let out a wry laugh as he put the smoking pan in the sink. "And here I was, trying to impress you."

Anna was touched—as well as tickled. "James," she told him, "you've already impressed me in a thousand different ways since I've first come to know you."

He looked so surprised, she almost laughed. "Have I?"

"Yes, you have. You're…" She paused as she cast about for all the ways she'd thought of him. "Thoughtful and kind and emotionally astute. Honest and caring and with a great taste in décor and mugs." She held her mug aloft. "I really like this one."

He laughed and shook his head.

"Sometimes," Anna continued, emboldened into an unusual recklessness, "I wonder what you see in me. Why would you even want to impress me?"

He glanced at her thoughtfully, the smile sliding from his face as he considered his response. "Anna," he finally said, his voice wonderfully gentle, "you've taken the hard knocks of life for a long time, so you might have forgotten—or maybe you never realised—just how special you are. Strong and resilient but also thoughtful and kind. Always thinking of others. And," he added with a devilish gleam in his eye, "incredibly beautiful, to boot."

Anna pressed her hands to her cheeks. "Now I'm blushing." And so, she was. No one had ever said such nice things about her…and so clearly meant them, as well.

"I'm only stating the truth." James held her gaze, a certain heat simmering in his eyes that he made no attempt to hide. The very air between them seemed to tauten with expectation, with *desire*. Anna had the sudden, mad urge to scramble right over the countertop, grab him by his well-starched shirt, and kiss him. *Kiss him.*

She couldn't even *remember* the last time she'd been kissed. Go that long without being kissed, and you basically forgot you had lips. Or a libido.

Yet she was feeling the fact of them both now, very much. They were positively roaring to life…and that was a little scary.

"Well, it seems we've formed our own mutual admiration society," she remarked lightly, knowing she needed to break the intensity of the moment, calm the intensity of her own feelings. She wasn't ready for them, not yet. "How about some toast?"

For a split second, James's face fell, and Anna feared she'd hurt him by backing away the way she had…and yet what else could she have done? Then he smiled and nodded. "Toast it is."

FORTY-FIVE MINUTES LATER, after two slices of toast and another cup of coffee, Anna decided she'd better get a move on. They'd both backed away from that intense moment—well, she had, and James had kindly followed suit—and kept the rest of their conversation both practical and light. As much as she knew she needed to sort out her car, her house, her life, Anna was reluctant to leave the comforting cosiness of James's house—as well as the man himself. She almost wished she *had* scrambled over the countertop, as ridiculous as that would have been.

It also might have been rather wonderful.

Clearly, the moment—if there even had been a moment—had passed, and after breakfast, they both launched into the usual script of courtesies, thanking each other, saying they must do it again—whatever it was.

At the door, James helped Anna on with her coat, and the feel of his hands sliding up over her shoulders ignited something in her again, that spark she'd long believed had flickered to cold ash. She turned around, and his hands dropped to his sides. He gave a smile that was clearly meant to be a farewell.

"See you soon, Anna," he said, and he leaned forward to do the kind of kiss where you simply hovered your cheek next to someone else's without actually touching. For a second, Anna just breathed him in. He smelled of woodsmoke from the fire, and coffee, and a hint of soap. Her senses swirled.

His cheek was still hovering near hers and he was about to ease back and suddenly Anna couldn't stand it. She'd stood on the sidelines of life, of her own marriage, for far too long. First accepting Peter's affair, and then living as quietly and unobtrusively as she could—yes, in part because she'd wanted to—but also because she hadn't believed she'd deserved anything else. Hadn't dared to dream she might ever find it.

And yet here was a man, a wonderful, amazing, handsome, *sexy* man, and his lips were an inch or two from hers.

Before she could overthink it, Anna moved her head. Moved her mouth, so her lips brushed and then bumped his. She felt James's whole body twang with shock and then go completely still, and with her lips still glued to his, she feared she'd made a terrible, terrible mistake.

In fact, she was pretty sure she had.

But in the split second of having that awful thought, things changed. James's hands came back up to grip her shoulders. His mouth fastened on hers with intent. And the brush-bump kiss that was more suitable for a thirteen-year-old than a fifty-three-year-old turned into something wonderful and passionate and intense.

Anna wasn't sure which one of them was deepening the kiss, who first walked who right up to the door so her back came against it and still James was kissing her, and she was kissing him. Her hands were in his hair, that lovely, white wavy hair, and her mind was reeling. Her body was on fire.

Then James broke the kiss, gasping, and they both stared at each other in wonder.

"Should I say sorry?" he mused aloud, and Anna let out a choked laugh as she pressed her hand to her tingling lips.

"*No.*"

He laughed too then, a sound of incredulity. "That's the first kiss I've had in fourteen years."

"Me too," Anna replied. "Well—twelve. Probably more, actually. I can't remember the last time Peter and I kissed, to be honest." She stopped talking abruptly because she didn't want to think about kissing Peter. She wanted, most definitely, to think about kissing James. Preferably again.

"I wasn't expecting that," James admitted with a sheepish laugh. He passed a shaky hand over his face as he shook his head. "But I'm very glad it happened."

"Me too," Anna replied, and knew she meant it. Utterly.

Chapter Eighteen

ANNA COULDN'T STOP smiling all the way back to Mathering. She felt guilty for feeling so happy when so much else in life was harrowing and sad, and yet…she *was*. And she knew she didn't want to feel guilty about it, because heaven knew she'd felt guilty about so much for so long. Right now, she just wanted to enjoy whatever it was that was happening between her and James. She wasn't even going to second-guess or catastrophise about the future. She just wanted to be.

Back at the house, Anna glanced uncertainly at Jane's front window; it was nearly nine o'clock on a Monday morning and yet the curtains were still drawn. Should she knock on the door, check up on Jane? She felt she should, but she knew it would mean a long conversation, and she couldn't exactly admit she'd spent the night at her father's and kissed him senseless, to boot.

A sudden, unhelpful giggle escaped Anna at the thought. No, now was definitely not the time to talk to Jane. She'd let something slip, she wouldn't be able to help it, and who knew how Jane would react. That was for James to handle; Anna supposed they would have to talk about it at some point. Some point soon, if things continued the way they had this morning…

For the next hour, Anna carted things from her car, so there was a big pile of boxes in the middle of her kitchen. She checked in with Rachel, who texted back to say Peter was sleeping, and Ben was bringing over lunch. Anna responded by saying she'd come by later that afternoon, which would hopefully give her enough time to unpack everything and sort her little house out.

She was coming to quite like this house, she reflected as she stacked some of her cookbooks on a slate shelf in the kitchen. If she sold her place in Stroud, she supposed she could buy something here, although she didn't think she'd mind staying in this rental. Of course if things became serious with James…

But she couldn't let herself think that way, not after just one kiss.

We're both in our fifties so there might not be loads of time to waste when it comes to a relationship…

James had said that, but he'd also said there was a reason people took things slowly. Anna neither wanted to presume nor rush. No, she just wanted to *enjoy*…as much as was possible, considering everything else going on in her life.

With everything unpacked, Anna changed her clothes, made herself a cup of tea, and then finally sat down with Peter's address book and her mobile phone to call Ruth Hatch. Outside the sky was a pale blue, laced with gossamer-like clouds. Pale sunlight had turned her little patch of lawn silvery, and a cluster of snowdrops had sprung up under the yew tree. Anna gazed out at the pleasant little scene, letting the moment's peace soak right into her bones.

I'm happy, she thought, and marvelled.

Then, putting down her cup of tea and squaring her shoulders, she turned to the address book and flipped it open to H. There were only two entries—a feed supplier and R. Hatch, in Peter's crabbed handwriting. Her heart lurched like a drunk staggering inside her chest. Did she really want to call this woman? *Talk* to her?

Then she thought of the look of wonder on James's face that morning, and decided that no, she did *not* want to ring Ruth Hatch but yes, she *could*—and would—do it. Taking a deep breath, she swiped her phone and then started putting in the numbers, her heart thudding harder with each digit she pressed.

When she finished, she put her phone to her ear, her mouth dry, her head light. She should have thought about what she was going to say, she realised. She should have had a script.

Instead, her head felt like it was full of cotton wool, and she had a legitimate fear that she might pass out. She waited to hear a ring, but there wasn't, just a funny click and then an automated voice stating rather firmly, *we're sorry but this number is no longer in service. Please try again.*

Try again? How? The call disconnected and slowly Anna put down her mobile. She hadn't been expecting that, but maybe she should have. How long since Peter had been in touch with Ruth? He'd mentioned years, and something about the way he'd spoken made her think it had been more than a few. It caused her a flicker of sorrow, to think that things had only ended between them after she had left. Why? Did it even matter now?

She glanced back down at the address book—Hatch Farm, Thorpe Willoughby, Selby. She could write, she supposed, but it would take a day or two for the letter to get there, and in truth she didn't know how long Peter had. Maybe another week or two, maybe less. Should she drive all the way out to Selby? It was about an hour and a half away, and something in her resisted a face-to-face confrontation with this shadowy woman who had caused her so much heartache over the years. She wasn't sure she could handle seeing Ruth Hatch in her own home, her *life*. And then, of course, there was Daisy to consider.

Daisy. Someone she had not let herself think about, at all, over the last thirteen years, because it was far too painful, but Anna recognised she deserved to know about Peter, too. There was no address for her in Peter's book, though. Had he even kept in touch with her?

Anna reached for her laptop and went on Facebook. She hardly ever scrolled on social media, but now she put Daisy Hatch into the search bar, held her breath.

Nothing relevant came up.

A gusty sigh escaped her, and she went onto Instagram, and then all the other social media channels she could think of, typing in Daisy Hatch. Lots of different random things came up, but nothing related to Hatch Farm, Thorpe Willoughby, or Yorkshire. She was, Anna realised, at something of a dead end, but she didn't feel like she'd tried enough.

She was just about to type Ruth Hatch into an internet search when her phone buzzed with a text, this one from Harriet.

Please come.

Anna slammed her laptop shut as she lurched up from the table. She would have to try to contact Ruth Hatch later.

Fifteen minutes later, Anna was pulling up to Embthwaite Farm, afraid of what she should expect. Rachel met her at the door, her expression sombre.

"The palliative nurse just came again," she explained quietly. "She said he's nearing the end. I didn't realise…I thought he was just sleeping a bit more deeply, maybe, after I gave him breakfast…"

Rachel's voice broke and Anna put her arms around her, murmuring soothing words.

"I don't know why I'm sad, exactly," Rachel said on a sniff as she hugged Anna tightly. "I mean, I will miss him, but you know we didn't have a close relationship. Not as close as I wanted, anyway."

"He's still your father," Anna reminded her. "And he was an important person in your life, regardless of whether the relationship was what you wanted it to be or not."

"That's true, I suppose." Rachel sniffed again and stepped back. "Harriet's in the kitchen, baking up a storm. Her way of coping, I guess. She spoke to Dad last night, but I have no idea what they said, only that she came down looking distraught."

"Oh, poor Harriet…" Anna murmured, her heart aching for her daughter. Had there been a reconciliation, she wondered, or had Peter been too far gone?

"Ben's gone out to get some lunch for us," Rachel continued, heading back towards the kitchen. "And Quinn is coming over soon. We all wanted to be together."

"Yes, of course… What did the palliative nurse say, exactly?"

Rachel glanced at her, her eyes filling with tears once more. "She said most likely not more than twenty-four hours."

Twenty-four hours. Even though Anna thought she had been expecting it, it felt like a punch to the gut. A single day left of Peter's life…and what then?

Back in the kitchen, Harriet was stirring a batch of cookie dough as if her life depended on it. Her eyes were red-rimmed, her face haggard. Anna didn't even hesitate as she went up to her youngest—and prickliest—daughter and put her arms around her.

For a single second, Harriet stiffened in shock and then, just as Rachel had done, she wrapped her arms tightly around her mother. "I'm so much sadder than I thought I'd be," she whimpered, her voice muffled against Anna's shoulder.

"I'd be surprised if you weren't," Anna replied, stroking Harriet's hair. "Death always feels like a wrench. Unexpected and shocking, even when you think you're ready for it."

Harriet let out a shuddery sigh as she eased back. "Yes, I suppose so." She went back to her mixing, her gaze on the bright red bowl as she said in a rush, "I spoke to him yesterday, like you wanted me to. He…he said he'd always known, really, that I was his daughter. He said he was sorry for the way he'd acted." She let out a choked sound, half laugh, half sob. "And then he said there was no one 'aught as stubborn as a Yorkshire farmer.'" Another sound escaped her, this one definitely a sob. "And then…and then we *hugged.* I couldn't remember the last time I'd hugged him."

"Oh, Harriet, I'm so glad," Anna said, and put her arms around her as her daughter broken down into tears.

"I just wish it hadn't come so late," she confessed between gulping sobs. "It feels like such a waste. A waste of so many years."

Anna knew there was very little she could say to that; it *was* a waste, and yet at least now they'd been able to move past it.

"At least it didn't end as a waste," Rachel said, putting her arms around them both. "We can move on, Hats, because we've made peace with it, and so has Dad. That's a gift. Truly."

For a moment they all stood there, their arms around each other, simply letting themselves soak in the sadness in a way that felt healing. Anna's heart was full of gratitude, that she'd been able to be part of this moment at all.

After a few more seconds, Rachel stepped back. "I should go check on him," she explained. "The palliative nurse said someone should sit with him."

"I can sit with him, if you like," Anna offered. "Or we all could. Or we could take it in turns."

"Let's all go," Harriet said, wiping her face. "Just for a bit."

They headed upstairs, crowding into the bedroom where Peter lay. At the sight of him, Anna experienced another jolt. He looked *shrunken*, compared to just yesterday, and so very still. His breath came in slow, laboured gasps, with enough space between each one for Anna to tense, wondering if it had been his last. It really was nearly the end.

"Before Dad got sick, I hardly ever went in here," Rachel said in a low voice. She pulled a chair up near the bed for Anna, and another for Harriet before she stood at the foot of the bed, her arms wrapped around herself as she gazed down at her father. "I didn't realise he'd kept all your clothes in the wardrobe," she continued. "I don't think he ever touched a thing." She glanced at Anna. "I didn't even realise you hadn't taken your clothes."

"I left in something of a rush," Anna conceded. A pang of unease assailed her. She needed to tell her daughters about Peter asking her to contact Ruth Hatch, and maybe also about Daisy. It would not, she knew, be an easy conversation.

They sat in silence for a few moments, the only sound the draw and tear of Peter's painful breathing. Harriet sniffed and wiped at her eyes, while Rachel looked resolute.

Then a noise from downstairs had them all turning.

"Ben, with lunch," Rachel explained, and slipped from the room.

Harriet drew a sniffly breath. "I don't know if you knew," she told Anna after a moment, "but Dad had changed his will right after you left. He left the farm to Rachel and ten thousand pounds to me."

"He…did?" Anna was startled; she had never thought about Peter's will, but she'd assumed he would have left his estate equally between his daughters.

"Yes, we found the will about a month ago. But he told me yesterday that he changed his will, just before he found out about the brain tumour. He said he wanted to do what was best for all of us." She gave Anna a watery smile. "So,

I'm glad about that. Not because of the money, but just because...he made it right."

"I'm glad about that, too," Anna replied. She hated the thought of Harriet feeling so singled out, so rejected. She glanced back at Peter with a sorrow that felt more like weariness than grief. *Why*, she wondered futilely. *Why were you so stubborn...about so many things?*

She heard the creak of the stairs and then Rachel poked her head in the door. "Ben's brought lunch...a big shepherd's pie that Diana made. Do you want to come down? I can stay up here, if you like."

"No, you both go eat, you look like you need something," Anna replied. "I'll stay."

She glanced back at Peter. *I left you thirteen years ago*, she thought, and *maybe I should have left you long before. But now I'm staying.*

THE REST OF the day passed in a surreal sort of dreaminess; they took turns sitting at Peter's bedside, going down to the kitchen for restorative cups of tea as they alternated spots. Around three o'clock Quinn came over, and Anna was glad to see both her daughters supported by such decent men. It gave her a sense of reassurance and security for their happiness.

And what about *her* happiness? She'd texted James to let him know she was back at the farm, had had a text back from him at lunchtime: *I must confess, I can't stop smiling. Hope you're holding up okay. xx*

She could hardly wait to see him again, and yet with everything happening here, she knew it would be some time.

During one of her breaks in the kitchen, she decided to make one more effort to look up Ruth Hatch. It might be too late for her to say her goodbyes, but Anna felt she needed to try. She typed Ruth Hatch, Hatch Farm, Thorpe Willoughby into the search box and waited for it to load.

Ben was making yet more tea for her and Rachel, and Harriet was sitting upstairs with Peter. Quinn had gallantly volunteered to walk Fred. Outside the sun was sinking behind the hill, casting dusky shadows over the garden as the last of the day's light was leached from the sky.

Anna glanced down at her phone, waiting with a weary sort of impatience for the search results to load.

"I don't mean to be macabre," Rachel said in a low voice, "but how long should we wait before we hold the funeral? It will just be locals, and I think I'd like to get it over with, if that doesn't sound too awful." She glanced at Anna. "And you probably want to get back to Stroud."

"There's no rush on my end," Anna replied. She supposed she should talk to both Rachel and Harriet about her tentative plans to stay in Mathering. She hoped they'd be pleased, but what if they weren't?

"A week or so is the usual time, if there isn't the need for an autopsy," Ben chimed in quietly as he handed them both mugs of tea. "That's what it was for my dad."

"I can't believe we're talking about this," Rachel murmured as she took a sip of her tea. "When will it stop feeling like a surprise?"

Just then, they heard the sound of Harriet coming downstairs, one slow step at a time. Rachel and Anna glanced at each other in apprehension; she'd only been up there for twenty minutes or so.

Harriet came into the kitchen, her face pale, her hair in a dark tangle. "He's gone," she said quietly. "I don't even know when. He slipped away so quietly…it took me a few minutes to realise there hadn't been another breath." She made a gulping sound. "I'm sorry. I would have come and fetched you if I'd known…"

"Oh, daring." Anna stood up and went over to embrace her daughters. "It's all right." She hugged her tightly. "It's all right."

"That's that, then," Rachel said. She sounded both shocked and numb.

Ben managed a crooked smile. "Whatever else you want to say about him, he was a good farmer."

Harriet gave a wobbly laugh and wiped her eyes. "Yes, he was that."

They were all silent for a few moments, absorbing the reality of Peter's death, and then Harriet went to the kettle.

"I need a cup of tea," she announced, and for some reason this elicited a watery laugh from Rachel.

Anna glanced down at her phone; the search results for Ruth Hatch had finally come up, and the first one gave her a jolt.

It was a notice of the arrangements for her funeral, three years ago.

Chapter Nineteen

THE NEXT FEW days passed in a muted flurry of activity; Anna had forgotten, from her own parents' deaths, how many prosaic practicalities had to be dealt in the midst of the daze of grief. A doctor had to be called, to sign the death certificate, and a funeral home, to arrange the removal of Peter's body. The church, to arrange the funeral, and various neighbours and acquaintances to let everyone know.

In typical Yorkshire style, casseroles and pies and Tupperware filled with scones or cookies came to the door of the farmhouse, sometimes left with a note, sometimes not. Within forty-eight hours, their fridge was completely full.

Anna had gone back to her house for some clothes and toiletries before returning to the farmhouse. She'd agreed to stay there until the funeral; it seemed silly not to, when there were so many different things to deal with, and the tensions that had meant they needed to be apart had eased or maybe even disappeared altogether.

Still, she found she missed the cosy comfort of her little house, and more significantly, she missed James. There hadn't been so much as a moment to see him since Peter's death, and while she knew he understood, she felt the uncertainty of their relationship like a tangible thing. They'd kissed, but they hadn't talked about it. Things were complicated, but they hadn't really explained how. She didn't know where they stood, or even where she *wanted* them to stand, or whether she would stay in Mathering. It was a lot of unknowns to be dealing with, Anna reflected, but right now her priority was her daughters, so she pushed all her own worries and doubts aside to focus on them.

After her absence in their lives for the last twelve years, it felt like a good and necessary thing.

THREE DAYS BEFORE the funeral, Rachel was contacted by Edward Hale, a solicitor in York who had managed Peter's estate, to talk about the will.

"He says he wants all three of us to come in," she said, sounding apprehensive. "As the will might not be what we expect. But we already saw it—"

"Dad told me he changed it," Harriet interjected. "Just before he died. He said he made it right, his exact words."

Rachel brightened. "Do you think he went back to splitting it between us fifty-fifty? You know I would have given you half anyway—"

"I know," Harriet replied with a small smile. "But maybe now you don't need to. And in any case, I'd want the sentiment to come from him."

It was a grey, wintry afternoon, with an unforgiving wind rolling off the moors, when they headed to York. Harriet had spent the morning making scones for the refreshments after the funeral, and Rachel had been filling out various paperwork regarding Peter's death.

"I cannot believe how many death certificates you need, to prove someone is actually dead," she'd exclaimed in frustration. "It feels like adding insult to injury."

Anna, in a bid to be helpful and because both girls had insisted it wasn't something they wanted to do, had cleared out Peter's bedroom, including her old clothes. She'd forgotten how many she'd left here, and almost every item held a memory—the dress she'd worn to her own father's funeral, the cardigan she liked for cold winter mornings. The dungarees she'd used when out in the garden. The colourful blouse that Harriet had always loved to see her wear. It gave her a pang of loss, to consider how much she'd left behind when she'd walked out of the door that day, yet twelve years later she didn't know if she could have done any differently. If she'd had the strength.

Which reminded her, she'd recalled uneasily, that she needed to talk to the girls about Ruth Hatch...and, more importantly, Daisy.

A sigh had escaped her as she'd sank onto the bed. She'd done another search for Daisy Hatch on the internet, but nothing had come up. As far as she could tell, Hatch Farm was no longer in operation. Ruth was dead, and Daisy had disappeared. Was there anything more Anna had to do?

The question was still rattling around in her brain as Edward Hale ushered them into his old-fashioned office, all mahogany and leather. He was in his sixties, with steel-grey hair combed into a severe side part, but his brown eyes seemed kindly behind his spectacles.

"Please, Misses Mowbray, Mrs Mowbray, do sit down."

They all took seats on the chairs drawn up in front of his desk; something about his expression was making Anna worried. It looked more serious than the usual I'm-sorry-for-your-loss face that most people put on in this situation. He looked, she realised, almost nervous.

"As I mentioned on the telephone, Mr Mowbray changed his will a few months ago, when he realised he had a terminal brain tumour. I believe you've seen a copy of his old will, which was made approximately thirteen years ago?" He raised his eyebrows, and Rachel nodded rather tersely.

"Yes, the one where he basically wrote Harriet out of it," she stated succinctly, and the solicitor winced noticeably.

"Yes, well." He coughed and cleared his throat. "He's changed the will significantly since then and I wanted to make you aware of it before the official reading, as I imagine its contents might be something of a…shock."

"A shock?" Harriet straightened in her chair, frowning. "But…that doesn't sound good." Mr Hale did not reply, and Harriet continued, her tone sounding both strident and pleading, "Dad told me he'd changed it right before he died. He said he was making things *right*. Those were his exact words."

"Well." Mr Hale cleared his throat again, and Anna was starting to feel seriously anxious. What, she wondered, had Peter done? How had he, in the tangled web of his own destroyed mind, made it *right*?

"Maybe you should just tell us what the changes are," Rachel suggested quietly. "We assumed he's split his estate equally between us, but I'm guessing that might not be the case?" Her eyes looked hard, but she chewed her lip in anxiety. Anna pressed her hands together.

"No, it isn't the case," Mr Hale agreed sombrely. "I'm afraid your father made a—a significant change to his will." He paused, and then in the resolute yet resigned tone of someone who knows he has to give unpleasant news and has decided to just say it: "He's left you, Rachel and Harriet, five thousand pounds each."

"What!" Rachel's face paled, her jaw slackening as she stared at the solicitor in disbelief. "You mean...that's it? What about the house? The land?"

Mr Hale's expression was turning rather wretched. "He has left the house and land, and indeed the rest of his estate, to Miss Daisy Hatch."

Anna felt as if she'd just been dipped in ice. "Daisy..." The name slipped from between her lips in little more than a breath of shock...but one Rachel heard.

"You know this person?" she demanded. "This *Daisy*?"

"I don't *know* her," Anna replied slowly. She should have told the girls about Daisy, she realised hollowly, to spare them this moment. But how could she have possibly known this moment was coming? She'd had no idea at all, not even the remotest inkling...

"She's...she's Dad's other woman, isn't she?" Harriet said slowly, realisation dawning across her face. "She must be. He's left everything to *her*." She spat the words, shaking her head. "I can't believe it. And he said he was going to make things right. What a bloody joke." Her eyes filled with tears, and she brushed them away angrily. "It's not about the money," she told the solicitor, "so please don't think we're money-grubbing shrews, angling for his inheritance, or something like that. It's…it's about the *relationship*." Her voice broke, and she had to wipe her eyes again, while Anna watched on impotently, her heart aching for her daughter, for all of them. "Or lack of it, really," Harriet continued. "I spent thirteen years of my life putting my own needs aside and looking after that man and that bloody, bloody *farm*—"

"I think there's been a mistake," Mr Hale broke in, sounding even more miserable at this outpouring of emotion. "About the identity of Miss Hatch—"

"Daisy Hatch isn't your father's…mistress," Anna interjected, her voice so low she wasn't sure if either Harriet or Rachel heard her, although they must have because they both went still. "She's…she's…" She took a deep breath, closed her eyes as she prayed for strength. "She's his daughter."

The silence felt shocking, endless. Anna opened her eyes. Harriet and Rachel were both staring at her, eyes wide and mouths agape. Anna stared back, having no words. What could she possibly say to them now?

"His *daughter*?" Rachel finally repeated, her voice hoarse. "You mean…"

"He had a child with Ruth Hatch," Anna confirmed, and now her voice sounded wooden. "Daisy. She was born between you and Harriet, I'm not exactly sure when. She must be about thirty, thirty-one now."

Another silence that felt leaden, awful. Anna longed to close her eyes against it all, but she didn't. She needed to face this—she knew she did.

"How long have you known about this?" Harriet demanded.

Anna glanced at the solicitor, who was looking, by this

point, as if he'd rather be anywhere else. "I think…I think we should have this discussion elsewhere," she stated. "And finish this one first."

"Is there anything left to say?" Rachel demanded, glancing between them all, her expression accusing. "He's left us five thousand pounds each. Did he leave you anything, Mum?" She turned to glare at the solicitor, as if this was all his fault.

"I wasn't expecting anything—" Anna began, only for the solicitor to take an envelope from his desk.

"He left you this," he told Anna. "A letter."

"He did?" Anna really hadn't been expecting *that.* She took it between fingers that felt numb. "Thank you." She could feel her daughters' curiosity like a palpable thing, but she was not about to open a letter from Peter in the solicitor's office.

"And everything else to Daisy Hatch?" Rachel asked flatly. "Right?"

The solicitor nodded. "Yes, everything else."

A silence fell on the little group. Anna thought about all the things Daisy would now own—all the furniture, the antiques and heirlooms passed down through the Mowbray family. All the knick-knacks she'd once dusted, all the mementoes Rachel and Harriet had treasured—or not. Daisy Hatch, this woman they'd never known, would be the sole proprietor of Embthwaite Farm. It felt inconceivable, offensive, *wrong.*

"Then I suppose there's nothing more to say," Anna said slowly. It was, she presumed, within Peter's rights to bequeath his estate to one of his children, and not the others.

And maybe something in his letter would explain it…or not.

She had the sudden urge to tear the letter up into bits, to never know what feeble excuse her ex-husband might have made, to cheat his two daughters of their inheritance. She'd made enough excuses for the man over the years. She'd been as forgiving and understanding and accepting as she knew how to be…but her patience was running out, now that he was dead, and it appeared as if he'd left only devastation in his wake.

Why, Peter? she cried silently. *Why would you do this?*

Mr Hale made some remarks that Anna couldn't quite pay attention to, and then they were rising with a scraping of chairs and a murmuring of both thanks and apologies—Anna wasn't sure which sentiment was more appropriate in this situation—and then they were wandering down the street, all of them feeling aimless, until Harriet guided them into a little tea shop near the Shambles.

"I've been here with Quinn," she explained. "They do lovely cakes."

She ordered them all a pot of tea and an iced bun while Anna and Rachel both seemed only to stare into space.

"Well, that's that, then," Harriet said finally, and she almost sounded relieved. "Five thousand pounds isn't something to sneeze at."

"Isn't it?" Rachel returned dryly. "I know Dad wasn't a millionaire, but a hundred acres of North Yorkshire moorland…the last time I looked, that would be valued at six or seven hundred thousand pounds, and that's without the house. With the house it's probably double."

Harriet winced. "Well, even so…" she managed before

she trailed off, shaking her head.

What really, Anna wondered, could there possibly be to say? Could any of them really understand why Peter had done what he'd done?

"Mum," Rachel said, sounding confused but also a little bit accusing, "why didn't you tell us about Daisy?"

"I should have," Anna told her daughters, grimacing in apology. Why had she kept it from them—to protect them or herself, and the inevitable emotional fallout? "I know I should have. I thought about it, especially in the last few weeks..."

"How long have you known?" Harriet asked, and Anna sighed.

Before she could formulate an answer, Rachel figured it out. "That's why you left, isn't it?" she exclaimed softly. "You must have found out about Daisy then."

Slowly Anna nodded. Thirteen years on, the memory was still painful, sharp enough to take her breath away. Time didn't heal that.

"How?" Harriet asked. "Did...did Dad *tell* you?"

"No," Anna replied after a moment, taking a sip of tea to steady herself, knowing how much this would hurt them both. "At least, he didn't mean to. It was just before Christmas, and a parcel came. It was addressed to him, but we'd had so many parcels coming for Christmas that I assumed it was one of the presents I'd ordered. I opened it—and saw it was a charm bracelet, with the letter D as one of the charms. Well, I knew it couldn't be for one of you girls. And it couldn't be for—for Ruth. At least, I didn't think it could, although by that point I wanted it to be. I confronted him about it, and he admitted Daisy's existence."

Rachel let out a huff of hard laughter. "A charm bracelet? I don't remember Dad ever buying me anything."

"Me neither," Harriet agreed quietly. Her expression was sombre as she stared down at her tea; Anna knew it would take a while for both of her daughters to adjust to this new reality. She was *still* adjusting to it, and it had been thirteen years.

"So, did he have a relationship with her?" Rachel asked. "I mean, he must have, to buy a bracelet like that."

Anna's heart ached, because she heard the child's question underneath the practical one—did he love her more than us? "I don't know about a relationship," she answered carefully, "but when he was visiting Ruth, he was visiting Daisy, too." She sighed. "I know that much."

Another silence, this one feeling heavy. "Why didn't you tell us before?" Harriet asked. "When you were talking about why you left?" She frowned. "If there hadn't been this thing with the will, would you have ever told us?"

"I..." Anna stared at them helplessly. "I didn't tell you for a long time because I didn't want to hurt you. And, really, it didn't feel like my news to share. I hoped your father might tell you, in time, but he never did."

"Well, he told us in his will," Harriet chimed in, unable to keep from sounding bitter. "Thanks a lot, Dad."

"I'm so sorry..." Anna began, but Harriet shook her head.

"Mum, we don't blame you." She sighed. "I don't even want to blame Dad, at this point. I just wish things had been different."

"Do you think there's anything in the letter he wrote you?" Rachel asked. "About the will and why he did it the way he did?" She clearly wanted Anna to open the letter right there and then, but she was reluctant to, in the busyness of a touristy tea shop, with her daughters craning their necks to catch a glimpse of what their father had written to her. Whatever it was, it had to be personal.

"Maybe," she replied. "I'll open it later, in private, and I'll tell you if there's anything relevant, of course."

Rachel sighed, deflated. "Fair enough." She slumped against the back of her seat, shaking her head slowly. "We have a *half-sister*. I can't even get my head around that."

"A half-sister who has our house," Harriet filled in. She paused, trying to organise her thoughts. "I know I keep saying it isn't about the money, but it sort of is, at least a little. I mean, we were Dad's daughters as much as this Daisy was. If he wanted to be fair, why not split it evenly between us all? I would have accepted that, absolutely."

Anna shook her head. "I couldn't tell you why."

"You must have known a little bit about what was going on in his head, Mum," Rachel pressed. "You were married to him for twenty years, after all."

"Oh, Rachel." Anna let out a broken laugh. "I wish. I don't think I ever truly understood your father. I let myself believe things about him that I'm just not sure were true, simply because I wanted them to be. I do think he loved you both, in his own way, but how much affection he was actually capable of..." She sighed. "He grew up in a family that didn't deal in emotions, pure and simple. A Yorkshire farming family from the 1950s... Well, you can imagine."

"We don't need to imagine," Harriet broke in. "We lived it."

"And when you left?" Rachel asked quietly. "It really was because you found out about Daisy…?"

Anna nodded. "It just felt like an even worse betrayal. I'd learned to live with his affair, even though I hated it. But a *child*…a whole life apart from me, from us…" She shook her head. "I don't really remember what happened that day," she admitted slowly. "Like I told you before. He told me the truth about Daisy, that he'd been visiting her all these years, and then he went out to the barn as if to say that was that. And something just…broke…inside me. I'm sorry—"

"We know, Mum." Harriet reached over to grasp her hand, and Anna gave her a rather watery smile of thanks. "You don't need to apologise anymore, trust us. This has all got to me a lot tougher for you than for us."

"Well, I'm not the one who was cheated out of my inheritance," Anna returned on a sigh, squeezing Harriet's fingers before she let go of her hand. "That makes a big difference to both of you."

"Yes, I could have used an infusion of cash for my business," Rachel agreed wryly. "But I won't be lost without it, and Ben and I have already discussed the future…" She blushed, dipping her head. "When—if—we get married, I'll move into the Mackey farm. I like their place better, to tell you the truth, and Diana is thinking of downsizing, maybe moving into Mathering."

"And Quinn and I want to buy a place of our own eventually," Harriet added. She had started to blush, as well. "I know it's early days, but we've already talked about it."

"Well." Anna smiled and sat back, shaking her head. "It sounds like neither of you have much need of a mouldy old farmhouse."

"No," Rachel replied after a moment, "we don't. But it still hurts."

"Yes," Anna answered quietly. There could be no denying that. "It does."

BACK AT THE farm, Anna sat at the kitchen table to open Peter's letter. Harriet had gone over to the hotel to see Quinn, and Rachel had gone to the Mackey farm, so she was alone in the house, save for Fred, in his usual position by the Rayburn. She gave him a small smile as she held the envelope in her hands. "What do you think, Fred?" she asked. "Is this letter going to explain everything? The big mystery finally solved?"

Fred, sensing her disquiet, beat his tail against the floor.

Anna sighed. She didn't actually think this letter would hold all the answers, but she still hoped it would shed at least a little light. "All right, here goes," she said, and she slit the envelope with her thumbnail. The letter, written in a painstaking, spidery hand, was unsurprisingly brief; Peter had always been a man of few words.

Dear Anna,

You'll be surprised to be hearing from me, I know, but I know I'll have ruffled a few feathers with the change in my will. You'll be thinking, no doubt, that I'm an or-

nery man who doesn't care about his daughters. All three of you have thought that, to one degree or another, and I'm not blaming you, because God knows I'm not an easy man, but the truth is, whether you want to believe it or not, I loved all of you. Not well, I'll grant you that, which might raise a smile from you—who knows?

As for why I changed the will…well, it's simple, really. Ruth lost her farm a few years back, and all Daisy has ever wanted is to be a farmer. It's in her blood, same as me. I was never a proper father to her, and I can already hear you saying I wasn't to Rachel or Harriet, but Daisy got even less of me than they did. I wanted to make it right with her before I died.

As for Rachel and Harriet…well, those girls of ours never liked the farming life. The house was a millstone around their necks, whether they realised it or not. Oh, I know they'd have liked the money from selling it—who wouldn't? But Embthwaite Farm has been in the Mowbray family for one hundred fifty years. Daisy will keep it, or try to, I know, and that's what I want both for the farm and for her. It might not feel fair, but I think it's right.

As for the money I've left for Rachel and Harriet…well, I'm not being stingy, but that's all there is, besides the land. Farming doesn't make you rich, not these days. I'm writing this to you because Rachel and Harriet barely speak to each other, although maybe that's changed by the time you're reading this. I hope it has. And I hope you come back for those girls, because they don't have a father now, not that they ever had much of one, but they always had a mother.

Peter

"Oh, Peter."

His name escaped Anna's lips on a trembling sigh, and she found she had to wipe a tear from her eye. He was a difficult, ornery man, she thought, but she understood at least some of his logic, and she hoped the girls would, as well. As for Daisy...well, Anna supposed they would all have to meet her one day, maybe one day soon. Mr Hale had told them before they'd left that he would be in touch with Daisy in regard to the funeral arrangements as well as her unexpected inheritance. Would she come? Did Anna want her to?

In any case, they would have to interact with her, get to know her, as she would most likely be living right here, sitting in this kitchen as Anna was doing now. How would Harriet and Rachel feel about that? How did she? Did she want to have a relationship with Peter's other daughter, who was now orphaned? She could hardly blame Daisy for existing, she knew, and yet it still felt difficult.

Anna rested her chin on her hand as the shadows lengthened outside and the kitchen grew dark. Despite the sorrows and surprises of the day, she felt unexpectedly at peace. Surely there were no more shocks ahead; everything was out in the open, and all three—or maybe even four—of them could find a way to move on.

Which made her think of James... Anna glanced at her phone, but there had been no messages or missed calls all day. He'd texted her last night, to ask her how she was holding up, and she'd responded, but she still hadn't seen him since their kiss, and she realised she wanted to. Why not right now? Harriet and Rachel were both occupied, and there was nothing for her to do. She could drive over to his house, have a cup of tea and maybe share a kiss…

Impulsively she swiped to dial his number, and then listening to his ring, already anticipating the sound of his voice, that hint of laughter, the alacrity with which he'd invite her over, the joy with which she'd accept.

But the phone kept ringing, and after a minute or two, it switched to voicemail.

Fighting a deep sense of disappointment—James had a life, *obviously*—Anna left a message.

"James, it's Anna. Just wondered how you were, and if you fancied a drink or a meal or—something. I…miss you. Quite a lot, actually." Embarrassed by the emotion in her voice and feeling like she'd revealed too much, she ended the call abruptly and put her phone back on the table. Hopefully that hadn't freaked him out. It would be good to see him again, she told herself, if just to figure out where they were.

But as the kitchen grew darker and darker, the screen of her phone remained stubbornly blank.

Chapter Twenty

THE FUNERAL WAS in one of Mathering's two parish churches, weak sunlight filtering through its windows of stained glass. Anna had been in the church for school harvest assemblies and candlelit Christmas Eve services, the occasional Easter. She'd never been there for a funeral.

There were a few dozen people present—the Mackeys and a few other farming families, Quinn, and some stalwarts from the town. Standing in the narthex of the church, Anna adjusted the black wool dress she'd bought online for the occasion as she gave Rachel and Harriet encouraging smiles. In the old, Anglican way, they would process into the church behind the vicar as he recited the familiar Bible verses of life and death. It felt like a rather archaic way to do things, but there was a comfort in the ritual, Anna thought, a certain peace. Death—and grief—were serious matters, and the service weighted them appropriately.

The last few days had been a flurry of funeral arrangements; Anna had gone back to her house only twice, and she'd knocked on Jane's door once to see how she was, but there had been no answer. There had been no answer to her voicemail from James, either a fact that was making her increasingly uneasy and even despondent. In three days, he hadn't so much as texted her, which felt very odd as well as alarming.

Was he actually *ghosting* her? He never had left a message this long before, and yet what experience really did she have to look back on? They'd spent so little time together. Yes, it had all become rather serious quite fast, but his blanking her now felt like a painful reminder that she didn't actually know him all that well, even if she felt as if she did. Why wouldn't he have at least texted her, especially knowing that the funeral was today?

There was, Anna feared, only one answer to that question—that he was no longer interested in her. Yet it seemed hard to believe, considering what she'd known of him. And their kiss…! Had he somehow started having second thoughts? Maybe he had decided she was simply too much hard work, and he wasn't messaging because he felt guilty for not being up for it, for her.

Whatever possibilities she came up with felt far too dispiriting. There was no explanation, she knew, that felt good enough, or even remotely reasonable. She hadn't seen him in nearly a week, and he hadn't responded to her text from three days ago. What else could be going on?

But she couldn't think about James now, Anna told herself, because Rachel and Harriet needed her. Although they'd both become stoical about the loss of their inheritance, the reality of the funeral—the sight of Peter's coffin, hefted by Ben, Quinn, and four pallbearers from the funeral home, at the church's lychgate had clearly shaken them. Rachel looked pale and grim-faced, and Harriet was fighting tears.

As the men brought the coffin inside the church, followed by the vicar, who gave them a kindly smile, they processed in behind.

"'I am the resurrection and the life,' sayeth the Lord," the vicar intoned. "'Those who believe in me, even though they die, will live, and everyone who lives and believes in me will never die.'"

Harriet threw Anna an uncertain glance and she smiled back in reassurance before reaching for both her daughters' hands and holding them tightly.

"We brought nothing into this world," the vicar continued, "and we take nothing out. The Lord gaveth, and the Lord hath taken away. Blessed be the name of the Lord."

Slowly, following the vicar, they walked down the church's aisle as fifty or so local residents, almost all whom Anna knew, watched them sombrely. She met the eyes of a few and saw only sympathy and kindness, and her own eyes stung. For better or worse, this was her community, she realised. Her home.

"The steadfast love of the Lord never ceases, his mercies never come to an end. They are new every morning; great is his faithfulness."

Anna led Rachel and Harriet into the front row as the pallbearers rested Peter's coffin on the bier and the vicar turned to face the congregation. "Blessed are those who mourn, for they will be comforted. Thank you for coming today to celebrate the life of Peter Mowbray..."

Anna found herself tuning out the rest of his words, not because she didn't want to listen, but because she suddenly felt overwhelmed by it all. She wanted to be strong for her daughters, but in that moment, it slammed into her that

Peter, her husband of twenty years, was dead. *Dead.* And although she'd made peace with it, with him, in that moment it felt like a terrible, gasping wrench. There was more she should have said, she thought. More she should have asked or explained. There would always be more, she realised. Death would always be a broken chain, an unanswered question. There could be no escaping the utter wrongness of it in that moment.

She sniffed, tellingly, and to her surprise, Rachel and Harriet, on either side of her, reached for her hands, just as she'd reached for theirs earlier. They remained that way through the whole service—holding each other's hands, holding each other up.

Ben had agreed to give the eulogy, and Anna listened, smiling faintly, as he spoke of Peter's love of the farm, the livestock, his dry sense of humour, his deep appreciation of a good cup of tea. He managed to find every good quality Peter had possessed and offer it up to the people who knew him well, and glancing at Rachel and Harriet, Anna knew they'd needed to be reminded of their father's better qualities. They'd loved him, after all.

As Ben reached the end of his eulogy, a slight commotion from the back of the church had the three of them—and quite a few other people—turning. A young woman, tall and slender with long, fiery-red hair, was sliding into the back row, a look of something like defiance on her face. There was, Anna knew, only one person it could be.

Ben clocked her, paused, and then continued speaking.

"We all know Peter Mowbray was a dedicated farmer," he stated carefully. "He loved this land like no other. But we also know he wasn't the easiest man to live with, and sometimes lacking when it came to his roles as husband and father. That doesn't take away from who he was as a person, and how much we all loved him. But it's something that he wouldn't deny himself, as he was a man who liked to say and hear it straight." He gazed steadily at the entire congregation before he cast his gaze heavenward. "So, Peter, God love you, I hope you're having a nice brew up there, in God's own country."

This caused a light ripple of laughter tinged with relief to move through the crowd; Yorkshire was known as God's own country, and the joke was appreciated. Nothing like a little levity in a moment like this, Anna thought, and glanced back towards the young woman in the back row, but she'd already gone.

IN THE COMMOTION after the funeral, while the pallbearers loaded the coffin into the hearse, Anna didn't see Daisy. She must have slipped out before the end of the service.

"It had to have been her," Rachel remarked as they travelled to the cemetery for the private burial. Afterwards there would be refreshments in the church hall, organised by the indomitable Diana.

"She looked like an Amazon," Harriet murmured. "Like a real force of nature."

"I guess we'll get to know her soon enough," Rachel replied with a shrug. Anna knew they were both apprehensive about meeting Daisy, as well as handing over the house. She was, too.

They buried Peter in a small corner plot of the cemetery, next to his parents and sister, all who had died before Anna had ever met him. They'd never been more than sepia-tinted faces in old photographs, but now, as she watched Peter's coffin being lowered into the ground, she was conscious of the history of his family in the place, and she understood a little more why he'd wanted Embthwaite Farm to continue, under Daisy. She'd shared the contents of his letter with Harriet and Rachel, who had been, in turns, tearful and furious, but also understanding.

"Truth be told, we would have sold it," Rachel had concluded practically. "And that would have been sad, although it's true we could have used the money. But maybe it is better this way…even though I don't particularly like it."

Back at the village hall, Anna was feeling exhausted and not particularly like she wanted to exchange pleasantries with half of Mathering, but she knew her duty, and she wasn't about to let Rachel and Harriet handle the crowd alone. In any case, everyone was kind and accepting; there were a few laughingly pointed remarks about how difficult Peter could be that, improbably, made Anna smile.

"To be honest," Judy, the wife of Peter's barber, whispered to her, "I'm surprised you didn't leave earlier. A *lot* earlier. That man!"

Anna looked around for Daisy, wondering if she might slip in, but she didn't see her anywhere. How did the young woman feel, entering this close-knit community as a stranger? It couldn't be easy.

By four o'clock, everything had wrapped up, and Diana

thrust a platter of sandwiches at Anna, insisting they take them home for their dinner, although Anna wasn't entirely sure any of them wanted to eat prawn salad sandwiches that had been wilting on a tray for the last six hours. She rather thought they'd have a takeaway, but she thanked Diana all the same.

"I don't know what we would have done without you," she told her. "In so many ways. You've been an absolute rock, Diana."

"Now, now," Diana replied briskly, blinking hard. "Don't set me off. You know where I am if you need me, but I hope you take a few days off, the three of you, to rest and recover."

"We have the will reading the day after tomorrow," Anna replied with a grimace. They hadn't told anyone about the surprising contents of Peter's will, but she supposed it would become common knowledge soon enough, if it wasn't already.

"That's a problem for another day," Diana replied, giving her a quick hug, and Anna had to agree that it was.

Back at the house, Rachel kicked off her heels with a groan. "I want a bath and then a sleep," she announced. "For about twelve hours. But first I want a very large glass of wine."

"I'm happy to go out and get a bottle," Anna offered, "and a takeaway. Chinese or Indian?" Mathering didn't have any other options.

"Chinese," Harriet stated firmly. "And red." Her expression softened into a smile. "Thanks, Mum."

It was, Anna reflected, moments like this that made it all

worth it. They were together in this, in a way she'd never dared to hope they would be.

On the way into town, she decided, quite suddenly, to stop by Jane's. She was uncomfortably conscious that she'd never had that talk with Jane, and maybe now she wouldn't even need to, considering James's radio silence, but she thought she ought to check in, and maybe she could work up the courage to ask about James, hopefully in a subtle way.

But when Anna pulled up to the house, she saw it was dark, the curtains drawn, and no car parked outside. She rang the doorbell, anyway, and there was no answer. Maybe they'd gone away for the weekend, Anna reflected uneasily. Maybe with James, which was why he hadn't rung or texted…except even on holiday you had access to your phone, and he hadn't contacted her for days. Something wasn't right.

A sudden, chilling thought occurred to her. What if something had happened? What if James was ill or injured or, heaven help her, *dead*? The thought filled her with dread. That had to be it! He would have contacted her otherwise, she'd known he would have…

Recklessly, her fingers trembling, Anna swiped to dial his number again. Again, she listened to it ring, and then switch over to voicemail. *Oh, no…*

She was just about to leave a faltering voicemail when her phone buzzed with a text. It was from James, and it was only two words.

I'm sorry.

Anna stared down at those words, trying to figure out what he'd meant, hoping he'd send another text to make it clear, but he didn't. Several minutes with her standing there in the cold and dark, and there was no further reply, which left her with one unfortunate conclusion. *I'm sorry* really meant *goodbye*.

She got the takeaway and two bottles of wine, because she had a feeling they'd need them, and then she headed back to Embthwaite Farm, feeling utterly flat.

"That smells amazing," Rachel remarked as Anna unloaded the cartons of lo mein and lemon chicken onto the kitchen table. "And wine!" She reached for a bottle, only to falter as Anna continued to methodically empty out the takeaway bag. "Mum, what's wrong?"

"Wrong?" Anna glanced up, forcing her lips to curve into an enquiring if rather brittle smile. "Nothing's wrong. I'm just tired."

"No, something's definitely wrong," Rachel answered as she studied Anna's face. "You look like someone just died, and I don't mean Dad."

Harriet, who had come into the kitchen, let out a huff of laughter. "That should *not* be funny, all things considered."

"Sometimes you just have to laugh, though, don't you?" Rachel was still studying Anna. "But what is it? Honestly? Have you learned something more?"

"No. That is, not about the farm or Daisy or anything to do with that situation." She hadn't, Anna reflected, told her daughters that James even existed. How could she explain how she was feeling now?

And yet…wasn't that what relationships were meant to be about? Not keeping everything in, saving it for a bloody letter after you'd died! Not putting a stoic face on it all and acting like a martyr when no one was actually asking you to. Maybe it was time to be honest…about everything.

"I'll tell you," she told her daughters, "but first I need a glass of wine."

"Oh, this sounds like a good story," Rachel replied, her eyes alight although she still looked concerned. "Are we going to get some serious goss?"

"Something like that," Anna replied on a sigh. "Although unfortunately, it's over before it even began."

"What's over?" Harriet demanded, and so, over plates of Chinese food and very full glasses of wine, Anna told them about James—seeing him at the quiz night, coming across him as her landlord, their day in Stroud and even their kiss.

"I know it probably all sounds ridiculously juvenile," she finished morosely, "and at my age! But I felt we had a connection, and it's…" She paused as she sorted through her tangled feelings. "It's hurtful as well as humiliating, to realise I got it so wrong *again.* I let myself believe all sorts of things about a person that weren't true. I made something out of nothing." She shook her head as she took a sip of her wine. "At least I didn't waste twenty years of my life this time. Not," she amended quickly, "that it was a waste. I have you girls—"

"Mum, please." Rachel held up a hand to stem the tide of apologies that always rose to her lips during conversations like these. "You don't need to say that. We get it."

"Yes," Harriet chimed in feelingly, "we do. And this James sounds like a real prat. I'm so sorry."

"But the thing," Anna remarked after a moment, "is that he really wasn't. He really did seem like such a lovely, warm, genuine person. I just…I just don't understand it."

"Why don't you call him?" Rachel suggested.

"I have called him," Anna replied. She hadn't got to that part of her story. "Twice. And tonight, he finally texted me back, with two words. 'I'm sorry.'" Both her daughters winced visibly, which actually made Anna laugh. "I know," she agreed. "Painful, right?"

And yet there was something rather wonderful about being able to share this heartache with her daughters, to chat and commiserate and just enjoy each other's company, despite the disappointment, the sorrow, the grief.

Small mercies, Anna thought. Silver linings.

"Why don't you text him back?" Harriet suggested, sounding rather bolshie after two and a half glasses of wine. "Ask him what he meant by his apology? Make him spell it out." She pointed a finger at Anna. "For your sake, Mum. You deserve a proper reply."

"Yes," Rachel chimed in. "You do!"

"I think 'I'm sorry' says it all…" Anna protested, admittedly rather feebly.

"No, it bloody doesn't," Rachel insisted. "It's a cop-out, and you deserve more. I mean, he ghosted you for three days, right when you were burying your ex-husband, and then texts 'I'm sorry' and nothing else? Like, what even is that?"

"When you put it that way…" Anna murmured. She was on a third glass of wine herself and was feeling a little reckless. Her daughters' determined vindication of her was a salve to her soul, and it gave her some much-needed courage.

"So, are you going to do it?" Harriet asked. "Text him?"

"I don't know…"

"What have you got to lose?" Rachel countered. "Especially if it's already over? Come on, Mum. I know you've learned that running away is never the answer."

Ouch. "I'm not the one running away here," she replied mildly, but she did take the point. When she'd kissed James, it had been because she'd wanted to take control of her life. Not be so darned passive all the time, letting things just happen to her. Maybe her girls were right…and she did deserve a reply.

"All right, fine," she said, and both Harriet and Rachel cheered.

Anna, knowing she was more than a little tipsy but still determined to do this, reached for her phone. Hesitated.

"Keep it brief," Rachel advised. "You don't want to do a big messy emotional thing over text."

"No, definitely not," Harriet agreed. "Succinct is best."

"And no emojis," Rachel warned. "That's so middle-aged."

Anna laughed. "I am middle-aged," she reminded them. "And so is he. But I'm not really in an emoji sort of mood." After a few moments' reflection, she finally typed out her response, recklessly pressing send before either Rachel or Harriet could weigh in.

What exactly are you sorry for? And don't you think I deserve more of a reply than that?

"Nice," Rachel approved as Anna tossed her phone aside. "That was very girl boss, Mum."

"Girl boss!" Anna let out a huff of laughter. "Well, I'm not entirely sure I know what that means, although I can guess."

"Were you hoping it would become something serious?" Harriet asked. "With you in Stroud and this guy up here..."

This felt as good a time as any to talk about what she'd been thinking. "Actually," Anna said, "I was thinking about moving up to Mathering. Permanently, I mean. Not because of James, but because of you two. I wanted to be closer to you...if you wouldn't mind that. I promise not to get in your space—"

"Mind?" Harriet repeated, looking both startled and pleased. "No, I wouldn't mind. Would you, Rachel?"

Rachel shook her head. "Definitely not. In fact, I'd quite like it." She ducked her head, seeming uncharacteristically shy. "We have a lot of lost years to make up for, after all."

"That's sorted, then." Anna smiled at them both. She wouldn't think about the possibility of running into James—or Jane—right then. Mathering was big enough for all of them...she hoped.

Just then, her phone pinged with a text, and all three of them lunged for it, laughing as they scrabbed for the phone. Rachel got it first, and she dutifully handed it to Anna without looking at it.

Anna swiped the screen and then wordlessly she showed it to Harriet and Rachel. It was a text from James, just three words.

Can we talk?

Chapter Twenty-One

IT WAS THE day after Peter's funeral, the morning after her wine-fuelled evening and James's text, asking her to talk. Anna still felt fuzzy-headed, but also firm. She'd had a good talking-to by Rachel and Harriet that morning, and it was one she'd needed.

"Mum, you've basically lived your life like an apology for way too long," Rachel told her as she scrambled eggs and Anna and Harriet sat at the table and sipped coffee. "And I know that's partly on us, because we forced you into it. Both Harriet and I were pretty good at the blame game, and we're sorry for that."

"Me especially," Harriet said, wincing as she sipped her own coffee. "I should have listened to you. Given you a chance."

"You were hurting…" Anna murmured.

"Still…"

Rachel held up a warning hand. "We are *not* going over all this again," she informed them both firmly. "The point is, Mum, don't be that way with this guy. You have nothing to be sorry for. He does. Remember that."

"And remember that you're worth it," Harriet entreated her. "And I'm not talking about a make-up ad. This guy is lucky to have you. To know you. And you need to make sure he realises that, no matter how it goes down."

"Yeah, because Dad never did," Rachel added, "or at least he didn't nearly enough. And a letter to be opened after his death doesn't count. If he'd been braver, he would have said all that before he died. *Way* before."

"I think he tried," Anna replied, recalling that poignant conversation with Peter, just a little over a week ago now, although it felt like so much longer than that. "I hear what you're saying, girls, and I agree with you…to a point. But something I've learned along the way is that *everyone* finds life hard. We're all struggling, and we all need to give each other grace. Maybe I just don't know what James's struggle is…and maybe he'll tell me." That was the conclusion she'd come to last night, when the wine had worn off and she'd been left staring at the ceiling, wondering just what it was he wanted to talk about.

"You're right," Harriet said after a moment. "We could have all given each other more grace over the years, I suppose."

"No more regrets," Rachel announced as she placed plates of eggs in front of them both. "Eat up, and then go get him, Mum!"

AND SO HERE she was, driving up the rutted track to James's house, wondering what on earth he was going to say to her. He hadn't offered any more explanation via text, just asked if she could meet him at his house at ten o'clock in the morning. He'd apologised for the lack of notice, and said he had to be somewhere in the afternoon. Where, he didn't say, and Anna didn't ask. But she certainly hoped she gained some more clarity after this conversation.

This time, James didn't throw open the door before Anna had stepped out of the car. In fact, she had to ring the doorbell—a first—and then wait a good thirty seconds before she finally heard the sound of the bolt sliding across and then the door opened.

Her first sight of James drew a startled gasp from her, and he managed a tired laugh.

"Sorry, I'm not at my best," he told her with an attempt at wryness. "I did shower, though."

"James..." Anna stared at him, the uncertainty and unease—and yes, the annoyance and hurt—she'd been feeling solidifying into a deeper dismay and concern. He looked dreadful...pouches beneath his eyes, deeper lines on his face, his clothes hanging off him. How had all this happened in just over a *week*? "What's happened?" she asked. "Because something obviously has."

He shook his head as he ushered her in, closing the door behind her. "It's a long story, and one I will tell you, but first let me take your coat. Coffee?"

Anna thought her stomach was churning too much to manage coffee, but she suspected they both could use something warm. "Herbal tea, please, if you have it," she said.

James went to put on the kettle while Anna ventured into the open space that had always been so cosy and welcoming before, but now felt weirdly unlived in. There was no fire in the fireplace, and there was a forgottenness about everything that made her wonder if James had even been home this last week. What on earth had happened?

"It's been a hell of a week," he told her as he put the kettle on and then riffled in a cupboard for teabags. "I've got lemon and ginger—is that all right?"

"That's absolutely fine." Anna walked into the kitchen area, resting one hand on the marble island to anchor herself. "What's happened, James? And why didn't you let me know what was going on all this time?"

He sighed heavily. "I should have. I know I should have. It was just…complicated."

"Is it still?"

"Yes." He turned to give her a rather wretched look. "Which is why, or at least part of why, I haven't been in touch. I was trying to figure out what was possible. But first, I should ask you about the funeral. I'm so sorry I wasn't there. I would have been, otherwise."

Anna gave a little shake of her head. "I don't know that I would have expected you to be there, all things considered." She paused before continuing clearly, "What this has made me realise, James, is how little we know each other. I know we *felt* like we knew each other, and that was wonderful, but it's not the same, is it? I rushed into a relationship—a marriage—once before. I know we're not remotely at that sort of stage, but I want to be honest. Whatever happened, I wish you'd told me about it. I wish we'd had that level of trust in one another, but the truth is, we didn't, and there was a reason for that."

"Maybe there was," James agreed. The kettle boiled and

he made them both tea while Anna watched in silence. Was this going to be nothing more than a post-mortem of possibility? she wondered. What could have been but now clearly wasn't? Was there even any point to such a conversation? She almost didn't want to have it. She'd had enough painful conversations already, and if there was no chance of them working through things…

But then she recalled how wonderful it had felt to kiss him, and how comfortable and happy she felt when she was with him…and how absolutely *wretched* he looked now. She thought of her own words to Rachel and Harriet, just that morning. *We're all struggling, and we all need to give each other grace.*

She wanted to do that now.

"Whatever it is, I hope you can tell me," she said quietly. "I want to understand. I admit I was hurt, but I'm not…I'm not angry. I want to be here for you…whatever happens between us."

James turned to her, his eyes damp. "Thank you," he said, his voice a low, heartfelt thrum. "That means a lot, Anna."

He took their cups of tea over to the table before sitting down on one end. He dropped his head briefly into his hands as Anna took her own seat, and then he looked up at her, resolute.

"So, what happened was Jane," he stated, and Anna felt a jolt of recognition. Of course, she should have considered that it had something to do with Jane—the darkened house, the fact that she hadn't followed up…

She swallowed dryly. "What…what happened?"

He sighed and took a sip of tea. "To explain, I have to go back a bit. I told you I was a workaholic, and that I made a deliberate decision to step away from that after Helen died."

"Yes..."

"What I didn't tell you," James continued resolutely, "was that I fell into a depression. It runs in my family, I'm afraid. My mother suffered pretty terribly at times. I staved it off through the years by keeping busy, but when Helen died...it felt as if my whole world had just...disappeared. I didn't have Helen; I didn't have my work. I ended up shutting down, in a lot of ways, and that wasn't fair on Jane. It's why she's been so protective of me. She doesn't want me—or her—ever to go through that dark time again."

"I understand," Anna whispered. More than he could possibly know.

"Four days ago," James continued, "Eric called me. He came home from work to find Henry in his high chair, screaming his head off, and Jane was gone."

Anna felt the blood drain from her face. Just like before! Should she have told James—or Eric—what had happened? She hadn't thought it too serious a matter, just the usual mummy blues, but now she saw how it had been a warning sign. "Where was she?" she asked.

"She was wandering through Mathering in her dressing gown and slippers," James replied bleakly. "Eric found her after twenty minutes of trawling the streets." His face crumpled before he smoothed it out, steadying himself with a quick breath. "Poor Jane. She's been coping so much less than I realised. And I, of all people, should have recognised the signs, because I was the same, back after Helen died—

not sleeping, not eating…"

Both of which she had noticed when she'd last been there, Anna realised. If she hadn't been so concerned about what Jane thought about her and James, maybe she would have suspected that something more serious was going on.

"I'm so sorry," she murmured. "Is she…is she all right now?"

"She's checked herself into hospital," James confessed with a ragged sigh. "Just yesterday. A psychiatric ward, just for a few days, to sort out some medication, and hopefully get some sleep. I'm proud of her, for knowing what she needed to do. It might have been what I needed, back in the day." He raked a weary hand through his hair. "In any case, the lack of sleep had led to some manic episodes—baking in the middle of the night, talking nineteen to the dozen. Eric's taken Henry to his parents, in Sunderland."

Anna thought of Jane coming out at nine o'clock at night, clutching the brownies, seeming a bit excitable. "Poor, poor Jane," she whispered.

"I know it sounds like an extreme situation," he continued, "but she *will* get her head on straight. I did, eventually. Not that it's that easy or simple, far from it, but there's such a stigma around mental illness, still…"

"Oh, James." Anna couldn't keep from giving a trembling laugh. "Trust me, I know that."

He frowned in confusion. "What do you mean?"

"I should have told you before, I suppose," Anna said. "And I know we're talking about Jane, but…when I left Peter, I had something of a breakdown. I just…walked out…on Peter, and on Harriet, who was still at home. Doing her A levels, like Jane was when Helen died. I've always regretted leaving her like that, and she's only just forgiven me. It has been very hard, for both of us." She paused, giving James time to absorb what she'd admitted. "I don't even think I was aware of what I was doing," she resumed after a moment. "Truth be told, I can't even remember doing it. But I ended up in a facility for three months. It took me that long to find a way to cope, to heal." She shook her head. "I was afraid to tell you, for a lot of different reasons."

His expression cleared and he smiled sadly. "Maybe we both should have been more honest with each other."

"Well, it's like I said," Anna dared to tease, her voice only a little wobbly. "These things should be doled out in medicinal sips."

"And we've both just had one big gulp," James returned with a small smile, before his expression turned serious once more. "I'm sorry for letting you down, Anna."

"You didn't," Anna assured him. "I was confused, it's true, and hurt, but I understand now why you went silent."

"Still." He glanced down at the table, tracing the grain of the wood with one finger. "Part of what was going on with Jane was she'd started to suspect there might be something between us. Something about a scarf."

Anna couldn't keep from wincing in acknowledgement. "I thought that might be happening," she admitted. "I wanted to talk to her about it—and you, as well—but then everything kicked off with Peter and there wasn't the time… I'm sorry. I should have dealt with it."

He shook his head. "You don't have anything to be sorry for. I should have spoken to her from the start. If I'd thought about it, I would have known she might get upset. It's been just the two of us for a long time."

"That's understandable, for her to feel that way."

He let out a sigh. "It's all part of the process, I think. A lot has come up for her, that I hadn't realised. Becoming a mother when she doesn't have her own around has been harder than I knew. And she never wanted to admit to me how much she was struggling, because she didn't want me to struggle. You were a godsend to her, Anna. Really."

Anna gave a small, rather unhappy smile. "But I was also part of the problem."

"We spoke about that, and Jane understands—in her head, at least—that I am perfectly entitled to have a relationship. She wants me to be happy. It's just harder in her heart, you know? In theory versus in practice."

Anna nodded slowly. "Yes," she agreed. "Most things are."

They both lapsed into a silence that felt reflective rather than disconsolate, although Anna still didn't know where they stood. Where they could stand, all things considered. Well, she told herself, she was trying to be proactive in all areas of her life, including this one.

"So," she asked James, giving him a direct look. "Where does that leave us?" Before he could reply, she continued, "You were honest about how you felt before. In fact, your honesty both humbled me and blew me away, and I was very grateful for it. So, without having any ideas how you're going to respond, I'll be just as honest with you now."

A faint smile played about James's lips and sparked in his eyes. He leaned back in his chair as he nodded his assent. "All right."

Okay, here goes, Anna thought and then launched in. "I like you," she told him baldly. "A lot. And I especially liked our kiss, which I don't regret at all." The smile that had been playing about his mouth deepened, giving her both courage and hope. "In fact, I'd like to kiss you again, soon. I've thought about that quite a lot."

"So have I," James murmured, his lips positively twitching with a smile he couldn't suppress. Anna found herself smiling back, even though she knew there was still a lot more to say. A lot more uncertainties to deal with.

"And I like being with you," she continued. "What you said about feeling like you knew me already? I felt the same. I know that's not necessarily real, but it's still something. Kindred spirits, maybe."

"Definitely," James chimed in.

Okay, this was going pretty well so far. And yet…

"But, like you said," she resumed, "life is complicated. My life is complicated—I've got two daughters who are both healing but still hurting, especially around Peter's will and some change and drama that will cause." She held up a hand to forestall any questions. "I won't talk about that now, but it's ongoing and will be for some time. I've told them I'm going to move up to Mathering, regardless of what happens with us, and they're pleased, so that's a good thing." She let out a breath, feeling a bit drained from everything she'd said, yet also excited, and glad she'd said it. "And you," she continued. "You have complicated factors too, in particular Jane and being a support to her, whatever that looks like. So, we've both got things—children, really—that demand our time and attention and might make having a relationship hard."

"Yes," James agreed quietly.

"But like you also said," Anna replied, "we're both in our fifties and life is short. There's no time to waste. These are early days regardless, maybe too early to say what might happen, but what I'd like to say is…I want to try to find out. Give it—*us*—a chance, amidst all the complications." There. She'd said it, as plainly as that, and she was glad, fiercely so. "But if you don't want to," she assured him, "then that's fine. No hard feelings, and I hope we still can be friends." She let out a self-deprecating laugh, deciding to be completely honest. "I mean, I'll be gutted, *obviously*, but honestly, I mean it."

James was shaking his head slowly, which made Anna's spirits, which had just started to soar, plummet right to the ground. She could almost hear his next words. *That all sounds amazing, Anna, and I really like you too, but I just can't do that right now. I'm sorry.*

"Anna," he said. She braced herself. "I completely agree," he told her simply, and she let out a trembling laugh of incredulous hope.

"You do…"

"Yes." He reached for her hand, drawing her up from her seat and across to him. Anna's heart beat hard as James stood, taking both her hands in his as he gazed down at her. "I think you're an amazing, incredible woman, and I want to find out where this goes, too, because I actually think it's going to go somewhere pretty fantastic. But I want to find out, like you said, amidst all the complications. Because if we wait for life to settle down or simplify, it never will, will it?"

"No," Anna agreed on a whisper, thinking of all that happened in the last few months. "It never will."

"So, here's to us," James said, "and here's to now." And then he kissed her, his lips settling on hers softly as his arms came around her and she pulled him even closer, deepening the kiss in the most wonderful way.

When he held her like this, she thought hazily, she felt like anything and everything was possible.

And maybe, she realised as they broke their kiss to grin rather foolishly at one another, anything and everything was.

A VERY PLEASURABLE hour later, where she and James chatted and laughed and kissed some more, Anna was driving back to Embthwaite Farm, her heart lighter than it had been in many long years. There was still some sorrow there, as well some uncertainty—what the future held still seemed alarmingly unknown, especially in relation to the farm.

Her relationship with her daughters, too, Anna acknowledged, was ongoing, in progress, but maybe that's how all of life was. Nothing ever felt truly finished or complete. It was ongoing until the end, which was why death could feel like such a wrench, an ending without the satisfaction, the sense of wholeness.

And yet in the midst of the uncertainty, the confusion, the heartache and disappointment…you found hope. You found strength. And you kept going.

She was smiling as she came up the drive, the sight of the farm lightening something inside her. A new story would be told in those dusty old rooms, she thought. She didn't know what it was yet, or whether she would be a part of it, but she was ready to find out. She was ready to embrace the future and all its changes…however it played out. She had her daughters, and she had James, and she had this community, ornery as it was, to help her.

As she pulled in next to the house, she saw a battered Land Rover parked in front. She'd assumed it was Peter's when she'd first come up the drive, but now she realised it wasn't. While just as beaten up and mud-splattered, it was blue rather than green, and Peter's car had been put into the barn. Had a local farmer come to pay his or her respects?

Slowly Anna got out of her car and walked up to the front door. She felt a sense of curiosity war with trepidation, although she wasn't sure why, until she opened the front door and saw the three women standing in the hallway, all glaring daggers at one another.

Harriet's hands were on her hips, and Rachel's mouth was pursed up like a prune. The third woman, with long, auburn hair and a statuesque physique, was looking down at her nose at both of them, her jade-green eyes sparkling with tears.

"Hello," Anna greeted them all cautiously.

The red-haired woman turned to look at her, lifting her chin just a little. "Hello," she replied in a voice that was determinedly firm, with a hint of challenge. "I think you might know this already, but I'm Daisy."

The End

Discover Daisy's story in the final Mowbray Sisters book, A Stranger at Embthwaite Farm*!*

If you enjoyed *Sunset at Embthwaite Farm*,
you'll love the other books in the…

The Mowbray Sisters series

Book 1: *Return to Embthwaite Farm*

Book 2: *Christmas at Embthwaite Farm*

Book 3: *Sunset at Embthwaite Farm*

Available now at your favorite online retailer!

More books by Kate Hewitt

Keeping Up with the Penryns series

Book 1: *A Casterglass Christmas*

Book 2: *A Casterglass Garden*

Book 3: *The Casterglass Heir*

Book 4: *The Last Casterglass*

The Return to Willoughby Close series

Book 1: *Cupcakes for Christmas*

Book 2: *Welcome Me to Willoughby Close*

Book 3: *Christmas at Willoughby Close*

Book 4: *Remember Me at Willoughby Close*

Christmas at the Edge of the World

The Willoughby Close series

Book 1: *A Cotswold Christmas*

Book 2: *Meet Me at Willoughby Close*

Book 3: *Find Me at Willoughby Close*

Book 4: *Kiss Me at Willoughby Close*

Book 5: *Marry Me at Willoughby Close*

The Holley Sisters of Thornthwaite series

Book 1: *A Vicarage Christmas*

Book 2: *A Vicarage Reunion*

Book 3: *A Vicarage Wedding*

Book 4: *A Vicarage Homecoming*

Falling for the Freemans series

Book 1: *Falling for Christmas*

Book 2: *Falling Hard*

Christmas Around the World series

Book 2: *A Yorkshire Christmas*

Available now at your favorite online retailer!

About the Author

Kate Hewitt wrote her first story at the age of five, simply because her older brother had written one and she thought she could do it too. That story was one sentence long—fortunately, they have become a bit more detailed as she's grown older.

She studied drama in college and shortly after graduation moved to New York City to pursue a career in theatre. This was derailed by something far better—meeting the man of her dreams who happened also to be her older brother's childhood friend.

Ten days after their wedding they moved to England, where Kate worked a variety of different jobs—drama teacher, editorial assistant, church youth worker, secretary, and finally mother.

When her oldest daughter was one year old, she sold her first short story to a British magazine, The People's Friend. Since then she has written many stories and serials as well as novels. In 2007 she received 'The Call' from Mills & Boon for her first Harlequin Presents novel, The Italian's Chosen Wife. Since then she has written over 25 books for Harlequin, and also writes women's fiction for Carina UK and Lion Hudson Press. She loves writing stories that both tackle tough issues and celebrate the redeeming power of love.

Thank you for reading

Sunset at Embthwaite Farm

If you enjoyed this book, you can find more from all our great authors at TulePublishing.com, or from your favorite online retailer.

TULE
PUBLISHING